# THE COSMIC KILLINGS

## A MALCOM WINTERS MYSTERY

THOMAS J. THORSON

Thorshammer Books
ISBN: 978-1-7358366-3-8
For ordering information, visit: www.thorsonbooks.com

Cover and internal design/Stephanie Rocha
Author photo © Stephanie Rocha
Front cover Image credits © istock.com, Freepic.com,
Gabriel Silvério/Unsplash.com, Velizar Ivanov/Unsplash.com
David Underland/Unsplash.com

Printed in the United States of America.

# DEDICATION

As always to my daughters Tierney,
Lourdra, and Gilleece, with love
and a warm cup of tea.

# ACKNOWLEDGEMENTS

The temptation is to copy and paste the acknowledgement from my last book, as I've been blessed with the continued support of the same group of loving and talented people. My daughters and my friends, who have to tolerate my random inaccessibility during those periods when inspiration hits and nothing else matters and whose praise, whether genuine or not, is music to my ears. My editor Kristen Weber, with whom I share a love of ice cream and mystery novels, and whose voice of reason I hear even as I type that dreaded first draft that eventually will make it to her desk so that she can work her magic. Steve Kirshenbaum of Looking Glass Books for his enthusiasm when I present him with my latest work and for being a sounding board of ideas. And of course Stephanie Rocha, whose incredible artistic talents are the first thing my readers see and whose covers and layouts force me to be a better writer in order to live up to her own high standards. I wouldn't be here without you, and I thank you all.

# ONE

"C'mon, Mr. 'Of Course I Know How to Skate.' Get out here and show me your stuff."

It's hard to be annoyed with the source of the taunt when she looks so adorable in a puffy white down coat that nearly doubles her small frame, her cheeks glowing as pink as the puffs of fur enveloping her ears, the cutest rear end on campus wriggling in anticipation as she readies to set off over the ice. I haven't lived in Chicago long enough to have any sort of history with the weather but was informed— many times—that the stretch of 60-degree weather leading up to the holidays wasn't typical. Two days ago, on Christmas Eve, Vinn and I were strolling along Michigan Avenue enjoying the millions of lights in spring jackets. As we exchanged gifts yesterday the wind battering the windows of my Ukrainian Village apartment led both of us to don gay apparel, meaning heavy sweaters. This morning dawned frigid enough to support a dusting of snow on the ground, which Vinn took as a sign that we need to quickly transition to winter activities to take advantage of the cold. A true Midwesterner.

Which is why I find myself languishing on a frozen bench at the Millennium Park rink nestled deep within the shadows of the buildings to the west. An ill-advised bout of bravado, combined with my desire not to disappoint my fellow professor and lover, led to my fib that I'm an old hand on the ice and would like nothing better than to go skating. In truth, I've never laced up a pair of skates in my life, which is why I'm initially stymied as to what to do when the eyelets transition to hooks. My brilliant powers of deduction eventually come to my rescue and I finish the job, stand up, and immediately have to grab onto the boards to steady my wobble. Hopefully she doesn't notice.

"A little rusty, are we?" She noticed. "Grab my hand and let's take a couple of laps together before you show me your double axel." Cute.

We link arms as I cautiously leave terra firma and step out among the throngs of people who seem incomprehensively cheerful as they propel themselves around in circles only one misstep away from breaking a limb. I match Vinn's smile, though, and we start off slowly. I'm not as bad as I feared and before long we're keeping up with the crowd, if you don't count the snotty eight-year-old girl who sees nothing wrong with mixing in leaps and twirls as she laps the rest of us.

"Vinn, this is nice. I have a confession to make, though. I've never actually skated before."

"I know," she replies before breaking away and dashing at full speed down the straightaway, weaving in and out of our fellow skaters, twisting to take the curve backwards, then gliding on a single blade as she lifts her left leg high, grabbing onto it with her right hand. I move to the boards to gawk at the woman who only moments before seemed to be awkwardly gripping my arm to avoid a painful spill. Seconds later, she comes to a sudden stop inches from me, spraying my lower half in a shower of ice, a sheepish expression on her face.

"Vinn, how in the—" I begin before she presses a colorful mitten over my mouth.

"I grew up in Minnesota, remember? I was skating before I could walk and gym class in the winter was figure skating. For the girls, anyway. Broom hockey for the boys." Vinn makes a face, this long-ago slight still stinging.

We set off again, slower this time, our arms wrapped around each other as we quietly enjoy the silence of each other's company. I'm not sure how I ended up dating a woman who sees winter as anything but a reason to bury oneself under five layers of blankets with a pile of books sitting on the nightstand alongside a steaming cup of fine tea, but at this moment at least there's no one I'd rather be with.

The sun disappears behind the tall buildings on the far side of the street, and as darkness begins to descend thousands of lights suddenly come to life on trees lining one side of the rink. Immediately afterward the skyscrapers of the city join in with their own light show. As we circle, we're treated to views of the city at its best, highlighted by the reflection of the lights in Anish Kapoor's Cloud Gate, known to locals as "The Bean," a giant, shiny steel monument rising up behind the restaurant adjacent to the rink.

Also rising up is a chilly wind, which may be fine for Midwestern farm girls but which cause this warm-weather soul to shiver slightly. Vinn looks up at me sympathetically. "Hot chocolate?" she asks.

"Sounds perfect. My double axel will have to wait."

One of us glides while the other stumbles to the exit, my feet thanking me as I plop down heavily on the wooden bench I recently deserted. Vinn packs up her skates then goes to find a table while I return my rentals. It takes five minutes before my body realizes that I'm not balancing on two thin strips of metal.

As I join Vinn at a table with a view of the other skaters, a waiter sets two steaming mugs of nirvana in front of us, a pool of whipped cream rapidly melting into the chocolate. Vinn's aware that tea is my drink of choice but also knows that few restaurants carry a selection that meets my refined (she says "snobby") tastes. In fact, sitting on my kitchen counter at this very moment is the nineteenth-century copper Tibetan teapot she got me for Christmas, a gift so thoughtful it would have brought tears to my eyes if I weren't such a manly man.

Demonstrating that I also have a sentimental side, my present to her was a top-of-the-line set of platinum professional lock picks. If you know Vinn, it wouldn't surprise you to know that my gift actually did trigger the waterworks.

My reverie is interrupted by reality as Vinn begins to speak. "You do remember that we're meeting Anna Gilcrest for coffee tomorrow, right? She's heard rumors about our past, um, exploits and has a friend who wants to meet us. Don't make that face—she's a colleague and it would be awkward to turn her down."

I've never met Anna Gilcrest, which isn't odd since the University of Illinois at Chicago is a fairly large campus and she's a professor in the sociology department, which doesn't overlap with my world as an English teacher. It's a matter of curiosity for others, and an annoyance for us, that these "exploits," as Vinn euphemistically refers to them, nearly got ourselves killed. It's also apparently no secret that we only got involved in these matters to help people we barely knew and could easily have stayed safe within our own personal worlds. But past training and experience for both Vinn and myself, former lives which we've revealed to each other but to no one else, combined with a lingering sense of justice, were too ingrained for us to walk away. In those matters, though, we initiated our involvement. The difference here is that for the first time we're being approached by an outsider. We agreed to hear her out without having been given a single detail of why our advice is being sought. It makes me more than a little wary.

"Yes, I remember," I say cheerily. "I can't wait."

# TWO

I'm on my second cup of tea and in the midst of mixing the flour and oatmeal for apricot hot cakes when a bleary-eyed Vinn stumbles out of the bedroom and plops herself down on one of the stools, pushing a plate aside to rest her arms and create a nest for her head on the island. I flip the switch on the coffee maker—its presence in my kitchen a concession to the growing number of nights Vinn sleeps over—then pour a dollop of sorghum I picked up over the summer at the tiny Amish grocery down the street into the batter. When I'm on my own cold cereal is about the limit of my effort for breakfast, although on special occasions I may go as far as toasting a bagel. Stepping outside of my culinary limitations in the morning is a holdover of trying to impress Vinn from when we started getting serious. Now she expects it and I'm not sure she'd be up before noon if Corn Flakes were on the menu.

I pour generous heaps of batter onto a sizzling-hot griddle and the kitchen is immediately filled with the aroma of apricots and molasses. My timing is impeccable, the pancakes hitting the plates at the exact time a bell goes off signaling that Vinn's coffee is ready. She looks at me through bleary eyes as I pour it into a large mug before reluctantly lifting herself up to make room for breakfast. I set a choice of pure maple syrup or fruit compote in front of her.

I know better than to be the first one to speak, waiting for the coffee to work its magic. Vinn finishes off two pancakes, drains the last of the java, then slides the mug over as a silent request for a refill. She's beginning to look mostly human.

"You know the only reason I stay over is this," she says with a slight grin forming at the edges of her mouth, pointing at her empty plate with a fork.

I pretend to pout. "And here I thought it was my dazzling intellect," I retort as I stack our dishes in the sink.

Vinn responds with a derisive snort and a smile, which would be hurtful coming from anyone else but frankly there are few people on the planet whose intelligence match hers, so I'm comfortable in the knowledge that the attraction may be based on something other than my brainpower.

She reaches across the island, gently takes my hands in hers, and pulls me forward for a light kiss. Her eyes, playful a second before, suddenly turn serious.

"I'm sorry about agreeing to meet up with Professor Gilcrest. She just sounded so desperate but wouldn't go into details over the phone. All she would tell me is that she has a problem and that we—I guess that's you and I together, Mal—have a reputation as people that might be able to help. I don't know what she's heard or what she wants, so I made no promises. Honestly, I'd prefer to just enjoy winter break and start preparing lesson plans for next quarter."

"What do you know about her? And do you have any idea what she wants to ask us about?"

Vinn makes a face. "I doubt a sociology professor is looking for advice about her love life from a couple of loners like ourselves." I raise an eyebrow at her but she doesn't seem to notice. "If I've met her I don't recall it. Follow me to the couch and let's see what we can find."

We snuggle close together as Vinn flips open her laptop and connects to the biography section of the UIC website. She snickers as she "accidentally" lands on my own page. She knows I submitted a fanciful summary which included a run for the Presidency I never undertook and a graphic description of the peak of a mountain I've never climbed, not to mention a reference to the book my namesake wrote which through mistaken identity and some creative fibbing got me the teaching job in the first place. I never thought the powers that be would print it. After the giggles die down, she gets down to business.

"Nothing here of much value. She's about our age, has been teaching courses in sociology and gender studies on campus for about eight years, is married and has two cats and a hamster. Seriously? She thinks students want to know about her rodent?"

"Calm down, superwoman. Stay on task." I read Vinn's own biography not long after we met in an effort to get some insight into who she is. It turned out to be a deep dive into her theories on molecular science. I never got past the third sentence.

She leaves the university website and Googles our fellow professor, but after twenty fruitless minutes where the most electrifying information we uncover is that Professor Gilcrest vacationed in Cancun two years ago and looks good in a bikini, Vinn gives up.

"I guess we'll just have to go in cold. Speaking of cold, I'll bet it's still plenty warm under the comforter." As she finishes speaking, Vinn grabs my hand and leads me back to the bedroom, making no effort to hide the mischievous grin spreading over her face.

Neither Vinn nor I have a car, but the thought of leaving the warmth of my unit for a cold walk to the el didn't appeal to either of us. As a result we pull up to our destination in a 1976 Gremlin. Our Uber driver claimed that it's a classic, but the loud exhalation of relief I hear coming from Vinn as we exit the car indicates that her opinion of our ride coincided with my own.

Professor Gilcrest lives in the suburbs but as an apparent courtesy to Vinn she arranged our meeting for a location in Lincoln Park not far from Vinn's condo. I've never been to the Heritage Bicycles General Store, which doubles (triples?)

as a coffee shop. Walking in, it's hard not to notice the bikes hanging from the wall and the ceiling, bicycles in various stages of repair off to one side, plants lining a shelf on one wall, and dark picnic tables sitting adjacent to a counter where I see Gilcrest placing her order.

As we approach and offer the usual greetings, a glance at the drink options reveals about half a dozen coffee options and one simple reference to "tea." Not willing to take the chance, I opt for a bottled drink out of the refrigerated case in the rear. I trail Vinn and our host as we're led to one of the tables, where I'm surprised to see a young woman already seated.

"Vinn, Malcom, this is Amity Fischer. She's the niece of a friend of mine and the reason I asked you here. Amity, these are Professors Achison and Winters. You can trust them." As she speaks, Gilcrest lowers herself next to her guest. Vinn and I take seats across from them.

Amity remains silent, biding her time and thoroughly checking us out as she first stares at Vinn before moving her eyes to me. I take advantage of the pause in the conversation to do the same. She's young, maybe eighteen or nineteen, with fair skin and blonde hair tied up in a bun. She's dressed simply in a cotton dress without any jewelry or makeup that I notice. Her hands have a death grip on a cup of coffee that is still filled almost to the top.

Vinn takes the lead and speaks softly, reassuringly, to the nervous girl. "Amity, I don't know what Professor Gilcrest has told you about us, but she hasn't said a single word about you or what type of issue you're hoping to find assistance with." I give an involuntary shudder at Vinn's ending the sentence with a preposition. I assume Amity doesn't care. "Since we don't know what your story is, we don't know if we can help. But as long as we're all here, why don't you relax, take your time, and when you're ready fill us in on the details."

Amity bites her lip, staring at the table as if it will tell her whether or not to reveal why she summoned us. Apparently it suggests she go ahead, as she begins speaking in a quiet and wavering voice.

"It's not me, I mean, not my story, not really." She pauses, uncertain how to proceed. "It's about my friend Rachel Yoder. I'm—we're—Amish. We live in Indiana. I mean, I do. She did. Rachel I mean." This isn't starting out well, but Vinn and I remain silent and continue to focus on Amity with what I hope are sympathetic expressions. Professor Gilcrest shifts uncomfortably in her seat.

"Have you heard of Rumspringa? That's the time, a kind of rite of passage the English call it, for Amish teenagers when we're allowed to see what life is like outside of our community. Amish people live simply and by a strict set of rules, so life can seem boring for young people. We're naturally curious about how other kids our age live. So when we reach a certain age, in our area it's sixteen or our junior year of high school, we're allowed to do things that are usually prohibited. We can dance, drink alcohol, ride in cars, and even visit the city. The idea is that we'll get all of our wildness out of our systems, recognize the benefits of a simple and pure life, and choose to remain in the community under Amish rules."

She pauses, longer this time, barely perceptible moisture forming in her eyes. When she resumes, the waiver in her voice is more obvious. "Rachel and I were in the same class, so we did Rumspringa at the same time, but not together. She was more curious than I was about some of the things other kids our age do. She wanted to see it all. Me, not so much. We were friends, but I'm different from her. I like my life the way it is. So I experimented a little bit, but still slept in my own bed every night and mostly kept living the way I always have."

Amity's voice cracks completely and she pauses, staring at a spot on the table. After an uncomfortable few moments, Professor Gilcrest puts her hand on the girl's shoulder, makes eye contact, and nods. Amity takes a deep breath and starts again.

"Rachel and a group of other kids decided to come here to Chicago to party and to really cut loose for a while." She swallows, tears now freely leaving a trail down her cheeks. "The rest of them came back. Rachel didn't."

A long period of silence, combined with Amity's silent sobbing, eventually clues us in that she would go no further in letting us know why we're here without prompting. I lean forward in her direction.

"Amity, do you want us to find Rachel, is that what you're asking?"

My question, which I assumed was the logical next step and completely non-threatening, brings on a near breakdown from the poor girl. Vinn and I both turn our heads to Gilcrest, who's only slightly less overtaken by emotion than Amity.

"No, you don't understand," she begins, taking over the tale. "The police already found Rachel. Dead. It's important to Rachel's family and her friends to know what happened. The police say it was just random violence, that she was in the wrong place at the wrong time. They say they're investigating, but it's clear that they aren't putting in much effort. We want you to find out why she died."

Vinn and I exchange glances, each of us sharing the same thought. Vinn's better at the gentle let-down than I am and she expresses what both of us are thinking. "Anna, as difficult as it is to hear, sometimes the cops have it right and this really could be just what they're saying. Senseless, but without any real reason."

Gilcrest closes her eyes tight, her lips compressed, then opens up both and stares at us as if we're uncomprehending idiots. "No. It's not. We didn't know this until we saw the coroner's report, but whoever killed Rachel did more than take her life. He also removed a bone from her forehead. It's missing and no one can explain why."

# THREE

"Crazy. Muy loco."

If I'd expected anything more than a terse muttering that reflected my own thoughts from Leo, the tenant in my basement unit, I had set myself up for disappointment. We sit in our customary spots across from each other at his kitchen table, the time somewhere between midnight and way too late to be up, the bottle of potent mystery booze that began full when we sat down and now down to its last gulp sitting between us. Since we first met when I bought the building with Leo already a fixture in it, much wisdom has been dispensed each way across this very table in the wee hours. Or at least it's passed for wisdom to alcohol-impaired minds, but on this evening I've drawn a blank. I shouldn't be so reliant on this ancient man who claims to be a Cuban in witness protection for trying to assassinate Fidel Castro even though he most certainly hasn't been within ninety miles of that island, but he's been surprisingly inciteful in the past. Usually when sewing or patching up knife and bullet wounds on my body, but if that's what it'll take tonight I think I'll pass.

"Muh friend," he goes on, either his mouth or my brain slurring every word, "you are best when you don't know what to do, when you let instincts work instead of your head. Follow your gut and you'll be okay."

That pearl of wisdom will apparently be the best I'm going to get today. I thank Leo, take five minutes finding the door and getting it to stop moving long enough for me to pass through, then head upstairs to my own abode. I must have made it, because the next thing I'm aware of is way too much light pouring through my bedroom window and a non-stop cacophony of annoying music playing somewhere near my pillow.

"That's the best he could do?" It was the ringtone I'd

programmed for Vinn that was responsible for the unwelcome concert that woke me up. My discomfort didn't get any better when I actually answered the phone, Vinn's derisive comments echoing loudly among the drummers beating heavily behind my forehead.

"I'm sure Hallmark has an inspirational card for this occasion that would be equally pithy and for $1.25 saved you a headache," she continues way too loudly. "Well you're in luck. I've got all of the ingredients for a hangover smoothie that'll make your troubles go away. Be here in thirty. It's time we did some research."

It's more like fifty minutes due to my efforts to try to look presentable before heading to her place, but if Vinn's giggles upon opening the door are any indication, the extra time was wasted. Not quite the sympathetic reaction I was hoping for, but she does take my hand, guiding me to the couch before heading to the kitchen, where I'm sure she intentionally runs the blender twice as long as is necessary. It takes all I have not to give her the satisfaction of seeing me wince.

The mixture in the large glass she presents me with looks vile and smells worse. I hesitate in bringing it to my resistant lips, but before I can react Vinn takes hold of my hand, guides the glass to my mouth, then with her other hand grabs my hair and tips my head back. Despite my sputtering and near drowning, she continues to hold me in that position until the flow of liquid evil stops. Not done torturing me yet, she produces a spoon and scrapes the overflow from my chin, feeding it to me like an infant. I don't trust myself to speak, but my feelings must show in my expression.

Vinn only smiles. "Trust me, I'm a scientist. That glop got me focused for my 8:00 genomic technology class many a morning. Close your eyes, relax, and count silently to twenty."

I follow her instructions, and sure enough the clouds

begin to clear and my headache fades. I look at her in wonder, she gives me a squeeze, then her face takes on the "it's time to get down to business" look that I know so well.

"Since Leo's demon rum didn't open up a path for us, I thought I'd do the next best thing and approach our problem logically." Vinn is never more in her element than when she's being sarcastic and subtly acknowledging her superior brainpower. "In this case, research. Before we start talking to Rachel's family and friends, let's see what we can learn about the Amish and in particular, Rumspringa. But before we get to that, we need to decide whether to go down this path at all."

We make eye contact, probing the other's inner thoughts, but we know each other too well to hold onto that facade for more than a few seconds. Despite our past brushes with death that began with an identical "let's just see what we can find" attitude, the challenge of an indecipherable puzzle combined with an ingrained desire to help people in need and egos that believe we're the only ones with the skill sets to do so, make our involvement a foregone conclusion. I'd be lying to say that Amity's tears didn't play a role as well. Besides, we can always stop if things get too crazy, right? A slight nod of my head and we're both headed to the couch.

Her laptop is sitting open and I can guarantee that she bookmarked the best informational sites she read in detail earlier this morning but will pretend that we're discovering together. Her fingers fly so fast around the keyboard that it would be impossible to prove my point, so I just play along for the sake of expediency and relational harmony.

Much of the information we see at first is already general knowledge for both of us and some reflects what Amity told us. The Amish culture is inseparable from their religious belief that God calls upon them to lead a simple lifestyle of hard work, discipline, and a strict adherence to their faith.

They value humility and a calm demeanor and believe that no one individual should stand out from the other members of the community. Many of them shun modern conveniences such as electricity and automobiles. While they don't isolate themselves from outsiders, they mainly socialize among themselves and school their children separately from the greater community.

I'm still on the section about school when Vinn snorts derisively. She reads faster than I do, so I skip ahead to find the reason for her disgust. It doesn't take long. The site describes the Amish belief that men are the heads of household and that the ideal roles for women are as wives, mothers, housekeepers, cooks, and gardeners. Many women do have businesses of their own but are clearly meant—at least officially—to be subservient to their men. Vinn reacts by closing out the page.

"I think we've seen enough about that," she says. "Can you imagine kids in today's world growing up in that environment? I'm surprised that any of them stick around to keep the Amish going. How can that be?"

"It's what they know," I say, trying to prove that even non-geniuses can have occasional insights. "And don't forget, without electricity they don't have laptops or computers, which means no internet and limited access to news from the outside world. And who knows how the non-Amish lifestyle is portrayed as they grow up. I'm sure someone who's been to an Amish school and listens to Amish preachers sees the rest of us as sinners and our world as the epitome of evil."

"Hmm." Vinn's thoughtful. "Still, they must see other kids their own age and at least be curious. And teenagers in any culture are just naturally rebellious. Which I guess explains Rumspringa. Let's take a look."

More flying fingers. Vinn brings up several websites, each with some information not contained in the others. Amity's brief description gave us a basic foundation. We discover though, contrary to the initial impression we each had, that Rumspringa isn't the Amish's blessing to go nuts. When kids reach the age of 16 or thereabouts, they're allowed to socialize much more often and openly. Since they're not yet members of the church, the rules observed by adults don't technically apply, so pushing boundaries, especially at that age, is almost a given. How far they push depends on the individual teenager. Some might simply wear flashy clothing, or dance, or try alcohol, or participate in sports. For the most part it's tame, but not always. Officially, it's also a time when the children should be considering who to settle down with in marriage. "Bundling," which consists of lying together on a bed fully clothed and talking into the early hours, is encouraged. Sex is not, but then again, their hormones are raging.

This period can last as long as two years. At some point the child has to make a decision to either get baptized and join the church, get married, and settle down in their own home, or to go their own way. Most choose the former, and their period of freedom from the rules ends. For those that don't, they can still keep in touch with family and friends but may be distanced from the community at large. I want to make sure I have this clear in my head.

"So if these articles are to be believed, when Amish kids reach their teens—the exact year varies—the restrictions they've lived under their entire lives are relaxed and they're allowed to do pretty much whatever they want, or at least the adults look the other way. Some of them treat it as a free pass to drink, have sex, drive a car, go to the movies, and so forth, for months or years, until they're ready to decide if they want to remain a member of the community or leave it behind."

Vinn frowns. "That's probably oversimplifying it, but yeah, it does seem like they're turned loose to sew their wild oats with the idea they'll get it out of their system, recognize the superiority of the Amish lifestyle, then return and get baptized, to sin no more. According to one of the articles we just read, they often form groups and go crazy together. Amity suggested that Rachel did just that, and apparently ended up in the big, bad city. I guess we have a starting point." She doesn't sound enthusiastic and I know why.

We've been here before. Each of us knows that once we step away from the computer and start an actual investigation outside the safety of our living rooms, we commit ourselves to finish the job no matter what difficulties we encounter. It's in our DNA, not to mention the conditioning we both received in the dark worlds we used to inhabit in prior occupations. Since leaving those lives behind and meeting each other on campus as mild-mannered professors, we've done it twice together and each time almost lost our lives in the process. It's a big step.

I turn to Vinn just as she turns to me. "Yep," I say. "We need to go meet the Amish."

# FOUR

At least she isn't laughing in our faces, although Professor Gilcrest must be wondering whether Vinn and I deserve whatever reputation she seems to think we have for getting to the bottom of someone's troubles. As brilliant as Vinn is, and as street-smart as I should be, you'd think one of us would have thought things through before calling to request the phone number for Rachel's parents.

To her credit, Gilcrest is making a mild effort to make us feel less foolish. "A few of them actually do have cell phones, mostly shop keepers or tradesmen who feel they're at too much of a competitive disadvantage if they can't be reached by suppliers or potential customers. But in those cases their use is restricted to calls related to their business. As far as phones, even old rotary models, in the home? Not a chance. There's a community phone in the Shipshewana general store where you can leave a message. That's how I reach Amity. It might take a day or two for them to get it, and there's no guarantee you'll get a call back."

Vinn mutters a quick thank you and hangs up without asking for advice as to other ways to reach the parents, most likely to keep the illusion going that we're sophisticated sleuths who have answers for every situation. She casts a sheepish look my way.

"Oops," she says with a slight smile. "Nothing like totally embarrassing yourself on the first full day on the job. At least I didn't follow up to ask for their email addresses. Any ideas other than the obvious?"

"Nope," I admit. "I can't imagine a worse way to meet the family than cold-calling as complete strangers who want to ask personal questions about the daughter you just lost, but I don't see that we have a choice. Unless maybe we pose as door-to-door butter churn salesmen?"

Vinn pretends she didn't hear me, which is probably the right move. She's already anticipated what I was going to say—minus the butter churn comment—and has pulled up Google maps on her laptop. "I knew there was an Amish presence in Indiana, but I always thought it was further south. Shipshewana is near the Michigan border, about fifty miles east of South Bend. A little over two hours. If we leave now, we can grab a late lunch when we get there before approaching the parents. Fortify ourselves."

Stall, is what she really means, which I'm totally behind. I rummage around her home office looking for a notepad while she arranges a Zipcar for the day. A notification on my phone chimes to confirm that I rented a Honda Civic and that it's ready and waiting for us. My surprise isn't at the efficiency of Zipcar, but at the fact that I didn't know I had a Zipcar account or that Vinn seems to have access to my credit card numbers.

Vinn brews her coffee while I steep some tea from the selection I keep at her place, in this case a Yunnan black tea for the caffeine. Unlike most black teas, it's golden in color, and soon the room smells of a hint of chocolate and honey. I rinse two thermoses out with hot water, we pour our beverages of choice inside, and we're ready to hit the road.

The Zipcar station is only about a ten-minute walk from Vinn's unit, but by the time we get there we're both praying that the heat works in the car. Vinn pauses and inhales deeply before taking off one glove to pull up the app that unlocks the car. She gets into the driver's seat, probably assuming that I would speed once we hit Highway 80, which is true, and also that if we get stopped last night's tippling would still be on my breath. Maybe true.

I adjust my seat, find the belt, and settle in as Vinn starts up the car. "Since you're driving," I tell her, "I'll navigate. I've got my GPS ready to go. What's the address for the parents?"

Vinn's blank stare tells me all I need to know. The super detectives strike again. It's going to be a long day.

We're quiet as we proceed east along the Indiana Toll Road past the belching and odorous smokestacks of Gary and on into the countryside. The scenery has nothing to hold my attention, mostly open fields and a never-ending parade of eighteen wheelers, but the lack of diversion gives me time to let my mind work, which it sometimes does. Discovering where Rachel's parents live will probably just be a matter of persistence in asking enough of the locals. There's always someone who's more than happy to be the first to spill a secret to a complete stranger. Once we get to the front door, though, is where I find myself stuck for an approach that doesn't seem morbid, insensitive, or just plain cruel. These people are living with a parent's worst nightmare and don't need a city man and woman to pour salt on those wounds.

Vinn's mind often works in ways totally foreign to my own, which can be both an advantage and an annoyance in working together toward the same goal, but today she's apparently on the same page when it comes to our first step once we reach town. We're close according to the highway signs directing us to take upcoming exit 107 and the ancient, faded wooden signs for the Shipshewana flea market.

"Let's head into town and find a place where the locals eat," she says, breaking our silent meditations. "If we order a generous amount of food, schmooze a little bit with the waitress, and leave a big enough tip, we may get directions to their home on our first try."

One exit and a few turns later, we're heading south on a rural two-lane road surrounded by endless fields that in the summer were bursting with corn, soybeans, and any number of crops that I probably wouldn't recognize. Three speed limit signs in close succession, each ten miles per hour lower than the one before, indicate we're on the outskirts of town. Just as the first few buildings come into view, we're caught up behind an open horse-drawn buggy. From behind, all we can see are the shoulders and head of a man in a dark coat and straw hat, the woman beside him wrapped up tight in a wool shawl, her head covered in an off-white bonnet. The tops of two small heads, mimicking the straw hat and bonnet of the adult in front of them, pop up periodically as the buggy bumps along toward town.

"Am I allowed to pass them?" Vinn wonders aloud, but the question almost immediately becomes moot as a line of cars traveling in the opposite direction force us to stay in our lane, plodding along at a horse's pace as we enter the metropolis of Shipshewana.

Our slow crawl allows both of us to scout for a promising place to eat. The town is no different from hundreds of other rural areas I've passed through over the years. One main street north and south, one more east and west. A smattering of shops line the two main drags, but look beyond them in either direction down a side street and it's a block or two of well-maintained homes. We pass the Shipshe General Store, a mercantile shop, two shops selling ice cream and fudge, and a couple of touristy gift shops. Looking ahead, it appears that the business district ends within the next block or two.

"Maybe we should just park and walk around to find a place to eat," I suggest. Vinn nods, and immediately angles into a space to the right. We're apparently on one of the few stretches that hosts parking meters, but at a dime for an hour it's not worth moving the car. Ten cents in Chicago would buy enough time to walk about five paces away. Not far from us we can spot the Blue Gate Restaurant and Bakery and head in that direction. A sprawling complex of food service, gift shop, and theater, it gives every appearance of the type of place Cracker Barrel tries to emulate, including the line of tourists waiting to be fed.

"Um, maybe not quite the local hangout we're looking for," I whisper to Vinn. In response she pulls out her phone, taps a few keys, and without a word spins around to head back in the direction we just came from. I hustle to catch up, but not before grabbing a flyer off of a small rack promising a guide to what to do and see in the area.

We take a right at the next block, walking away from the bustle of the main shopping district, then a left at the next intersection. Vinn suddenly stops and looks up from her phone, confused. We're in front of a large, four-story building and can hear the faint sounds of carousel music filtering out from inside. We approach the front door warily. At the same time a family exits, allowing us to peer past them to see what lies within.

"It's a mall, kind of," Vinn states, leading the way. We catch the door before it shuts and step inside, our noses immediately assaulted by a not entirely pleasant mix of scented candles, popcorn, perfume, body odor, and, from somewhere, cooking food. Casting caution to the cold winter winds, we wander around like bloodhounds trailing the scent of our next meal. It might have been easier to look at a directory, but we eventually find ourselves on the third floor outside of Millie's Market Café. Glancing inside, the simple tables with mismatched chairs host a few touristy types, but tables filled with groups of teens and farmers from central casting predominate. This is the place.

No line here. We're escorted to a table by a middle-aged woman who neither smiles nor frowns at us, making me think we're being evaluated before she makes up her mind whether to be pleasant or not. Menus are quickly placed in front of us, water glasses filled. Time for operation "Charm the Locals Into Revealing an Address While We Stuff Our Faces" to begin.

Gone are the lists of Amish foods, or foods that the Blue Gate wants tourists to think that Amish eat, such as fried chicken, meatloaf, beef and noodles, and fried fish, and in their place are about a dozen sandwiches and wraps that do anything but excite the imagination. The menu promises homemade soups and pie, though, so that seems a direction worth going. We decide to order a bowl of soup and a sandwich to split. Need to leave room for the pie.

Our server is a young blonde woman with the clearest complexion I've ever seen, either still in high school or recently graduated. She introduces herself as Renee, pulls out her pad with pen poised, and waits. Before I can exhibit my charms, or perhaps acting quickly to prevent just that, Vinn addresses the woman in her best "helpless woman in distress" tone.

"Hi Renee, I'm Vinn and this is my friend Malcom. We just kind of stumbled onto this place and don't know anything about it. What's good here?"

Poor Renee has heard this before and offers the company line. "It's all good, it just depends what you like." That's it, she's said her piece.

Vinn isn't ready to give up. She leans in Renee's direction, lowers her voice, and speaks in a conspiratorial whisper. "No, Renee. I'm sure everything is just wonderful. But what do you eat? Or what do the locals come here to eat? You can tell us, really." As she finishes, Vinn gives a broad, friendly smile that she uses on people when she wants something or likes them a lot. She's never used it on me.

Renee looks around nervously, a sure indication she's about to reveal the establishment's deepest, darkest secrets. When she talks, it's hard to hear her. "Don't order any of the sandwiches on there..." she gestures to the menu, "If you like noodles the cook sometimes makes a cheesy dish with lots of vegetables too. I can ask him if he'll do it for you."

"That would be great, Renee, thanks!" The poor girl beams like she's won the lottery. "And bring us each a bowl of your favorite soup."

Renee hustles away to the kitchen while I appraise my companion. "You're shameless," I tell her. She only shrugs in response.

Within minutes, we're presented with two bowls of chicken corn soup, followed almost immediately by the famous chef's special. The soup is fabulous, especially when some of the fresh bread from the basket on the table is dipped into it. The noodle dish is, in a word, horrid. We can see Renee casting glances at us as we eat, so making faces other than those of extreme pleasure are out of the question. We do our best.

The lunch hour is long past and the place is emptying out, but we stick around and order a slice of pie each, blueberry for me and lemon for Vinn. Vinn asks Renee if we can buy her a piece and if she would sit with us for a minute to tell us a bit about the town. I'm shocked when the girl returns with three slices, hers being a banana cream, along with our check.

"So, Renee, what sights shouldn't we miss while we're here?" Vinn's laying it on thick. "We don't have a lot of time today but may come back. We're from Chicago, so not that far away." As Renee responds with a few shops and the flea market, I glance at the flyer I picked up as if I were following along. One detail is hard to miss. There's the Yoder farm, the Yoder Department Store, Yoder's Meat and Cheese, and Yoder Hardware, among others. It may be hard to track down the right Yoders without some help. I refocus on Vinn pretending to be transfixed by every word Renee says.

Renee won't see it, but I notice the slight changes in Vinn's eyes and her tone of voice. She's about to get to why we're really here.

"Renee," Vinn says quietly, looking around as if she's concerned about being overheard. Conspirators again. "The real reason we're here is to talk to Rachel Yoder's parents. I'm sure you knew Rachel or at least heard about what happened to her. Her friend Amity asked us to help, which we want to do, but we don't know where they live. Can you help us?"

A sudden freeze hits the table. Renee's face changes instantly from friend to foe, her head rapidly turning in every direction to make sure no one overheard Vinn's request. She's clearly frightened, or nervous. Without saying a word, she stands and exits the table, leaving a half-eaten piece of pie behind.

Vinn sighs. It's only now that I realize that I didn't open my mouth once in our entire exchange with Renee. Would my manly charms have made a difference? There's a first time for everything.

I reopen the flyer. "Maybe we try the general store next. Isn't that where the gossips in small towns supposedly gather around the pot-bellied stove?" I pause as Renee sweeps by to take my cash for the meal. For her troubles, and to cover her angst, I leave a hugely generous tip. Not her fault there's apparently a code of silence for all things Rachel.

We're putting our coats on when Renee returns with our receipt, handing it to me in silence before instantly retreating. I begin stuffing it into my pocket when Vinn stops me, holding onto my arm.

"Mal, wait. Pull that back out."

I do so, looking at the itemized total for our food. Does Vinn think we were overcharged? As if reading my thoughts, she slides her hand up to my wrist and twists it gently so that the back side of the check is visible. There, in blue ink, is a hand-drawn map to the home of Rachel's parents.

# FIVE

The map is greatly appreciated but crudely drawn, seemingly based on the assumption that we're familiar with the area. Once back in the warmth of the car, we take some time to compare the sketch with a Google Map that Vinn brings up on her phone. By doing a mental overlay of the two, we at least figure out the first third or so of the journey. We have to hope that the topography makes sense or that a couple of the landmarks Renee wrote in help us the rest of the way.

Turning right at the main intersection of the town, it takes us about four seconds before we leave the shops behind and another two or three before we find ourselves once more in the midst of snow-dusted fields. The dashboard clock says there's still some afternoon left in the day, but already tinges of darkness are casting shadows, an unnecessary reminder that nightfall comes early this time of year. I need to use the flashlight on my phone to follow the map.

"It looks like we're going to be turning left at a T-intersection where a dragon is perched at the southeast corner."

Vinn doesn't take her eyes of the road but her lips compress, which is never a good sign. "Well that should make it easy to find then." I think she's being sarcastic.

With few roads of any type bisecting the endless fields, we travel along at a good clip, our eyes focused ahead searching for any signs of a fire-breathing beast. Even the navigator himself is beginning to think we missed a turn somewhere, but where? Just when I'm ready to admit defeat, Vinn's eyes, much better than mine, catch something up ahead.

"The dragon!" she exclaims excitedly as she starts to slow down. Sure enough, we approach an intersection where the only way to turn is to the left. Nestled in the field on the far corner is an ancient wheat harvester, a double-sided feeder looking everything like a pair of folded wings, the platform and engine that serves as its body supported by metal wheels for legs, and a long conveyor ramp stretching up as the neck, bent back down at the end to emulate the head. It's probably been sitting there rusting for forty years, which is why Renee felt comfortable using it as a marker.

We make a slow turn onto a dusty dirt road. No traffic to worry about here, so Vinn turns to me to seek guidance. "So what do we look for now, a herd of unicorns?"

"No, you missed those while you were focused on the road earlier. Now we turn right at the box with an apple on top."

I won't repeat the word she utters, which offends my sensibilities, but within a few seconds a roadside farmstand appears on my side. No fruit in sight, although an orchard behind it filled with apple trees is what we in the profession call a clue. Without prompting from me, Vinn turns right.

This road is barely wide enough for one car and well-worn ruts keep us from drifting into the fields that threaten to envelop us on either side. The jostling and bumping make it impossible for me to read the small writing on the map, so Vinn stops and taps her foot impatiently.

"Eggs," I tell her. "On your side. All it says on the map is eggs."

We start moving slowly, our eyes scanning the roadside for eggs, which sounds as absurd as it feels. After about a mile a driveway appears on the left. On one side sits a black covered buggy, a large cardboard sign fastened to its rear facing the road. In a large scrawl, the last 's' smaller than the other letters and squeezed in to fit due to poor planning by the sign-maker, is the word "EGGs." Vinn eyes me, shrugs her shoulders, and turns in. In retrospect it makes a lot more sense than finding a large pile of them.

About a hundred feet down the driveway sits a weathered white farmhouse, overdue for a paint job by about thirty years. A front porch with two rocking chairs and a swing adds to the Midwestern rural stereotype. The yard around the home is neat and uncluttered. The drive continues to the right, ending at a small barn with a buggy similar to the one we passed on the road resting outside. Vinn parks the car a short distance from the house. I wait for a porch light to come on as recognition that the home's occupants know we're here. It's several long seconds before I realize my error.

"It'll be dark soon and farmers eat dinner early. We came all this way to see them, we can't sit in this car forever. I'm not looking forward to it either, but it's show time."

With those words, Vinn leaves the car, pressing the lock button by habit. I catch up to her, grab her hand more for my own comfort than hers, and together we walk to the door. I still have no idea what we're going to say.

After my mental lapse with the porch light, I know not to look for a doorbell. Taking a deep breath, I rap loudly on the door. The sound echoes within the home before everything falls eerily silent again. I'm about to try again when I hear faint footsteps approaching. Vinn is biting her lip, an unconscious habit she does when extremely nervous. She claims she only started after she met me.

A girl of about twelve dressed in a dark blue, long-sleeved dress that falls to just above her ankles and a white apron answers the door. Her hair is wrapped neatly in a bun, which in turn is covered by a lace cap. She stares at us with what appears to me a mix of uneasiness and curiosity but remains silent. They may not get many visitors outside of the local Amish community. After a few awkward moments, Vinn finds her voice.

"Hello. My name is Vinn Achison and this is Malcom

Winters. Are either of your parents at home?"

Just as she finishes her question, a solemn-faced woman dressed identically to the girl, down to the blue dress and bare feet, steps behind her daughter and examines us from toes to head as she makes up her mind what to say. The resemblance to the girl, even apart from their apparel, is uncanny. Clearly mother and daughter.

"Jacob is out back. What is this about, if I may ask?" Her tone doesn't reveal if she considers us friend or foe. My guess is that the jury is still out but leaning toward the latter.

I instinctively decide, perhaps without foundation, that they might consider a man to be more of a voice of authority, so I jump in ahead of Vinn. "We're, uh, investigators from Chicago, Ma'am. Are we speaking with Mrs. Yoder?" An almost imperceptible nod encourages me to go on. "First of all, I'm so sorry for your loss and can't imagine how you must feel. We're looking into the circumstances of Rachel's death and wonder if we could have a few words with you and your husband."

Her expression unchanging, Mrs. Yoder makes a decision and nods us through the door, escorting us to a room immediately to the left. Simply furnished, it consists of a plain-colored couch with a quilt neatly folded over the top, several wooden chairs, and an unfinished wooden coffee table. Vinn and I claim the couch.

"Esther, go fetch your father," Mrs. Yoder tells her daughter before moving in the direction of lamps fastened to the door frames on either side of the room. I watch, fascinated, as she lowers a lever on the wall fixture, then pulls a match off a nearby table and strikes it, raising it into the glass lamp from beneath. Instantly a small light appears then increases in intensity until it's blinding to look directly at it. A faint odor of propane drifts in our direction.

I'm so distracted by the lamp-lighting process that I don't see Esther return with her father until Vinn pokes me. Mr. Yoder is tall and husky with an unkempt beard falling six or more inches from the lower part of his face but no mustache. His shirt, mostly hidden under a black jacket, is a dark gray but from the waist down the black reappears, including his workman-like shoes. I can't help but notice the button fly on his pants and the lack of belt loops, which would explain the suspenders.

He stands hovering above us, staring without saying a word—a family habit. Before he addresses us he turns to his daughter. "Don't you have chores to do?" No sass here as the girl immediately exits the room. I watch her as she goes, wondering if she bears a resemblance to her sister. It occurs to me that we were never provided with a picture of Rachel. I look around the room and notice there isn't a single photograph anywhere.

Mr. Yoder waits to hear the back door slam then turns his attention to me, as if Vinn doesn't exist, his face even more dour than his wife's. "Well?"

"Mr. Yoder, as I explained to your wife, we're investigators from Chicago looking into the circumstances of your daughter's death. To start, we're wondering if you could tell us a little bit about her, about what she was like." I wait for him to ask for identification or to challenge us in some way, but instead face a wall of silence. It drags on long enough for me to debate whether it would help or hurt to bring Amity's name into the mix. I decide to meet his silence with my own.

His eyes are piercing and send a deep chill throughout my soul. I begin to fidget, and I never fidget. This was meant to be an easy question as a prelude to asking for details about Rachel's behavior during Rumspringa, which might be more uncomfortable for him to answer. It shouldn't take this long to describe your own child.

"Difficult." Mr. Yoder's body doesn't move and the one word seems to be all I'm going to get. Time to try a different tact.

"Maybe a little more detail. Was she a good student? Did she have a boyfriend? Did she get along with her sister?" I try to include Mrs. Yoder in the conversation but she's sitting in a far corner of the room, her hands knotted tightly. She looks away when I glance in her direction.

"No." I'm not sure which of my questions he's answering, or if he's telling me that he doesn't care to go on. He quickly and directly answers my unspoken thoughts by standing up and sending a signal to his wife. "We have work to do. Goodbye."

With that, he leaves the room. Mrs. Yoder motions us to follow her to the door, and without so much as a word or a change in the frown that first greeted us and has been there ever since, opens it for us. Reluctantly, Vinn and I step out into the chill. We're not going to get anything more here today.

As we move toward the car, a flash of movement from behind causes Vinn and I both to turn around. Esther is hurrying toward us, looking nervously in all directions as she walks. We pause and wait for her to approach.

"I doubt you got what you came for," she acknowledges, a little breathlessly, her eyes constantly moving between us and the house behind her. "Our...my...parents aren't much for talking, especially with strangers. Rachel was a good girl usually, but she and our parents had been fighting a lot. She was shy and didn't think she was as smart or pretty as others her age, so when anyone would pay attention to her she would do anything they asked just to feel like she belonged. That's how she fell in with some other kids who weren't exactly saints. She changed. Ma and Pa noticed but they didn't really know why or what she was up to. If you want to find that out, you need to talk to Rachel's friends, especially the ones she hung out with for Rumspringa. Seth, David, and Margaret. If they'll talk to you."

Before we can follow up, Esther lifts the hem of her dress and hurries away as fast as she can. Vinn and I look at each other, sharing the same unwelcome thought. We're going to have to come back.

# SIX

"Am I the only one that felt unprepared?" I ask Vinn over breakfast. Nothing elaborate today, just some store-bought bagels, farm-fresh cream cheese, and a fried egg over the top. I sip an Indian black breakfast tea infused with lavender and lemon grass, which claims to have a calming effect on whomever consumes it. A well-intentioned present from a gift exchange in the English department before the break for the holidays, it's not something I would buy for myself. It tastes like I'm drinking a floral garden. The calming element must be working, though, as I refrain from throwing my mug across the room. Vinn, as always, opts for coffee.

"Not to your liking?" she taunts, a smile betraying the pleasure she takes whenever my fine tea obsession works against me. She rightfully calls me a snob, but adamantly denies she's the same way with coffee despite the fact that we've spent an hour at a local coffee roaster sampling various bean combinations before she committed to buying a pound. "No, I felt the same way. I guess doing our homework for half an hour online before running headlong into a culture that's so foreign to us wasn't enough. Maybe we could have been better educated on how to connect with the Yoders, but I doubt they would have spoken with us under any circumstances."

"Agreed. Nevertheless, before we go back and try to engage the kids Rachel hung out with, both her long-term friends and the three she hooked up with during Rumspringa, we should be a little more thorough. Not only on the Amish, but we don't know the first thing about how Rachel died or if the cops have a theory about who did it or why a bone from her forehead was removed."

Vinn tops off her coffee, glancing with amusement at my still-full cup. "We did seem to jump into this investigation at second base without touching first." I make a face. She hates most sports and it's not like her to make a baseball analogy, and a poor one at that. I say nothing as she continues. "You know what we need to do, right? How are you getting along with Jenkins? You've always had a better relationship with him than I have."

London Jenkins is a detective with the UIC campus police force. I get along with him better than Vinn does primarily because the first time we met when Vinn wanted to report a missing person, she questioned if he was old enough to be a cop and threw forms he asked her to fill out back across his desk. Granted, his baby face does make it look like he should be in high school, but Vinn's never acknowledged her behavior might have been a little out of line. They've made up since but are still wary of each other.

"We get along fine. He really appreciated the tube of acne cream I gave him for Christmas." Okay, it was a bottle of scotch. "The real question is whether he's got any pull with the Chicago cops left. They may still think he has some connection to the severed head that was left on the doorstep of that precinct captain."

Vinn lets out an involuntary giggle. The cops had good reason to think we were involved in that incident, which we were, and brought us in for questioning. Jenkins got pulled in as well simply because he had assisted us in getting some information on the unfortunate headless man. Both he and Vinn were perfunctorily examined and released in minutes. I was grilled for six hours. They had no hard evidence to back their suspicions, and as far as I know the case remains open.

Despite the early hour I make a call to Jenkins and leave a voice mail asking if he can use his connections to get us the police file or murder book on Rachel Yoder. While I'm doing that, Vinn moves to the couch and opens up her laptop.

As a scientist there's nothing she likes better than the chance to do research, and she's good at it. I flop down beside her.

"Let's start with seeing what we may have missed on the Amish, then we'll see if we can pull up any news articles on Rachel's death. Move closer, Mal." I snuggle close and put my arm around her. "That's better."

Most of what we're finding repeats what we read a couple of days ago, although we do learn that there's a wide range of how stringently various communities follow the rules. The 25,000 Amish in the area around Shipshewana, the third-largest congregation in the nation, are stricter than most. Even within that one area, some families adhere to a more conservative lifestyle than others. The Yoders are clearly on that end of the scale.

We read on. It's a set of principles grouped together under the term "Gelassenheit" that discourages the use of modern technology such as electricity, cars, and electronics based on a belief that they would do more to divide a community than to bring it together. That, along with a religious belief that God wants them to isolate themselves from those with different outlooks, dictates that they mostly keep to themselves within the Amish community.

Vinn and I sit and digest this information for a while. The arm I have wrapped around her is falling asleep, so I decide to make one of my smooth moves and pull it away while turning toward Vinn as if to say something. Now all I need is something to say.

"That was instructive, I guess," I begin, an obvious stall while my brain is searching for the right combination of words to string together. "And goes a long way to explain the reception we received. But where does it get us in solving Rachel's murder? We already know that she used Rumspringa as the reason for distancing herself from her old friends, latch-ing instead onto some ne'er-to-dos and coming to the big, bad city."

Vinn looks thoughtful. "Yeah, we're getting the big picture and becoming more educated about the Amish in general, which I guess is useful in some respects. I mean, at least we know now not to ask if they have a picture of Rachel." True. While not strictly prohibited, most Amish prefer not to be photographed and a portrait-style picture is thought to be an exhibition of vanity. It explains the lack of photos in the Yoder home. "But I feel like we're looking at the community from a distance. It's like the difference between reading someone's Facebook page and actually talking to them. Before we go back, it'd be nice to speak with an insider personally."

"All right, I'll concede that. But I don't think meeting with us is an experience Amity would want to repeat and we don't have any Amish connections. Do you have any ideas?"

"I do have one thought." The mischievous sparkle in her eyes sends warning signals through my brain. "Since we're still kind of lost and could use any sort of help from anyone, maybe we should try to find someone who grew up Amish who'd be willing to talk with us. I don't know anyone, and I assume you don't either or you would've mentioned it. Now..." she's dragging this out with obvious glee... "who do we know that seems to have personal connections with an incredibly diverse group of people and just might be the right person to ask?"

It's clear she has someone in mind and that the question is rhetorical, but I'm drawing a blank. Then suddenly it hits me what she's suggesting and I blanch. "Vinn, no, I really don't think that's a good idea. I mean, we're not that desper—"

Vinn hands me my phone. "Why don't you give her a call?"

When I bought my three-flat after deciding to set down roots in Chicago, I inherited Leo as a tenant in the garden apartment. Ted, the businessman in the unit between Leo and my top-floor home, I found on my own. Business major to business executive aggressively climbing the corporate ladder with no qualms about squashing anyone who stands in his way. I have mixed feelings about my decision to offer him a lease. On the one hand, he pays rent on time and, unlike Leo, pays in U.S. currency instead of faux-Cuban delicacies. In the negative column, he's loud, obnoxious, arrogant, and just an unpleasant person to be around. I never would have renewed his lease if Leo and I hadn't discovered his alter ego, Rebecca. Ted used to hide his feminine side from us but once we let on that we knew, he sheds his suit the moment he gets home from his job and transforms into a kinder, somewhat more tolerable soul. Rebecca at times tries to emulate women as seen through Ted's eyes, which could border on insulting to the female gender if she weren't so sincere.

"Hello, darlings," she intones as she flounces by me and on to the living room, where she sits in her usual chair across from where Vinn is perched on the couch. It's a rarity to see Rebecca in anything but a dress, even in winter, but today she's a vision in a red pantsuit with a green blouse underneath, her apparent nod to Christmas past. She's holding a holiday cookie tin, which I pray holds makeup, sewing materials, or anything but cookies.

"These are for you, Malcom," she says sweetly as she extends the tin out in my direction. "Macaroons are just to die for, don't you think? For my first try, I think they're just divine."

A smirk that only I can see crosses Vinn's face as I hesitantly take possession of Rebecca's offering. One of Rebecca's many hobbies is to try to recreate dishes that she's eaten without the benefit of recipes. I'm not sure what her success rate is on this endeavor, but I've never been given anything but her failures. I quickly deposit the tin on the kitchen island.

"Thanks so much, Rebecca. It's a little early in the day

for sugar, but I'm sure Vinn and I will delight in sampling them later." I take satisfaction in seeing Vinn's smirk instantly disappear. She tries to hide it by jumping into the conversation.

"Rebecca, Mal and I are looking into a situation involving a young Amish woman. You've shown in the past that you have connections with a, let's say, diverse spectrum of local people. The individuals you assembled to help us when we needed assistance with the Chinatown murders were as invaluable as they were, um, unconventional." With this, Rebecca sits up alertly, repositions herself to the edge of her seat, and almost drools in anticipation. Vinn picks up on this and smartly moves to tap down her expectations. "No, don't get excited Rebecca. We don't need that kind of help, at least not yet. We're just getting started and think it'd be helpful to get some first-hand information on the Amish lifestyle, in particular habits of younger people and how their minds work. Do you know anyone in the city who used to be Amish that would be willing to talk with us?"

Rebecca slides back into the couch, clearly disappointed. She saved our asses on an earlier adventure, in part by putting together a team of assorted fringe personalities that indicated how wide her social connections are. Being asked to tap into that same pool of locals without getting her hands dirty is obviously a let-down.

She sighs as she rises from her chair, glancing over longingly at the tin of macaroons, apparently in the middle of an internal debate. Please, I say wordlessly, take out your disappointment in us by reclaiming the tin. Do it. No such luck.

"I don't know of anyone offhand, but I'll ask around and let you know." Without so much as a goodbye, she saunters out the door, slamming it loudly.

Vinn shrugs her shoulders and smiles. "Cookie, anyone?"

# SEVEN

The café and bakery on the main drag of Greektown isn't that far from campus, but neither Vinn nor I have been here before. She orders a double espresso to take off the chill while I look around to locate Jenkins. I finally find him in a far corner, several tables away from the nearest customer, but he's not alone. The man sitting next to him isn't a familiar face.

Vinn grabs her coffee and also appears puzzled as we approach the table. They're certainly an odd-looking couple. Jenkins with his dark complexion, youthful appearance, and skinny physique topping off at maybe just over five and a half feet tall, his companion a head taller, with the look of someone who's been on the job too long. Hispanic, maybe of Mexican descent. Jenkins rises as we approach, extending his hand.

I grasp it warmly while Vinn pretends not to see as she lowers herself into the seat directly across from the stranger. I can tell we're being evaluated as the man's eyes take us in. Under the microscope first with the Yoders, now here. Hopefully we'll find a better reception than we did with Rachel's parents.

"Vinn, Mal, this is Officer Mendez of the 18th District. He's one of the officers assigned to investigate Rachel Yoder's case. He's heard of you from when you helped solve the Chinatown murders. The top brass may not approve of you, but Officer Mendez appreciates your results. Also, I've vouched for you."

Mendez gives a slight nod, his facial features remaining impassive. He may be appreciative but that's still a far way from accepting. Still, there must be some reason he's here. He wouldn't be if Jenkins didn't think he'd pass on something of use.

Vinn decides that a female's touch is needed and takes the lead. "Officer Mendez, thank you for meeting with us. Just so you know, we have no intention of stepping on your toes or hampering your investigation. We don't even know yet that we're getting involved at all. A colleague asked us to look into Rachel's death. We at least want to be able to tell her that we covered the basics."

Mendez stares at Vinn as she speaks, glares at me, then relaxes his shoulders, a decision having been made. His voice, when it comes, is deep and low.

"There's not much of an investigation for you to hamper. It's been a couple of weeks since she was discovered and we've got squat. From all appearances, it was a random act of violence. Her body was found behind the monkey house at the zoo by an unlucky couple who were there for the Zoo Lights festival and thought they'd find a quiet place away from the crowds to grab a quickie. She'd been there at least a couple of hours. Strangled, probably with rope or a cord. It was rough but clean, suggesting the guy knew what he was doing. Not sexually assaulted, no signs of anything out of the ordinary, except..." Mendez stops, uncertain if he should go on.

"We know about the bone from her forehead," I tell him.

Mendez nods. "Yeah, about that. Clean cut so it wasn't like a lion escaped, but then a sloppy removal and he didn't even take the whole frontal bone. Just a small piece. No idea if that was intended or due to the perp being in a hurry or maybe he got interrupted. Nothing in the database to connect it to other victims anywhere in the country or to tell us what that was about. We don't even have any plausible theories."

"Were you able to get anything out of her family or friends? We met with her parents and got about three words."

Mendez makes a face. "Three more than we got. They

wouldn't talk to us. Not that we thought they'd be much help anyway. There's no reason to think they were involved and with a kid that age, chances are the parents didn't know what she was up to anyway." He sees me about to interject and puts up his hand. "Yeah, we know about Rumspringa. There should be a series. Amish Gone Wild...

"We did track down the kids she came here with. There's a hostel up on Arlington not far from the zoo where Amish kids who come to the city have been staying over the years. Cheap, clean, and in the heart of the action. We were able to get to them there before they fled town to the safety of the country. Lots of false bravado but they were clearly scared, naïve, and totally ignorant of what happened to Rachel. They claim that she left them after the first couple of days and that they never saw her again. No reason not to believe them, and the front desk seems to support their story."

Mendez reaches down beside his seat to grab a folder that must have been sitting in a backpack or bag of some sort. He takes a sheet of paper out of it and slides it across to Vinn.

"These are the names of the kids. Boss doesn't think it's worth us driving three hours to Indiana to talk to them again. He's probably right. From what I hear you've had some success in getting to the bottom of a couple matters after we stalled. Good luck if you decide to try with this one. There's not much more I can tell you. And I hope it's not necessary to say, but don't tell anyone that we met and I'm not your source, so don't call me at the station. If anything pops I may or may not tell Jenkins here, but don't count on it. This file is already headed for the unofficial inactive pile."

Mendez doesn't offer a hand as he stands and leaves us without another word. Our mood discourages Jenkins from sticking around and making small talk, so after a few moments of awkward silence he rises as well.

"See you back on campus in a couple of days" he says as he walks away. Shit. I had completely forgotten that I have a job and that I need to be ready for my first class. I had unconsciously put my lesson plans on the unofficial inactive pile.

"He's right," Vinn confirms, peering at me over the top of her laptop. "Not that I didn't trust him, and he's obviously got better access to resources than Google gives me, but I can't find any information on cults, cultures, or serial killers where removing a piece of the frontal bone is a thing. I'm beginning to wonder if an animal carried it away, but for that to happen it would have had to be exposed, so it gets us nowhere."

Vinn's frustration is evident as she thinks aloud. Our conversation with Mendez provided a good number of negatives but very little in the positive column. Combined with Rebecca informing us that she's put word out looking for anyone Amish or Mennonite without any success so far—"but will a salesman of Amish furniture suffice?"—we're looking into a great void of nothingness. There's some consolation in our history of having been in this position before, but not much.

I'm spreading peach rhubarb jam on an English muffin when I stop with my knife in mid-air, do a double take at the label on the jar, and close my eyes while I mentally give myself a well-deserved lashing. I've been so focused outward that I missed what was right before my eyes, or at least sitting on the top shelf of my fridge.

"Vinn, I'm an idiot," I begin, hesitating for a moment to admit my failure, which gives Vinn a chance to jump in.

"If you think that's a revelation to me, think again," she smirks. "Now are you going to tell me how your mental deficiencies manifested themselves this time?"

In response I pick up the jar of jam, screwing the top on as I move to my living room, and hand the jar to Vinn. Her jaw may have hit the ground.

"You've got to be kidding me." She stares at the jar, with its simple label touting the freshness of this product straight from the kitchens of Yoder's Meat and Cheese in, where else, Shipshewana, Indiana. "Where did you get this?"

"There's a tiny Amish grocery down the street on Western, only a few minute's walk away. They carry health foods and some jams, honey, and other provisions from local farmers and artisans. I go there occasionally to find foods I can't find anywhere else. They also serve some kick-ass ice cream." Time to try to save face. "This has been in my refrigerator for so long I never made the connection."

"Are they open now?" she asks. I nod. "Okay, genius, get your boots on. Time we take a walk."

The short stroll was still long enough that by the time we enter the shop under a tinkling bell, I can't feel parts of my face and I think I left my nose somewhere around the last corner. The wind has been gradually increasing in strength over the last day, bringing with it a fierce cold snap. The store is miniscule compared to the mammoth chains, a simple box slightly longer than it is wide. Two aisles were created by placing portable shelving stocked with food in the middle. A glance or two is enough to take in all that it has to offer, which makes up in variety what it lacks in volume.

Vinn immediately heads toward the jam and jelly section. I'm not surprised when the young woman who always seems to be here when I drop in hustles up from the back. For the life of me I can't remember her name, but I've been coming here for over a year and at this stage it would be humiliating to ask. On the bright side, I'm sure she doesn't remember mine either.

"Mr. Winters, welcome back." Dammit. "Can I interest you in a freshly-baked gooseberry cheese bar?"

"Sounds delicious." I mean it. "Maybe on the way out to take with us. This is my friend Vinn. We're looking into a tragic event that took place a couple of weeks ago, the death of a young Amish woman here in Chicago. I was wond—"

"Oh, you mean Rachel Yoder! Yes, that was so terribly sad. Of course all of us in the community are heartbroken." She turns her head toward Vinn, who was drawing closer, jar of jam in hand. "Hello, I don't believe we've met. My name is..."

At that very moment a semi-trailer rumbles by outside, blowing its air horn, and I don't catch her next few words. Vinn has a memory far better than mine, certainly good enough to be able to fill me in on our way back to my place. By the time my ears stop ringing, she's picked up the conversation, holding the jar of jam out for my nameless friend to see.

"Do you know the Yoders? Mal and I made a trip to Shipshewana a few days ago and got kind of a chilly reception. We need to go back, and it would be helpful to have someone put in a good word for us. Or maybe you could just help us understand how an outsider can approach the Amish without appearing disrespectful or intrusive."

"I don't know them personally, no. At least not these Yoders. It's a very common name among us. I'm actually from Iowa, and we have Yoder families there too. We place our orders for the jam online..." She must see the surprise on my face because she feels the need to explain. "Yes, we can use computers for business—and it's delivered to our door. I've never been to Shipshewana so I don't know anyone there. Who is it you want to talk to?"

"Rachel's classmates and friends," I interject. "We just want to get a sense of who she was, and maybe some details about her visit here."

"Ah, I see. With younger people you might have more

luck than with the older generation. Their curiosity about the English—that's what anyone not Amish is called—is at its peak with teenagers, before they commit to the church. You may find that they want as much information from you as you do from them." She pauses and blushes before continuing. "In some ways they're not too much different from other teens. Not suspicious enough of strangers, and easy to bribe with food. Treat them to a couple of Big Macs or some Oreos, and you should buy enough of their attention to give you what you need.

"Now, about those gooseberry bars? Only two? I think you need at least four, just give me a minute."

She disappears into the back, giving me a chance to whisper to Vinn and ask what the woman's name is.

"You don't know?" she giggles. "How long have you been coming here? Maybe you should ask her yourself some time."

I'm about to respond, not kindly, when the subject of our exchange returns, paper bag in hand. "Here you go. I don't know if it will help, but I also wrote a short note asking whomever you meet to cooperate with you, that you're friends of mine. It's in an envelope inside the bag. Now, did I tell you that we just churned some brittle chip ice cream this morning?"

Back in my apartment, Vinn takes possession of the envelope before I can open it to see what it says and, just as importantly, to seize the opportunity to see the signature. She's stubborn, and the more I push about the name—which has become more important to me now that it really should be—the harder it'll be to convince her to tell me. I'll just need to steal the note at some point.

Vinn does at least tell me what it says. "Not much, just vouching for us personally as good people and asking whomever to help us if they can. That was nice of her."

"Yes. When do you want to go? I'm not sure what's open on Sunday there and then we have meetings the next couple of days before classes start on Wednesday. Next Saturday, I guess?"

"I hate to wait that long, but I guess we'll have to. Anyway, I've got to review my notes and finish preparing my syllabi. Are you all set? Ready for a new semester?"

The last time I lied to Vinn I ended up risking severe bodily harm on a pair of ice skates. This time, I choose to remain silent.

# EIGHT

Institutions of higher learning as a general rule do an adequate job of providing an education to their students, but if there's one thing that they inarguably do better than anyone else, it's hold meetings. At the beginning of every semester UIC sticks to a pattern of starting with a general lecture by the President to all staff, then proceeds through a series of ever-narrower groupings. After the first assembly yesterday, a pep rally which was identical to the one in August with a few word changes to the speech, we were separated into various colleges, then into schools. Today we're further divided into departments, then majors, and soon will probably be sectioned off by height. Yesterday it was easy to hide in the back or skip a meeting entirely. Today, not so much, which means I'll no longer be able to avoid my boss, Stuart Vanguard.

Stuart hired me under the mistaken impression I was someone else. I needed a job at the time so while I didn't do much to encourage his error, I also didn't correct him. Sometime during my first semester of teaching he began to suspect the truth but couldn't admit it to his higher-ups without looking foolish or incompetent. The fact that it's hard to spend more than five minutes with Stuart without concluding that he's both a fool and incompetent, so that the administration already must see him in that light, totally escapes him and serves to protect my job. Besides, my English classes have been wildly popular and are actually used by the school in marketing campaigns to high school juniors, so he's stuck with me. That still hasn't prevented him from looking for any justification for sending me on my way.

The English department meeting, our last of the day, is being held in the same classroom in which I've taught creative writing to freshmen. I decide to sit in the same seat that was the favorite last semester of Cindy Meyer, who planted herself in the very spot my eyes seemed to focus on as I lectured, just to get the perspective she had of me. Other bleary-eyed faculty members filter in, none looking overly excited to be here. I'm slouching down in my seat and biting the end of my pen while I play with my hair as Cindy used to do when I feel a presence behind me, which is quickly followed by a familiar, squeaky voice.

"Mr. Winters, welcome back. I trust you had a good break?"

I respond without turning around. "It was outstanding, Stuart. Four of the world's highest peaks in three weeks. Only eleven more for the top fifty. How about you?"

If he's impressed by my fictional climbing exploits, he doesn't say so. Instead he leans down and whispers in my ear, his tone defiant. "I was very tolerant of the riff raff that traipsed in and out of your office last fall and of your general misbehavior, you and that Professor Achison, but be aware that this year I'm going to draw the line."

Without waiting for a response, he hustles down the aisle to take his place at the lectern. He has the lights dimmed and begins a power point presentation on academic excellence and how to achieve it in which he reads the words on the screen, which are identical to those on the handout, so I let my mind wander.

If I were an Amish Cindy Meyer, eighteen years old and newly exposed to the world at large, what kind of an approach would it take by someone twice my age to encourage me to cooperate? I glance around at my colleagues, most of whom are also mimicking our students by ignoring Stuart and watching YouTube videos on their laptops, and try imagining that some of them need Cindy's help. I quickly realize that wearing a suit like Clive has on gives off too much of an authoritarian vibe, while dressing too young like 40-ish Victorian literature specialist Marian, whose cleavage leaves little to the imagination, would only subject the adult to ridicule. Vinn and I will need to be casual but grown-up enough to command at least a little respect, and steer Rachel's friends into thinking they're helping us of their own volition rather than because we're asking them to, and to avoid pulling the adult card. And most importantly, as my friend in the Amish grocery suggested, to make clear that if they don't cooperate they don't get treated to French fries.

My mind snaps back to attention as the lights come back on. At least two of Stuart's audience were so rapt that they're having trouble waking up. Stuart is oblivious and shows no sign that he's ready to call it a day as he concludes his presentation with the obligatory "Are there any questions?"

I raise my hand and speak at the same time, another habit picked up from my students.
"Do you believe that King Lear offers a nihilistic vision of humankind devoid of all hope or do you see the king's reuniting with Cordelia at the end as Shakespeare's offering a glimpse into the possibility of relief from despair such that Lear's death is actually a moment of triumph?"

Stuart is momentarily stunned, which gives my co-teachers the chance to contribute. "Yeah, I've always wondered that." "Great question." "Is there a power point for this?" As one, we all sit up and move to the edge of our seats. Stuart, in typical Stuart fashion, blushes six shades of red, each deeper than the last, before he mutters "class dismissed" and hurries to the door.

Saturday morning finds Vinn and I once more driving east to Shipshewana, this time with an actual agenda which in theory will produce better results than our last visit. With so few hard facts to push us in a particular direction, or to get started at all, our best bet is to find out as much about Rachel as possible in the hope that some small, otherwise insignificant fact about her life will be the thread that helps us unravel the circumstances of her death. What were her interests, who did she hang out with, what kind of young woman was she? Maybe somewhere in answers to these questions there'll be insight into what she got herself into in Chicago.

Having met her parents, neither Vinn nor I think that their daughter would confide in them, especially about her baser desires and dreams. That, and the fact that they've already said all that they're going to say to us, leaves us with her friends. Despite this obvious next step of our inquiry, it's also where we face our first hurdle. Other than the names of the kids who she accompanied to the city, who we prefer to save for last, we don't know who her friends were or how to reach them, or even if they'll talk to us. Before we left Vinn reached out to Professor Gilcrest to give her an update and ask for Amity's assistance, but Gilcrest seems to think that her job was done after making the introductions and only stayed on the phone long enough to tell Vinn that Amity's parents put the kibosh on any further meetings with the English. We're left hoping that inspiration will hit us during our drive, but so far no ideas have miraculously appeared. Our confidence level is not high.

I pull out the local chamber of commerce's flyer I picked up on our last visit and start reading it over. "None of these businesses sound like places that kids, Amish or not, would hang out at. The closest mall is probably a hundred miles away. This will be a little more difficult than dropping by the food court."

I glance over at Vinn, who appears to be deep in thought. Underneath her down coat, she's got on a pair of jeans and an MIT sweatshirt, which is her idea of appearing approachable. She insisted that her look is exactly what we discussed: casual, but in such a way that young adults will respect her for the brain she obviously has. I'm not so sure. My own choice is dark khakis with a denim shirt. Kind of a restrained cool. Vinn wasn't thrilled with my selection either.

"And what are the odds that any kids we do find will be Amish and were Rachel's friends?" she asks rhetorically. "I don't know how big the local pool of Amish teenagers is to begin with, and the only kids that will be allowed to speak with us anyway would be teenagers on Rumspringa. It may be not only be an impossible task going from place to place looking for them, it won't produce results. Like it or not, I think we have to approach them through the adults. Appeal to their sense of justice. And make use of the letter from your friend in the jam store."

She's right, I don't like getting the grown-ups involved, but unfortunately what she's saying also makes sense. I stick my nose back in the brochure. "I think our two options are Yoder Meat and Cheese, which is on the south edge of the downtown area, for no other reasons than I like their jam and it's probably a busy place on the weekend. Number two is the Shipshe General Store, on the north side of downtown across from the feed mill. Also two reasons: my stereotyped perception that in small towns the general store is a gathering place for locals, and also their Facebook page says that they have, and I quote, 'neat stuff.' Who doesn't like neat stuff?"

Vinn makes a sour face but probably realizes that unless she has a better idea, it's at least some sort of an approach, one more than we had a few minutes earlier. We're shooting in the dark anyway, so starting out at two random locations based on illogical reasoning has just as good a chance as trying to think this through. Armed with our new plan, we drive in silence toward town, successfully doing our best to hide our super high spirits.

We park outside the general store, opting to make it our initial stop only because driving in from the north it's the one we come to first. Stepping inside the door, we're immediately confronted with a sensory overload of goods of every sort jammed onto shelves stacked nearly to the ceiling. Shirts and pants, slippers, books, music, packaged foods, candy, Presidential salt and pepper shakers, toys, greeting cards, purses, and more, including special after-Christmas sales on ornaments and garlands. It's what dime stores used to be decades ago, a place full of everything where you could spend hours browsing but never finding whatever it was you actually came there for.

Contrary to our expectations, the store isn't crowded. It probably had its pre-holiday rush and now people are happy to hide from the cold near a fireplace and to postpone any purchases of Disney Princess wristbands. Vinn takes the lead and approaches a middle-aged Amish woman straightening stacks of postcards behind the counter. The woman looks up, surprise showing on her face, before adopting the universal fake smile of all salespeople.

"Hello, may I help you find something?"

"I'm hoping you can help us. We're from Chicago and are investigating Rachel Yoder's death. We're wondering—"

"I'm sorry," the woman interrupts, suddenly abrupt and stern, the smile gone, "but I meant can I help you find an item from our store. That's what we provide here."

Vinn persists. "Yes, I understand that, but we're hoping that you—"

"I'm sorry, but I'm quite busy. You can certainly look around, but perhaps it would be best if you went on your way. Goodbye and have a safe trip back to Chicago."

Vinn stands stunned as she stares at the back of the woman hustling her way to a curtain leading to the safety of a back room. She turns to me, open-mouthed and wordless. I gently take her elbow, leading her past the display of commemorative cookie tins and out the door.

Once inside the car, Vinn lets loose with a string of words that we don't teach our children. For once, I need to be the calming influence.

"Vinn, you couldn't have done anything differently and gotten a different result. But maybe we've learned that the direct approach isn't going to work. Take a couple of deep breaths, and when you're ready let's head down to Yoder's Meats. My turn to give it a try."

Vinn starts the rental car, closes her eyes, her lips counting to ten, then opens them up with a new look of determination. She may swear like a seasoned sailor in taking out frustration, but doing so somehow seems to infuse her with new life and the motivation to keep going. She pulls into traffic. Well, into the street. We appear to have this portion of town to ourselves.

We travel the few blocks down to Yoder's Meat and Cheese Company and pull into the nearly empty front parking lot, easing into in a space close to the entrance. Unlike the general store, the first impression here upon entering is one of a well-maintained, clean, organized delicatessen, with a welcoming scent of cured meat lingering in the air. Like the prior store, this shop also is virtually empty, which might explain the eagerness with which a woman approaches us, a friendly smile leading the way. We might be her only customers so far today. Except for her warmer demeanor and lack of Amish attire, she could be a twin of the woman from Shipshe's. Vinn tenses, expecting the worst.

"Hello, welcome folks. My name's Francis. We have some of the finest meats and other products in this area of the state. Cheeses you won't find anywhere else. Locally-made jams and candies. Please, take your time and look around and let me know if I can be of assistance."

Vinn still appears suspicious as Francis retreats and I

need to pull her in the other direction. We browse. I'm surprised by the wide selection of coffees, which also hold Vinn's interest, but the teas are limited to a few nationwide brands of bagged leaves. I pull a jar of Harvest Jam off the shelf and head to the counter.

"Francis, we're from Chicago and you may not believe me, but a little store in my neighborhood carries a few flavors of your jam. I've grown to love them and wish they had as many flavors as you do!" Francis beams. "I want to take some home, but you have to help me. What is harvest jam?"

"Oh, you picked one of my very favorites. It's like spreading the holidays on your toast. It's got cranberries, orange peel, apple, pecans, and cinnamon. I might be forgetting a few, but that's most of them. Would you like a taste?"

Before I can answer, Francis produces a spoon from a hidden pocket, wipes it on her apron, then opens the jar and dips the spoon in, holding it out to me. She's right, it's an explosion of flavor and I tell her so. Vinn arrives at my side with coffee bag in hand just in time to get her own spoonful, same spoon, and she also offers the highest complements. Francis seems beside herself with joy. Time to keep the momentum going.

"Francis, one thing I noticed," I say as I nod at the bag in Vinn's hands, "is that you don't seem to carry a lot of tea."

I appear to have killed the mood, as poor Francis all of a sudden deflates. "You know, I love tea myself but there's just not much call for it in this area. People around here drink what we call meadow tea, which is an iced tea made from mint. Coffee's the preferred drink I'm afraid. There are times, especially in weather like this, where a good Earl Gray would hit the spot."

Time for Operation Cheer Her Up. "Francis, I tell you what. I'm kind of a tea nut myself, as Vinn will attest." Vinn nods, playfully whispering "snob" behind her hand. "I used to travel quite a bit and have teas from China, Japan, India, and others that are nearly impossible to find anywhere. I may even have some Earl Gray. Why don't you write down your name and address for me while I go grab a jar of apple butter, and because you've been so kind, when we get home I'll send you some."

Francis looks like she's going to cry with joy. I tuck the paper she offers into my jacket pocket, place a jar of apple butter on the counter, and tell her we're ready to be rung up. As she's doing so, a broad grin brightening her visage, I know it's now or never.

"Francis, I don't know if you could help us, but Vinn and I traveled down here today because we're looking into poor Rachel Yoder's death. It would be ever so helpful if we could talk to a few of her friends to give us some background. Do you know how we might go about that?"

Francis freezes, a fierce internal debate obviously raging. As she returns my credit card, she looks around the empty store and says softly, "Well, I don't know..."

Vinn leans closer. "Maybe this will help." She pulls out the letter we got from the Amish shop and hands it over. Francis reads it slowly, then goes back a second time before giving it back.

"I guess it wouldn't hurt. Rachel was a distant something to the owners of this store. My daughter knows a few of her friends. I'll see if she can get them together—one of them uses a secret cell phone. About a block up from here is the Wana-Cup Restaurant. Why don't you go have some lunch there and I'll see what I can do."

Vinn leans over the counter to give an awkward hug, an unusual gesture for her, and I squeeze Francis' hands with thanks. We gather up our jams and coffee, an optimistic buoyancy in our step.

# NINE

The Wana-Cup markets itself as an "Amish-style" restaurant, which if true means the life expectancy of the Amish must be somewhere in the 40s if they subsist on pizza, cheeseburgers, and chili dogs. I'm scraping the bottom of my second bowl of soup watching Vinn push her fried fish sandwich around on her plate when girlish chatter draws our attention to the door. Three teenage girls, two in jeans and sweaters and one in traditional Amish garb, giggle loudly as they make their way to our table. We're not hard to find, as the only other customer left thirty minutes ago.

The young woman in front, tall and blonde, speaks for the group. "I'm Ashley. My mom said you want to talk to some of Rachel's friends. This is Hannah and that's Ruth. They both went to school with Rachel."

Vinn changes seats to be next to me while the two friends shed their coats and sit opposite us. Ashley grabs the closest chair from the next table and draws it near.

"Thanks for agreeing to meet us on such a cold day. I'm Malcom and this is Vinn. We—"

"Ashley's mom said you'd buy us ice cream," Ruth interjects. The other two throw puzzled looks her way before nodding their heads vigorously. I know when I'm being conned, but what the hell. I rise and lead the way to the counter. Five minutes, one sundae, and two waffle cones later, we resume our seats.

"As I started to say," I pause and wait but there are no further interruptions, "we're looking into Rachel's death. As part of our investigation, we'd like to find out as much as we can about her. I don't have any specific questions right now but would just like to hear from you."

"Wait, I have one preliminary question," Vinn puts in.

"Ashley said both of you went to school with Rachel. But Ruth, are you Amish?"

Ruth looks momentarily confused, then catches on. "Oh, you mean the way I'm dressed. We're both on Rumspringa, so we get to dress however we want. Hannah's a bit of a dweeb…"

"Am not!"

"…but I couldn't wait to try some English clothes. Rachel was the first of us to put on pants, which surprised me a little. We grew up together and she's always been the reserved one. Shy I guess. The three of us were tight, at least until recently. I don't think Rachel ever made a decision on her own when we were together. It was always like, 'I don't care, you guys choose.'

"She was definitely a follower," she adds, her mouth full of cookie dough. "I think that's because of her parents. They're really, really strict."

"We've met them," Vinn says.

Ruth grimaces. "Then you know. Rachel probably was always told what to do at home and that made her into who she was. She was pretty, and smart, and would have been popular if she tried. But she had self-esteem issues and I don't think she thought much of herself, so she assumed no one else would like her either."

Hannah's been nodding in agreement at Ruth's description but decides to contribute her own thoughts. "There was one time, though, a couple of months ago. Remember, Ruth?" Ruth bobs her head. "We were walking home from school and Rachel started talking about how she hated her parents and her life and that they never gave her a chance to do anything or to be anyone other than who they wanted her to be. It was the first time I ever saw her angry. We were shocked. But then her house came into view and she looked scared, like her parents could overhear her from that far away. She shut down, fast."

Both girls look sad all of a sudden. "That was one of the last times we saw her. I miss her."

The mood has become solemn, but I need to keep things going. "I know this is hard for you, we won't be much longer. You say you were close friends, but then she traveled to Chicago with some other kids."

Ruth again takes the lead. "You have to understand that during Rumspringa, you see a lot of weird things. You can't predict how kids our age will react to all of a sudden being given freedom they've never had before. Hannah, here, has flirted a little with drinking and rode in a car once, and she's here talking to an English adult, but like many Amish kids, her life isn't that much different. I've gone a little further than she has. But Rachel..."

She lets her sentence hang. After a moment she picks it back up. "She went a bit crazy. I guess rebellion had been building up in her for years. She didn't see Hannah or I as the kind of kids who would break off completely, and if that's what she was thinking she was right. So she hooked up with Margaret and those idiots, David and Seth. They've never been straight Amish and they just carried her with them. Of course she followed, because that part of her hadn't changed."

Hannah points to a hidden spot under the table, probably indicating the clock on the contraband cell phone. "Look, we need to get going. Thanks for the ice cream."

"One more question before you go," Vinn quickly says. "Do you know what happened when the four of them came to Chicago?"

Hannah this time. "There's been so many stories and no way most of them could be true. You'd need to talk to those three. I can pass on a message if you buy me a cone to go."

We've clearly created a monster. "Okay fine. Tell them that if they meet us by the carousel between 4:00 and 4:30, we'll drive them to McDonald's for a Big Mac."

All three girls look crestfallen. They only got ice cream and missed out on the grand prize.

The promise of fast food must have been a powerful lure. The second hand has barely ticked past 4:00 when we see all three of our target teenagers as they top the stairs of the third floor of the same mercantile building where we ate lunch the first time we were in Shipshewana. At least I assume it's them. Two boys and a girl, dressed in a manner clearly intended to be the exact opposite of the plain Amish fashion: part punk, part goth, and all screaming "look at me, I'm a rebel." I try to keep my expression impassive, but Vinn can't help but roll her eyes.

In the time since I made my impromptu offer of forbidden burgers, we debated the propriety of transporting underage children out of town without parental consent, but were eventually swayed by the fact that they took an unaccompanied 130-mile road trip to the one of the largest cities in the country. Their affectations give us some assurance that they're well on the way to adulthood, although as they draw nearer the youthful faces that show through the layers of makeup on two of the three and past the nose ring on the third still give me pause.

Their swagger and effort to be too cool for the room could be an issue if they use it to try to take control of the interview. Vinn's on the same wavelength, and with an unspoken glance we both turn to watch the wooden horses continue their circular path and pretend not to notice the trio as they approach.

A voice comes from behind, barely audible above the obnoxiously repetitive calliope music. "Hey man, we heard you're looking for us."

We don't react. A few seconds later, I feel fingers tapping me on my shoulder, and another "Hey man" from behind. I turn, scowling, raising myself to my full height and try to make my eyes appear piercing. I'm not even sure quite what that means, but it sounds like it could be intimidating.

"Did you just touch me?" I growl, slowly turning my head to take in all three teens. Color drains from their faces and the initial look of confidence is rapidly replaced by uncertainty, a little fear, and maybe even some regret. Piercing, indeed.

"Um," the kid with the nose ring begins with the slightest tremble. "I didn't mean anything by it. I didn't know if you heard me. We were friends of Rachel. We heard that you wanted to talk to us. And that you'd take us to McDonald's."

I don't soften my features or my tone. "Maybe. We got most of what we need from some of her other friends earlier. I'm not sure there's much you can add."

The girl speaks up for the first time, her voice years younger than the appearance she tries to pull off. "We can! Lots! They weren't with us in Chicago. They couldn't have told you about that."

I do my best to appear indecisive before Vinn the good cop jumps in. "Mal, let's give them a chance. If they don't come through, well, then..." She lets it hang. All three pairs of eyes grow wide as they picture who knows what if they don't cooperate.

"Fine," I finally say in exasperation. "The car's out front."

I take the lead heading to the stairs while Vinn hangs back in the rear. I hear snatches of conversation between she and Margaret about fashion as Vinn continues to soften her up for later.

We didn't anticipate a full passenger load when we rented the Zipcar, so with the bulky winter coats it's a tight squeeze in the back seat. We may have to ration how much our guests eat or they won't fit on the way back. The closest McDonald's is in the next town, about a fifteen-minute drive. It's a quiet ride.

To the supposedly tough, worldly teenagers who pile out of the car, arriving at the golden arches is like Christmas Day. For many of us who've been exposed to wider culinary experiences, especially in a city known for its diverse and outstanding restaurants, it's difficult to see things through the eyes of teenagers who for their entire lives have been banned from the evils of English fast food and been limited to less imaginative, and the Wana-Cup notwithstanding, certainly healthier, fare. They've now crossed into forbidden territory and a Big Mac is enough to induce broad smiles of joy. The kids order value meals with extra apple pies and both Cokes and milkshakes. I ask for a cup of water while Vinn gets coffee and fries to share.

For the first time today there are people around, so we guide our prey to a table away from the other diners where we can speak openly. We wait until the teens each have the chance to devour half their burgers in a few massive bites before getting to the point.

"Take your time," I begin. "We need at least one of you to have a mouth free of food once in a while. Let's start out with how you knew Rachel and how it came about that the four of you decided to go to Chicago together."

The boy with the makeup, who I assume is David because he looks like a kid in my high school Spanish class named David, speaks for the first time. "The three of us, Seth, Margaret and I..." Bingo. "started hanging out together in eighth grade. I mean, the other kids are so lame, you know? But we're cool. Then when school ended—for us eighth grade is the last year of school—we just kind of kept together. None of us were friends with Rachel. She was one of the lamest."

Seth's turn as David crams a massive handful of fries into his mouth. "Yeah, I mean most Amish kids act just like their parents but they're okay. But she was super conservative and kept to herself. It surprised us when she ran into Margaret at Shipshe's and said she heard we were going to go to Chicago and that she wanted to come with. At first we didn't really want her to, I mean we don't even know her, right? But then we figured it would be cheaper to have a fourth tag along and share the cost. Plus then it would be two boys and two girls, you know?"

I swear David blushes a bit at the sexual undertone of Seth's last statement. I realize then that he's the third wheel and that Seth and Margaret are together. Seth may have thought that with Rachel along, he and Margaret could get more alone time. Worth looking into.

"So tell us what happened in Chicago." Vinn directs her question at her new best friend Margaret.

"Rachel didn't say much on the drive to the city, except to rag on her mom and dad a little and say how she felt like she'd been a prisoner her whole life. We can relate to that and thought maybe she'd be okay, but it didn't really work out like we thought. We got some beds at a hostel and started talking about what we wanted to do. You know, things we could never do in our little town. Nothing really over the top. See the lake and the zoo, try different foods, shop, try to sneak into a bar or grab some beer. She didn't want to come with us and hung out in the hostel the first day.

"The next day we were going to go to the Nike store on Michigan Avenue, maybe go to the top of the Sears Tower—do you know how expensive that is though?—and try to find an escape room or a club with music. She got kind of nasty and said you mean we came all the way to the city and that's all you want to do, and she accused us of being lame! Anyway, we left her in the hostel and when we came back she wasn't there. She came back late at night when we were in bed, didn't say a word to us, and then was asleep when we went out the next morning. That became the pattern for about a week, until one night she didn't show up. Didn't bother us and no way we thought anything bad happened to her. It was mostly just 'good riddance,' you know? We never saw her again and didn't know what happened until the cops told us."

The food is almost gone, and once it is their cooperation will end as well. "Did she say anything about what her plans were? About what she wanted to do that wasn't lame?"

The three exchange glances as if seeking answers in the others' eyes. "Nope," they say in unison. Seth adds, "Looking back we think she was just using us for the ride. She must have had her own agenda, but we have no idea what it was."

The last of the pies get consumed and the slurping of the bottom of the cups of milkshake indicate that the meal, and the interview, is over. The total cost of feeding the hoard was under $20.00, but I'm not sure we got information justifying even that expenditure.

We drop the teens off at David's home, a farmhouse with workshop attached just outside of town. As they walk away Margaret turns with a slight wave goodbye, but the boys never look back. It's dark now as we head for home. I drive in the direction of the highway, ready to discuss what we might have learned from our venture out here today. A rhythmic, steady breathing from the passenger seat postpones that talk. Just as well. It wouldn't have taken long anyway.

# TEN

Bright and early Monday morning, I join Vinn at her usual spot by the window in the campus cafeteria. I drop off my trusty thermal container of Keemum Mao Feng tea at the table and head to the cashier, where the muffin of the day awaits me. To start off the new year Manuel, the café manager, and I came to a truce. He lets me bring in my own tea as an alternative to the swill produced by the bags he sells and I purchase a muffin. I don't really care what flavor he chooses, as Vinn usually eats it anyway.

She wastes no time in breaking off her first piece while I unscrew the container, savoring the smoky, slightly floral scent rising from within. A deceptively mellow variety, it can pack a wallop of caffeine, making it one of my favorites for Monday morning before class. Vinn watches me with a bemused expression as I pour. She's not above making a snarky comment about what she calls my obsession, but today manages to refrain.

"Now that we've had a day to digest our trip out to Amish country," she begins, "what do you think? Did we gain anything at all?"

I did in fact spend a great deal of Sunday scrutinizing our talks with the kids from every perspective, trying to find some glimmer of a lead as to where to take our investigation from here. I try to put the best face on it. "I think so. We've now got some insight into Rachel's state of mind at the time she came to Chicago. If we can trust what they told us, we've also established when she disappeared. I wish I didn't believe them that Rachel basically deserted them and didn't accompany them on their ventures around the city, but I do."

"Yeah, me too," Vinn sighs. "They try to give the impression that they're hard-asses, but all I see beyond the surface are some scared, naïve kids. Still, they were the last people we know of that saw her alive, so I'm not quite ready to give up on them. They may know more than what they're telling us. We should at least try to verify their story before writing them off. That gives us a starting point."

"Right. The hostel. It's not all that far from your place, so we could hit it after classes today. When's your last one?"

"I have a lab that ends at 2:30, but then office hours until 4:00. You?"

I guess I should have been prepared for that question, but being the first Monday of the semester I'm not actually sure what my schedule is beyond my freshman American Literature class that starts in about twenty minutes. Being the twenty-first century, it's easy to post my class schedule for every day of the week on my phone. I wish I had done that. Instead I pull a scrap of paper out of my pocket. "Um, I'm done at 3:00. I'll swing by at four."

I cap off my mug, grab the muffin wrapper with only a few crumbs remaining, and make my way out to meet my new students. The first class is no time to have my mind drift to other topics, so I put Rachel out of my mind temporarily and try to remember what I might know about American literature.

The day gets off to a rough start, which isn't entirely unexpected. My freshman classes are always populated with kids pursuing degrees in science, business, engineering, and other areas but who need to fulfill a certain number of hours in the arts. They don't want to be in the class and don't mind showing it. It takes a number of weeks and the realization that the grade I give them counts just as much against their GPA as a course within their own major before they buckle down and take it seriously. Today when I ask random students to name their favorite American novel I get answers ranging from Japanese graphic comics to French poetry to "does online fan fiction count?" Rough start, indeed.

Things do get better after that. I find time between my Introduction to Writing Science Fiction class, referred to as "drafting for dweebs" by my colleagues in the department, and my History of the Short Story seminar to mail off a selection of teas from my personal collection to Francis in Shipshewana. I manage to avoid Stuart and even have time to look up the exact location of the hostel in Lincoln Park. I think about calling to let them know that we're coming but decide that doing so might get us a manager more interested in protecting themselves from liability than a desk clerk who might have useful information.

Students don't realize that the school day can drag just as much for the faculty as it does for them, but 4:00 does finally roll around and I'm eager to get out of Dodge and to head up north. I arrive at Vinn's office a few minutes later but pause when I hear quiet sobbing coming from inside her office. Only a few minutes pass before a student with puffy eyes exits, turning her head away from me as she hurries down the hallway.

"Happens every semester," Vinn explains as I pass through the door. "Top of her class at a small high school downstate, things always came easy for her. One class and one lab into her college experience and she feels lost and overwhelmed. Smart young woman, though. She'll be okay. You ready?"

Just west of Clark Street in the heart of the toney Lincoln Park neighborhood, the three-story brick Getaway Hostel belies the image that jumps into my mind when I hear the word "hostel." Envisioning a rundown hovel crammed with mattresses lined side to side resting on floors on the verge of collapse with every step, I'm astonished to discover a clean, spacious accommodation that would rival hotels charging five times the going rate in the area.

The young man behind the counter is busy with a group of travelers laden with backpacks when we step into the lobby. As we get closer we can hear them trying to communicate in a mix of German and broken English, apparently without great success. He looks frazzled but manages to make eye contact with us.

"I'll be tied up for a few minutes more. Why don't you take a look around and I should be able to help you by the time you get back." His attention immediately returns to the others and the cacophony resumes.

We wander the halls and my level of surprise and admiration continues to rise. They have a game room, a communal kitchen that wouldn't be out of place in a fine restaurant, a coffee bar, and computer stations complete with printer. Glimpses into a few of the rooms where the doors are ajar reveal a range of accommodations ranging from simple dorm-room style boxes with any number of bunk beds to more comfortable and spacious set-ups with rugs, writing desks, and private bathrooms. Flyers for weekly social events line a bulletin board above a small display case of tourist brochures. Vinn whistles through her teeth. "Where were these kind of places when I was young and carefree?"

I let slide that I don't believe the highly-driven Vinn was ever carefree, but I still get the point. To Amish kids used to simplicity, access to complementary coffee and computers and even the ability to flip on a light switch at night must be an awe-inspiring introduction to life away from the farm. I ponder what kind of reactions they must have to even these basic features and to the overwhelming unfamiliarity with modern living. Would they be intimidated, such that they would adopt a cautious approach to their time here, or would they flip their own switch, adopting an attitude that could mute any sort of sensible wariness of danger? I don't know the types of crime they have in Shipshewana, but I doubt it prepares them for what they could encounter in any large city. In the back of my mind, despite having written off her travel companions as suspects, I also wonder if it's possible that it could release behavior in themselves that might lead to violence against one of their own.

As we head back toward the lobby, the desk clerk approaches from the other direction, leading the tourists to their room. He raises a finger and then uses it to point behind him, signaling that he'll meet us there momentarily. He wasn't wrong.

"I'm so sorry you had to wait," he says wearily. "Now then. Have you stayed with us before?"

"I assume you have to deal with that a lot here," Vinn sympathizes. "You must be very patient."

The young man sighs and relaxes his shoulders, happy to find someone that understands the stress he encounters on a daily basis. "It's part of the job. Now how can I help you?"

Since he and Vinn are now simpatico, I let her take the lead. "I'm afraid we're not here to rent a room. We're investigators looking into the murder of a young Amish girl several weeks back. We'd like to ask you a few questions. I promise we won't take up much of your time. If you don't mind starting with your name?"

If he's flustered by the change of direction, he doesn't show it. "Dan. Daniel Hickman. I'm not sure I can add to anything you guys asked me the last time, but go ahead. Shoot."

"Do you remember the group she came in with?" I ask.

"Sure. Not that it's that unusual for Amish kids to be here. I think word gets around that we're economical and a decent place to stay when they make their trip to the city. That group kind of sticks in my memory only because of what happened. They were typical—excited, totally unprepared, lots of questions about the city. How to get around, things they can do, bars that might let underage kids slip in. We get that a lot but don't pass out that kind of information. They'll end up finding those places on their own anyway from talking to the other guests staying here."

He scribbles a few names on a scrap of paper and grins as he hands it over to Vinn. "These are the ones I've heard mention that are nearby. I figured that would be your next question."

"Good, we appreciate your diligence. Did they mix much with the other guests?"

"Not that I saw, but that doesn't mean it didn't happen. They stayed in one of our basic, cheapest rooms. Four beds, bathroom down the hall. So they had a room to themselves."

"Did you notice if all four of them stayed together?"

Daniel shakes his head. "I was going to mention that since you were asking about them mixing with others. I only noticed it because it was a little odd. When groups of travelers check in together, they almost always stay in the same pack when they go out for the day. They often join up with people they meet here, but rarely break off from their own group. It was different with those Amish kids. Almost from the start, it was three and one. Two of the males and one female would leave in the morning and come back together at night. The one girl left later and came back later, always on her own."

"Tell us about her, whatever you can," Vinn asks.

"Not much to tell. Young, but then to me they all look so young. Pretty in a juvenile kind of way. Reserved, at least to me. I don't think I ever heard her speak for the first three or four days, and she hung back when they checked in. She'd go out an hour or two after the others left. She wasn't with them when they came back either. She must have re-turned at night after my shift ended. The only time she ever asked me anything was when she wanted to know how to get to the zoo. I gave her a flyer and directions. It's a short walk from here. Come to think of it, that was the last time I saw her." I begin to ask if he knew that the zoo was where her body was found when a sudden explosion of noise drowns out my words.

The German travelers emerge from the door leading back to the rooms, speaking loudly and excitedly, crowding the front desk as we talk with Daniel. He asks them to hold on just a moment and turns his attention back to us. "Look, I have to get back to work and that's really all I can tell you anyway."

We say our thank yous and back away from the crowd as we head to the door. After only a few steps, though, Daniel calls out to us from above the noise. "Wait. I was going to call but as long as you're here I might as well ask. Is it okay to toss the stuff that girl left here?"

# ELEVEN

"We really should have called Mendez, or at the very least Jenkins, to collect Rachel's belongings directly from the hostel. They'll throw a fit." I could remind Vinn that she was as enthusiastic about taking possession of the box as I was if not more so, but I don't think she's genuinely having second thoughts.

"We can tell them that we took the box home for safekeeping and, as long as we're careful, swear that we didn't go through it. Besides, we didn't know if they would take five minutes or five hours to show up, or maybe not at all today. Five minutes and we wouldn't have had time to examine it, more than a couple of hours and we'd have had to give it back to Daniel before we left. He'd wonder why we didn't take it to the station ourselves and might have raised that issue with any real cops who showed up. In that case they'd do more than throw a fit, they'd charge us with impersonating police officers. No thanks, I'll take my chances this way."

We're sitting on the floor in Vinn's living room. Her condo is not only an easy walk from the hostel, in the event Daniel realizes we never showed him badges or represented that we were on official business, the cops wouldn't take long to figure out who we were but would descend on my place first because my name is already in their system highlighted with arrows and stars. That would still give us time to go through Rachel's things.

There isn't much. A few receipts, a small, cheap notepad with a few scribbles inside, a brochure from the zoo identical to those on a stand at the hostel, and four pieces of candy. For this kind of task Vinn and I would normally divide up the pile and then give summaries to each other, but with pickings this slim we took positions side by side, backs resting against the couch. Being the seasoned investigators that we are, we quickly push the candy and the flyer to the side. Vinn picks up the receipts.

"Mostly places she ate," she notes as she riffles through them on her initial pass-through. "In fact, that's all there are. Let's look at them chronologically."

The first several are quick service places near the hostel for the day she arrived and the day after, showing an interest in trying new cuisines ranging from Middle Eastern to Peruvian to Chinese, which may have been a shock to her system if the Wana Cup was considered adventurous eating back home. The only thing of note is that all of the receipts for the first two days are for a single portion. Either the group ordered separately, or she ate alone. They don't really tell us anything significant. Vinn sets them aside and picks up another.

"This next one is for the third day and it's the first receipt from outside the neighborhood. From Lou Malnati's pizza in River North. I guess it took her a few days but like every other tourist she had to try deep dish."

"Yeah, but there's something not right about this" I suggest. "Why did she go all the way downtown for it? There's an almost limitless selection of great pizza places within a short distance of the hostel. In fact, there's a Lou Malnati's about a ten-minute walk from there. What was it about this one that drew her there?"

Vinn studies the receipt for a minute in silence but the answer isn't there. "Right. It could be nothing. Or it was nearby something she wanted to see down there, although this location is up near the river away from most tourist sights other than the boat rides, and it's winter. Plus it's for dinner after most everything is already closed in the Loop. Could she have met someone there? Got cold or lost? Worth thinking about."

The next receipt jumps way over to the Humboldt Park neighborhood just to the west and north of Ukrainian Village.

It's named for the large park within its borders boasting two lagoons joined by a river, a fabulous old boathouse, a fieldhouse, music venue, and lots of open space. Recently it's been gentrifying as professionals priced out of nearby Wicker Park and Bucktown head west, although it remains a Puerto Rican area at heart. This is reflected in several of the receipts.

"Lots of Mexican and other Hispanic places here. From what she spent each time, probably just cheap little local dives. She could have done worse. Good food and interesting variety without spending much." Vinn sorts through them as she talks, going back to the beginning several times. "What they tell us is that she spent a lot of time in Humboldt Park. These are spread out over four days, with both lunch and dinner receipts on the same days. She could have just liked the park, but I can't see a young Amish girl from the middle of farm country coming to the city to watch the geese all day. There's a reason she was there."

"Agreed. But just as with the pizza place, I don't think she went there specifically to seek out the places she ate. It was something else, something the receipts alone won't tell us. Maybe we need to move on to the notepad."

"Hold on, Mal, we'll get there. Hand me the zoo brochure, would you?" She opens it up to reveal a map of the exhibits, brings the flyer close to her face, then asks me to verify the hours for Zoo Lights. A gleam in her eye indicates that she may be on to something. "Do you see this little 'x' and scribble next to the sea lion pool? Rachel wrote down a day and time, 5:45. The day matches the day she was killed, but the time is random. Zoo lights opens well before then. What's the one reason you would mark a time and location on a map? Mal, I think she was meeting someone."

Vinn hands me the map to see for myself. I admit that seeing Rachel's handwriting seemingly indicating a meetup sends a tingle down my spine. Only one issue. "If that's the case, why didn't she bring the flyer with her?"

Vinn sighs in exasperation. "She's a kid, Mal. She forgets things. Besides, these brochures are everywhere. She could have picked up another one on the way out of the hostel or at the zoo itself. It's not that hard to remember "sea lions 5:45.""

I concede her point, but the adrenaline rush from the map immediately crashes when we open the notepad and find nothing useful. A few random times of day, the name "Scott" underlined twice, and crude sketches of local landmarks. Could Scott be who she was meeting at the zoo? No way to tell. Vinn takes pictures of the entries and the receipts with her phone and places everything back in the box, making sure that there are no neat piles that would indicate anyone examined its contents. I take out my own phone, staring at it for a few minutes before pushing the number of someone who will not be happy to hear from me.

"You didn't think that maybe this was important enough to call Mendez as soon as you were told about it?" Jenkins is scowling at me, just as I thought he would. The box is sitting on his desk in the campus police department office.

"Actually that did occur to us, but we thought that perhaps you'd like to be the one to produce it and to take credit for finding it. Might be some brownie points in there from your Chicago compadres."

His sour face remains unchanged but I notice a flash of interest pass through his eyes. Jenkins has made no secret of the fact that he doesn't feel like he gets the respect he deserves from his colleagues, which is partly due to his being the new guy on the force and partly because he looks like he should be looking forward to tenth grade next year. He's scored some grudging respect due to his affiliation with Vinn and I when we solved the killings of two young Asian women recently, but not enough to noticeably bolster his status even with the other campus cops. I suspect he'd also love to have his name become familiar with the Chicago police, where the real action is.

"Yeah, well I'll make sure he gets it. By the way..." he lowers his voice to below a whisper and looks around the room with nervous eyes, even though it's empty other than the two of us, "how's it going? Anything else I should know?"

I shake my head. "We're spinning our wheels. Drove all the way out to Amish territory twice and have nothing to show for it. We were able to talk to the three kids that Rachel came here with. We don't have anything definite to write them off as suspects, but they don't seem capable of murder and we don't see any way they would carve up her forehead. I guess it's possible that they know something, but neither Vinn nor I think they killed her or know anything that'll help us find out who did."

Jenkins sighs and leans back in his chair. "That's what Mendez' report says too." I raise an eyebrow. "Yeah, he let me read it, and no, he didn't let me copy it. It's pretty thin, though, I could almost recite it from memory. Other than using some really poor-quality fake IDs to get past a sympathetic bouncer and into a bar, they seem like they toed the line while they were here." He chuckles. "The bartender asked them if they wanted to run a tab and they had to ask him what he meant. They were a lot of show and no substance. That, and they have an alibi for the night the girl was killed."

A small upturn at the corners of his mouth tells me that Jenkins is baiting me and wants me to beg for it. Instead I remain impassive and even have to stifle a yawn as the seconds pass. He gives in first.

"Time of death was sometime between when Zoo Lights began at 4:30 and when the body was found around 8:30." I don't tell him that the note in the brochure might narrow that even further. "Security cameras show the other three were eating dinner at the Rock and Roll McDonald's from 5:00 to just after six and they had tickets to see Blue Man Group after that. I guess they could have bought the tickets and torn off the stubs themselves, but for Amish country teenagers that would be an expensive alibi. They could have come up with something just as good for a fraction of the price."

"Dammit," Vinn mutters when I drop by her office to bring her up to date on what I found out from Jenkins. I don't think the news of the alibi was much of a surprise and probably not that upsetting to her, otherwise she would have chosen a much more colorful word from her impressive storehouse of creative profanity. She goes on to prove my point. "I mean, it's not like we suspected them, not seriously. But it never helps to have a door shut in our faces, especially when we don't exactly have any other doors to open."

"What about social media? We haven't checked to see if Rachel posted anything on Instagram, or Facebook, or whatever kids are using today. A hint about what she's doing while in Chicago, a picture of herself in front of the lion house at the zoo, that kind of thing."

Vinn doesn't seem impressed at my suggestion, in fact she seems to be staring at me as if measuring me for a dunce cap. Rather than give voice to her thoughts, she turns to her computer and taps out a series of commands, stopping after only a few minutes before turning her attention back to me.

"Let's see, no electricity, no laptop, no cell phone to take pictures, and no friends to speak of outside the two we met, who had one ancient non-smart phone between the two of them. What are the odds Rachel's posting online?"

I sheepishly but silently have to admit that my idea was, in fact, stupid under the circumstances, but I need to save face.

Time to open my mouth, ramble, and hope something resembling genius pops out by pure chance. "Well, sure, maybe not her social media. But what about someone else's? If she went to any tourist sights, and especially at the zoo, there must have been around a zillion people taking selfies, pictures of friends or polar bears, and so forth, where Rachel either photobombed them or was in the background."

Vinn's eyes narrow as she stares at me. "Are you suggesting we use facial recognition technology?"

"Yes." Well, no. I need to find a way to Google it on my phone to see how that would apply here without Vinn noticing. She does seem deep in thought.

"That's definitely a long shot. But the only direction we have to go is our belief, with hardly anything to support it, that Rachel was meeting someone there. It's a million to one, but maybe the two of them would show up together in a picture a complete stranger took at the zoo. Do you think J.J. could run a scan for us?"

J.J. is my contact for all things IT, especially hacking. If he can't do it, nobody can. Two problems, though. First, he knows he's the best and charges accordingly and I'm not sure my bank account can take the hit. Second, from what I've heard on the grapevine, he's gone dark. Something about needing to keep a low profile after breaking into the records of Russia's Foreign Intelligence Service.

This time, Vinn uses a word so new to me that I'm not even sure it counts as a swear word. Maybe it's synonym for "darn," or something similar. Whatever its meaning, it's clearly meant to show her unhappiness with J.J.

I try to salvage my idea that I didn't know I had. "Vinn, this doesn't sound like it needs someone with J.J.'s skills. I'm guessing that the main requirement is the right equipment. We teach at a major university in one of the country's biggest cities. Somewhere in the student population here there must be a geek with the ability to help us out."

"Yeah, possibly. It's worth a try. I'll look into it and see what I can come up with. Good idea."

She smiles at me as I head out the door and off to class. If I hustle, I'll have time to do a little research on how facial recognition technology could apply here and evaluate just how good an idea I unknowingly produced.

# TWELVE

"I thought it would be best to keep our interest in this off the radar," Vinn tells me as she slides into one of the two student chairs across from my desk, which takes up about eighty percent of the floor space in my postage stamp of an office. "I don't know enough about the use of facial technology to be sure, but I'll bet there are ethical questions involving privacy and intrusion into people's social media postings meant only for select friends and family members. If I used a faculty member to find someone to help us out, that might have led to more oversight than we want. Instead I tracked down a student who took one of my general physics classes last semester as an elective. She needed the science credits for her computer science major and told me that she's the head of the Women in Computer Science student group. Physics wasn't easy for her but she tried hard enough that I curved her grade up, so I figured she'd be receptive."

Vinn lets the conversation hang as she notices my new hologram of Edvard Munch's "The Scream" hanging from the bookshelf behind me. The face she makes indicates that she has no taste for fine art. "And..." I prompt.

"And she doesn't know enough about it to help. But she did give me the name of a woman from her club who she thinks might be able to. She'll be here any minute."

Right on cue, a soft knock on the door is followed by the entrance of a woman dressed in the typical student garb of blue jeans and a sweatshirt, but more noticeable is the colorful hijab wrapped around her head. What appears at first to be random lines of color becomes identifiable as patterns of computer code as she draws nearer. My instincts tell me that we may have struck gold.

"Excuse me," her voice is very soft, even timid. "Are you

Professor Achison? My name is Malika Kumari."

Vinn stands and slides her chair over to make room for Malika to take the other seat. "Yes, please, do come in. This is Professor Winters. We need some help with a computer search and you came highly recommended."

Malika casts her eyes down, not comfortable with the compliment. This simple sign of humility has me liking her already. Time to see, though, if she's willing and able to push the limits of technology and ethics. "Malika, before we go on, I'd like you to know that what we want you to do could be very exciting in terms of the use of cutting-edge computer technology, and we believe it's perfectly legal"—I'm hoping that's true—"but it might also make some people uneasy on the invasion of privacy front. If that's the case, feel free to turn us down. All we ask is that you don't talk to anyone about this."

It's subtle, but I notice a slight upturn at the corners of her mouth. Vinn must see it too, as her eyes take on a new sparkle as she goes in for the kill. "One more thing," she says, "this is part of our investigation into a young woman's murder. We don't see any risk at all to you, but we want to be upfront about what you'd be involved in." Vinn may have couched her comment in terms of concern for Malika's safety, but I know better. She's appealing to the woman's sense of decency in helping track down the killer of someone in her age group.

"What is it you want me to do?"

"Do you know anything about the use of facial recognition software to scan random social media accounts looking for images of a particular individual?"

Malika sits up straight, her eyes gleaming with excitement. "Are you serious? I've read all about that and even put together what kind of programs it would take in my head, but have never had the chance to test my theories. I would do anything to try this!" I have the feeling that's some sort of record for the number or words Malika has strung together at any one time. Her enthusiasm is contagious, but my heart falls when I see her face take on a sad, serious look.

"But there's a problem. The software that's available to do this is proprietary and not available to the public. I could emulate it by combining a few other programs, altering their code a little, and then adding some of my own so that it recognizes the right commands, but I would need to buy the software and it's expensive."

"How expensive?" I ask, wondering if we've gotten so close only to have our progress pulled back due to insufficient funds.

"Let's see," Malika uses her fingers to count as she stares at a point past my shoulders, probably admiring my hologram. "I can try to find some used ones, but if we bought them new they'd cost around $250.00."

Vinn and I exhale our relief in tandem. "You're right, that's quite an expenditure," I tell Malika solemnly as Vinn grins in the background. "But it's for a good cause. Email me the information as soon as you can and I'll pay for it. And for helping us out, you can keep it when we're done."

A non-stop stream of questions suddenly erupts from our new recruit's mouth. Vinn does her best to provide the relevant details, in particular the date and time frame that Rachel visited the zoo. Eventually all is answered and a much more energetic Malika stands and takes two steps toward the door before stopping, slapping her forehead with the palm of her hand, and turning back to face us.

"I can't believe I almost forgot one of the most important things. Can you please give me a picture of this woman?"

Vinn and I look at each other, neither of us wanting to admit to once again jumping ahead without thinking this through. I finally speak just to hasten Malika's departure. "Um, we're working on it. Give us a day or two." Malika gives us both an odd look, shrugs her shoulders, and leaves without another word, leaving Vinn and I with egg on the faces we have buried in our hands.

"According to Mendez, the only photos they have of Rachel are post-mortem. He emailed a couple to me and I just forwarded them to you. They didn't have any luck tracking some down from the family. Amish, you know."

"Thanks, Jenkins, I guess they're better than nothing," I tell him as I hang up. I'm not sure that's true when a computer is trying to make a match between two images. I'm at a loss and fruitlessly brainstorming when my cell phone brings me out of my funk. I don't recognize the number. I'd usually ignore it but decide I deserve some self-flagellation in the form of a spam call and punch the button to answer.

"Mr. Winters? Is that you?" The voice is vaguely familiar but I can't place it. "This is Francis from Yoder's Meats. Remember, we met when you and that lovely woman were here asking about Rachel. I just wanted to thank you so very much for the teas that you sent to me. I thought you were just being nice. I never really thought you would do it! I've only tried one of them this morning—something needles, I don't remember the exact name. But it was a revelation! If the others are even half that good, it'll be such a treat. I just wanted to express my appreciation and tell you that you've spoiled me for life now. I don't know how I'll go back to what we sell here."

I finally have the chance to get a word in. "I'm so happy that you like them, Francis. And please call me 'Mal.' When you've gone through all of them just let me know which were your favorites and I'll be happy to send some more along."

"Oh, you're just so wonderful, thank you! If there's ever anything I can do for you..."

Her words are like a sledgehammer to my brain. "Well actually, Francis, there may be. Would you mind asking your daughter something for me?"

"Not quite a school portrait, but there are a couple that might work," Vinn comments as she gazes over my shoulder at the images on my computer. Frances' daughter came through and was able to pull up about half a dozen pictures she took at last year's holiday lights celebration and this past summer's quilt festival, where Rachel was her family's designated member to auction off a quilt her mother had made. The winter photos were mostly too dark with too many other people in them, but several of the pictures from the auction feature Rachel in front of the crowd. She was a pretty girl, tall for her age with a clear complexion and blond hair drawn up into a bun, some sun freckles dappling her cheeks. She doesn't look happy but mood is probably irrelevant for our purposes.

We're both quiet as we stare at the images, the unspoken knowledge of what would soon happen to this girl hanging heavily in the room. Once we break out of our reverie, it doesn't take long for Vinn and I to agree on the two to forward to Malika. I type up a quick note and press send. We move to my kitchen to make a dish we call "Pantry Raid." It's our go-to when we don't have a meal planned and don't feel like ordering out. We find any number of food items close to their expiration date and try to combine them in a way that is at a minimum palatable. Sometimes we surprise ourselves. Sometimes not.

Today the creative juices aren't flowing, but neither one of us has an appetite anyway. We're in that uncomfortable zone where there's nothing we can do to further our investigation except wait for someone else to provide us with information. It's a helpless feeling. We can only hope that Malika's enthusiasm translates to a quick turnaround.

Four days later, Malika and Vinn are back in their same chairs in my office. Malika, wearing a plain hijab this time although in a blindingly neon green, brought her laptop and is bursting to tell us every detail of her adventure with her new software. Each of us is more interested in the results than the process, but artists are entitled to be able to explain their genius if it means getting what we want.

"Well, if I had to scan millions of accounts, that could take forever, right? I mean, I did this on my laptop, not a supercomputer. So I had to find a way to narrow down the search. It helped so much that you gave me that small window when Rachel was at the zoo. You said that it might be okay to bend ethical boundaries..." I glance at Vinn with concern. I'm not sure that's quite what we said. "...so I hacked the zoo's financial records and downloaded information on anyone who had used a credit card to get into the Zoo Lights festival that night. After that it was a piece of bosbousa to trace the family and get the names and ages of their children too. If the kid was over ten, I figured they at a minimum have a Facebook account, maybe Instagram or more.

"So I ended up with maybe between ten and twenty thousand social media accounts, which is much more manage-able. After eliminating any accounts that didn't have photos from the zoo that night it was a lot less and that's when I ran the program I created. By the way, thanks for the software. It's awesome. It isn't as sophisticated as the real thing, so I still ended up with about five hundred pictures to go through myself of people that bore some sort of resemblance to Rachel. That festival looks pretty cool, by the way. Did you know they use over 2.5 million lights?"

She gets no reaction from us and continues on. "After culling, I had eighteen pictures. In seven of them it just wasn't clear if it was her and they were fuzzy or too far away anyway.

Seven more you can see her but she's alone and the picture doesn't show enough of where she is or anything that you'd find useful. That leaves these four."

Malika turns the screen so that both Vinn and I can see, presses a button, and the first photo fills it. An expressionless Rachel in front of the seal pool, the back of a man's head behind her. The next one must be from the same camera, as it's nearly identical and still no shot of the man or any indication that they're together. Third one shows Rachel passing by an outline of a lion made of lights. A man wearing the same jacket as in the other shots is walking in the direction of the camera holder, side by side with Rachel, but his face is cast in shadow.

That leaves one more. Malika knew all along that this was the money shot and kept it for last. With the great ape house in the rear, and a frightened-looking Rachel in profile, we're looking straight into the eyes of a thirtyish, white, buzz-cutted, cold-eyed son of a bitch. Is this the face of a man who was minutes away from killing his companion or just a sour temporary companion having a bad day? Scott, is that you? As exciting as this is, we still have work to do.

Malika gives us a few minutes to stare at the photo before taking back the laptop. "I just sent both of you the photo. I did try to find out who the guy was, but he must keep a low profile because I came up empty. Sorry. I hope this still helps."

Me too.

# THIRTEEN

The last remnants of the Christmas season, including the Zoo Lights festival, have finally passed, making the chances of our tracking down a volunteer docent who might recognize and remember the man with Rachel even longer than they would otherwise be. I'm not sure what useful information we can expect to get anyway, as it's not likely the photograph will produce a sudden memory of witnessing the killing or remembering the man carrying a length of cord or rope or overhearing Rachel call him by name, but it never hurts to visit the scene of the crime anyway. Especially when we're rapidly running out of ideas on what else to do.

"Good news," Vinn announced a couple of days ago. "Zoo Lights may be over but the zoo has a series of adults only night affairs. Part outreach and part fundraiser. My guess is that the volunteers who work at these events have their favorite places to be, so that the same people who worked the polar bear and great ape exhibits for Zoo Lights would also work there for the..." she pauses to look back at her screen, "'Post-Holiday Beat the Blues Pre-Valentine's Wine and Cheese Extravaganza'. And lucky us, it's this Saturday night. I just ordered the tickets."

It did seem like good news at the time. The bad news is that, as we leave Vinn's condo to walk over to the zoo after dinner, it's about 150 degrees below zero with a nasty wind coming off the lake throwing pellets of snow and ice into our faces. Even dressed for the elements, I'm frozen within the first three minutes and having serious thoughts about taking a hiatus from the investigation until, say, June.

Trying to put a positive spin on our outing that has an almost zero chance of producing results, I shout to Vinn over the gale, "We'll probably be the only people there. More wine and cheese for us."

I couldn't have been more wrong. Fighting the wind as we trudge east on Webster, we keep our heads down in a fruitless effort to stay warm. Looking up out of necessity to cross Stockton Drive and the beginning of the park to the entrance, I'm startled to see a mass of down jackets and stocking caps huddled in line waiting to get in as the gate keepers scan tickets one by one. I don't know if it's the animals or the wine that's the bigger draw. The real question, though, is who are these people?

"Unbelievable," Vinn mutters as we take our places in the queue. Fifteen long minutes later, we're inside. The sea lion pool is the first animal exhibit inside the west gate and a line of around fifty people extends out from the underground viewing area. Not the ideal situation to corner a volunteer to ask questions about a murder from weeks ago, but the primate house may be no better. We once again take our place at the end of a line that moves forward at a glacial pace, which somehow seems appropriate.

Just inside the door, a young man and an even younger woman stand behind a platform littered with small plates of cheese and crackers. "Red or white?" they ask in unison, each one proffering a small plastic cup with at best a sip of wine. I pretend to take my time deciding, giving Vinn a chance to act friendly.

"You look familiar. Were you here for Zoo Lights?" Her focus is somewhere between the two, allowing them both to think the question was directed at them.

"Nope." "Not me." We move on, miniature cups cradled in thick winter gloves, downing our drinks in one swallow. We each passed on the cheese as that would have required exposing our hands to the elements. Visitors press themselves close to the glass to get a better view of the sea lions as they make their passes. We retreat to the far wall, where an older woman with an ID badge suggesting that we "Ask me anything" stands forlornly, watching the crowd with a scowl on her face. She must be there to make sure no one has too much fun.

We stand a few seconds eyeing the pool before I turn to woman and with as cheery a tone as I can muster with a frozen jaw remark "Not quite as crowded tonight as it was for Zoo Lights, is it?"

"I wouldn't know," she replies as she moves sideways to put distance between us, establishing her new position ten feet away.

"You do have a way with the ladies," Vinn smirks. We scan the crowd for a few seconds more looking for any other official-looking person but come up empty. Strike two.

Frigid air slaps our faces as we exit and climb the ramp to ground level, encouraging both of us to increase our pace. Fortunately we've been to the zoo a few times and know where to go without having to consult a map. We pass by the lion house and whatever delicacies lie within and hasten down the path to the primate house. Much larger that the tiny sea lion area, this time there's no line to get in.

The line inside is short, so it only takes us a few minutes before we're offered wine by clones of the earlier couple. Unsurprisingly, the answer Vinn receives is also identical. Same story with the first docent we find, an elderly man half asleep on a portable stool. Our next stop is with a middle-aged woman with a Jamaican headdress standing near the lemurs. Vinn asks the now-familiar question.

"Yes, but then Lights always does draw a larger crowd than these events for adults, and given tonight's weather I don't blame people for staying home." She has a slight lilt in her voice that suggests she may in fact come from the island. More to the point, we finally located someone who worked the festival.

Vinn makes small talk and confirms that she was working this exhibit the night Rachel was killed. Removing one glove, she pulls two photographs out of her coat pocket. "I know you're busy, but we're looking into an incident that occurred here on that night. Can you tell me if you remember this man or this girl?"

As if this were an everyday occurrence, the docent carefully studies the pictures without any questions. She takes her time, but eventually shakes her head. "No, I'm sorry. But you might try asking someone at the African Ape Exhibit. I can tell from the background that that's where the picture was taken."

"Someone needs to tell Mendez that monkeys and apes mean two different things," I grumble as we exit the warmth of the primates into a wall of icy air. Our destination is visible and seemingly within easy reach, but the path between the two buildings takes a circuitous route that allows time for my fingers to grow numb.

The out-of-the-way location of this exhibit may work in our favor, as there are only a smattering of visitors scattered about. The air is warm but heavy with the scent of primates, making the thought of partaking of the cheese unpalatable. We skip the lonely couple holding out cups of wine, much more liberally filled than at the sea lion pool, and make a direct line to an elderly woman holding court with a small group of imbibers in front of the gorillas. We wait patiently as she finishes her talk and the group moves on.

"Hello, may I help you? Would you like me to tell you about our gorillas or some of our other great apes?"

"Actually, no, sorry," I say gently.

"Thank god," she sighs wearily. "I mean, sometimes people ask the most dumb-ass questions. Read up on the damn animals before you come here or just shut up and drink your wine."

For a moment Vinn and I are startled, then can't help but start laughing. The release of stress feels good.

"I'm sorry," the woman continues, smiling at our reaction. Her badge identifies her as Madge. Of course it is; it suits her. "But I think I've done too many of these events lately."

"Does that include Zoo Lights?" Vinn asks. "That's actually the reason we're here. We're investigating the unfortunate death of a young woman during the festival a few weeks back." She pulls out the pictures. "Do either of these people look familiar?"

Madge doesn't need more than a glance. "Of course. I remember them because of what I heard later. You're not from the police, are you? Incompetent boobs, they never even asked me a single question. That couple drew my attention because I thought how sweet it was that a father and daughter were spending time together here at the zoo, but then as they got closer I started to have doubts because they weren't really, well, together. She didn't seem to be paying attention to the animals, and the apes we have here are pretty impressive, hard to ignore. She was just wandering. Her eyes may have been damp. He stayed a few feet away from her until they got near the exit, then he took her by the elbow and led her out. We see people arguing all the time, so it wasn't really all that suspicious, I was just disappointed that they didn't seem to be enjoying themselves. It wasn't until I found out what happened that I wondered what was really going on."

I could have kissed her, but then I'd be the story for the next set of visitors. We just got confirmation that the man in the photograph was in fact with Rachel that night and is either the killer or one of the last people to see her alive. We give our thanks to Madge and start to move on before she calls out in a stage whisper.

"If you want to know where it happened, it was in the trees to the left as you exit. About twenty feet in and around the side of the building."

We nod our appreciation. As we push past the door into the cold, we both look to our left. All we see is dark, and our faces are starting to freeze in place. A quick glance at each other and we silently agree. No need, as a warm apartment and some real wine is calling. We head for the exit.

Vinn and I agree that we've taken our investigation about as far as it can go with our own limited resources, so Sunday morning I call Jenkins' direct line expecting to leave a voice mail. To my surprise, he picks up. Still low man on the campus cop roster, he must work a lot of weekends. I tell him that I've got an update and a photo of the possible killer and that I'll be by later today. He insists that we set a specific time, I assume to make sure that he won't be out on a call helping a coed find her lost library book, so after some back and forth we settle for 1:00.

I'm not surprised to see Mendez sitting in one of the chairs at Jenkins' desk when I arrive. I'd have heard if they had solved Rachel's murder and their investigation is most likely stalled, having encountered the same dead ends that we have, and unlike Vinn and I they have other cases that need their attention. A possible visual identification of the killer would be one of the few things that would entice him to make a per-sonal appearance. The fact that he's in jeans indicates he's not on duty today, which really shows how desperate the Chicago cops, or at least Officer Mendez, are.

"Mmph," he greets me, as ebullient as always. "Sit and spill." So much for preliminaries.

I pull out prints of the four better photographs Malika uncovered, the best shot at the bottom, and hand them over to Mendez. Jenkins shoots me an irritated look, but it's his own fault. If I had known he was inviting company, I would have made an extra copy.

Mendez takes his time with the first three, but stares at the last one for so long that I wonder if he's still awake. Without saying a word, he goes back through them again, quicker this time, then hands them over to Jenkins as he turns to face me.

"Where did you get these?" He doesn't sound happy and I don't appreciate being treated as an adversary. He's not going to like my answer.

"From a social media search. We were able to get a picture of Rachel and ran it through a facial recognition program focusing on the night she was killed. We didn't do anything illegal, but that's all I'm going to say about it."

Mendez gives me the evil eye, then much like the first time we met seems to remember we're on the same side and the tension leaves his face as he sags back into the chair. He holds his hand out to Jenkins, who reluctantly passes the photos back. "Okay, that'll have to do. For now. I don't suppose you were able to attach a name to this face?"

I put on my best sorrowful expression. "Sorry, no, and we did try. He could be the Scott mentioned in Rachel's notebook but that's pure guesswork. Look, we don't have the resources that your department does and we did the best we could with what we had. Giving you these pictures is our passing the baton. As far as we're concerned, we're done." For once, I think I mean it.

Mendez stares at me, wheels turning inside his head, something on his mind and clearly torn about whether to share it. "Yeah, I get it. And these will help, at least give us a jump start. But like I told you last time, this case isn't getting much attention. Most of the guys I work with are good cops, but there are a few higher-ups who find it easier to assume a random act of violence, put a file at the bottom of the stack, and move on. Now they'll have to put a little effort into it. But that's not why I'm here, at least not completely."

He looks at me like he's sorry for me, which is unsettling. "You're not done, at least you may not want to be. Here's the reason I gave away tickets to the Blackhawks game to be here today. Early this morning a body was found down by the Planetarium. White male, twenty-three years old, lived with his parents in Skokie. Strangled."

He pauses waiting for a reaction, but I don't see the relevance and say so. "I'm sure you get a lot of deaths by strangulation. That doesn't mean it's connected to Rachel."

Mendez' face grows dark. "By itself, no, it doesn't. Two things though. First, the vicitm's name is Scott Kaufmann." He sees me open my mouth to say something and holds up his hand. "We're not stupid, Winters. That's why I said you may not want to be done with this, the name thing. Rachel's Scott? Maybe, maybe not. Second, we're still waiting on the coroner's report, but according to the cops on the scene and the sergeant who got me out of bed this morning, the kid appears to be missing a piece of his frontal bone."

# FOURTEEN

"Why is there always a second victim?" I vent to Vinn later that evening. "Why can't we ever figure things out and catch the bad guy before he strikes again? And is this the 'Scott' that Rachel referenced or does the killer have the same name? If it is the same Scott, how did they connect? And why?" In response she simply places her hand over mine and snuggles closer. She knows I'm just expressing frustration and don't expect an answer. During the periods of our lives we prefer not to discuss, we each either directly or indirectly put our skills to work investigating, identifying, tracking, and sometimes terminating some very bad people, and have admitted to each other that we were good at it. But in those days we had the very deep resources and backing of an entire govern-ment to support us rather than an undergraduate computer science major with a laptop. It makes a difference.

We sit in silence for several minutes before Vinn expresses what we've both been contemplating. "Well, what now?"

I can't keep the irritation out of my voice. "Two minutes after Mendez suggested that we continue helping out unof-ficially, he told me in no uncertain terms that we were to stay away from the boy's parents, not to interview potential wit-nesses, and that if anyone was going to do 'the facial recog-nition thing,' as he called it, it would be his department. I got the impression that he wouldn't mind a little help, but what he expects us to do I have no clue."

Vinn considers this. "Look, we both agree that the two murders have to be connected. What are the odds there's two killers out there who would risk getting caught by taking the time to do some cranial surgery on a body lying where a bystander could wander by at any minute? And that's even assuming that this is a common thing, which it's not. Plus it's a safe assumption that Rachel either knew or was planning to meet up with someone named Scott. Two victims, one killer. Right? Mendez has put crime scene tape with a big "Do Not Cross" on it around every possible avenue of inquiry regarding the male. That doesn't mean we can't keep looking into Rachel's death and by association work on both. We already have a picture of the prime suspect. Unless we hear otherwise, we can assume that the cops can't identify him. Maybe we can."

What she's saying would be encouraging except for that one qualifying word. "Maybe." We already had this conversation and agreed that the police are far more capable of tracking the guy down than we are, which is why I met with Jenkins today in the first place. Nothing between then and now has changed my opinion on that nor provided sudden insight into what actions we could take to find out who he is. Vinn senses my doubts.

"Let's talk this out. Malika already tried to identify him through the same facial recognition search that helped us find him initially with no luck. In addition, Mendez told you that they'd be trying it with the new victim. So that's out. What sources do we have that might be even better equipped than the Chicago cops?" I can tell she's already got someone in mind. "What about Carlotta?"

I wince at the name. Carlotta is a former associate of mine who helped us out previously, albeit under her own terms. She and I have a somewhat complicated relationship. All professional, just a bit odd.

I shake my head. "No, as of a month ago she told me that she'd be off the grid until further notice and that to try to contact her could put her in danger. Besides, her contacts would focus on individuals trying to take down a government or who travel the world to go after a high-profile target. Rachel and a suburban kid living with his parents don't fit the bill on the victim side, and I have a feeling the killer here is local and hardly a national threat. He's only taken out two people in the city several weeks apart. So far anyway."

Vinn doesn't seem discouraged. "Yeah, I thought the same thing but wanted to hear you say it. But if we're right and the guy is local, someone we know may know someone who knows someone who might know him or at least of him. Ideally, we could put the word out through an individual with dark connections even if they won't admit it, or through someone who seems to be able to broadcast this kind of need out through an odd and diverse network." She is clearly smirking now. "Or both."

It only takes me a nanosecond to realize what she's proposing and the very idea fills me with dread. "Vinn, no. I mean—"

"Mal, I don't see that we have any other options if we want to keep our hands in this. Desperate times call for..."

"Don't say it," I interrupt. Vinn looks so earnest, even as the devious grin she's attempting to hide spreads wider. "I'll set it up."

Leo and I have an unspoken agreement that we won't probe into the past life of the other, which doesn't mean that I haven't spent time speculating what dark secrets he'd rather not reveal. I don't believe his Castro story and have doubts about his claim to be in witness protection, but I'm sure he either attempted or succeeded in killing someone somewhere and that he's very much in hiding, even if not government sanctioned. He's deduced that my former career shared some similar traits, and despite our mutual lack of disclosure it's created a bond of sorts. The same goes for Vinn despite her general absence from our periodic alcohol-infused talks late into the morning. Leo has a sixth sense about her that accurately tells him that she's one of us.

The same can't be said for Ted. The totality of his adult

life is an open book, but one which would put anyone to sleep by the second chapter. The only secret he holds close is his desire, or compulsion, to shed his male persona and transform to a gentler if not entirely tolerable semblance of a woman. Once we discovered Rebecca, Ted essentially disappeared, and all of our interactions since then are with his alter ego. She can be frustrating and headstrong but is by far the preferred option.

They've each assisted Vinn and I in prior investigations and hopefully will be able to do so again, although preferably in more of a consulting role than as active participants. We believe Leo has connections to a seedier segment of the city's citizenry while Rebecca, notwithstanding her failure on the Amish connection front, has shown herself adept at gathering information through marginalized people who have skills not readily advertised. Not that we truly believe that either will put us on the path to identifying the killer, but as Vinn so rightly and depressingly pointed out, we're desperate.

Normally we would gather in Leo's apartment when the clock says we should already be asleep and even then hold off any serious conversation until we were well lubricated, but that would best occur when we could sleep off the effects the next day. Under the circumstances this time, though, we're not willing to wait until Friday. As an alternative, I invited them to my place for dinner tonight, Tuesday, reversing the trip down the stairs to Leo's garden apartment and asking them to climb up to my top-floor home.

Vinn sidles up to me as I grimly study the array of platters crowded on the island of my kitchen. "Did you say that this was potluck?" she whispers under her breath with alarm. "Please tell me you didn't ask them to bring this food." The reason I believe that Leo is running from a former life is that despite owning the Kuban Kabana, his tiny dive that never seems to have customers, he has shown no evidence that he knows how to cook. Memories of lingering gastric distress from the first and only time I ate there are even now causing stomach pains. Still, his efforts qualify as Michelin notables compared to Rebecca's.

I continue to stare at the various cuisines competing to overshadow my simple plates of crab-stuffed potatoes, classic bruchetta, and pulled pork sliders. Leo brought one dish that appears to be meat and smells of cumin and another that is completely unidentifiable and smells of alley cat. Rebecca's contributions boast neon colors that are probably meant to distract from whatever flavors they hold. "Take small amounts of each and slide them around your plate to make it look like you've already eaten some of them," I suggest.

My strategy is simple. I plan to do the talking, and the more I talk the less time I have to eat. Leo and Rebecca are already indulging next to each other on the couch. Leo, as always, looks like he just came from the restaurant and has grease stains in interesting patterns over everything he's wearing. Rebecca chose a lime green leather skirt and pink angora sweater that probably looked better together in her mind than they do in reality. Vinn and I take chairs across from them. I push something purple around my plate then start right in.

"Thanks for coming. I have no words for the fact that you were able to put so many dishes together on such short notice. It's a work night, so I'll get right to the point so that you can get back home quickly. You both know that Vinn and I have been looking into the death of a young woman for the past few weeks. I won't go into detail, but we were able to secure a photograph of the man we believe to be the killer." As I speak, I place printouts of the pictures on the coffee table, one for each of them. Vinn takes advantage of my pause to jump in.

"You know," she starts, "it may be useful for you to have an electronic copy as well. Let me email it to you before I forget." She rises and takes her plate with her in the direction of the kitchen. I guarantee that when she returns most of the food that was there when she left will be gone.

I resume in her absence. "Anyway, neither we nor the cops have had any luck in identifying him. Each of you has a web of connections that may extend into parts of society where its members rub elbows with the likes of this guy." Neither of them is insulted by my suggestion. On the contrary, they appear proud of themselves. "The task is simple. Please spread the word that we're looking to find out who he is, but do not under any circumstances try to actually corral him or ask anyone to do the same. He's killed a teenage girl and another kid barely an adult, so while he's worth getting off the streets, we can let the police handle that. Any questions?"

Vinn returns, and sure enough her plate is empty of all but the food I prepared. She adds her two cents. "We don't really expect results so don't be too disappointed if nothing happens. We know you like to help out and we thought we'd give you a shot. We really appreciate it."

Neither Leo nor Rebecca have any questions, not that we expected them to, so we concentrate on eating or, in my case, not eating. I do notice that Leo and Rebecca took generous portions of their own offerings but that there's little evidence of anyone else's on their plates. We munch silently for several minutes before Leo stands and, as if by signal, Rebecca joins him.

"Thank you, darlings, this was such a lovely idea," she coos. "We'll have to do it more often." I start to object before Vinn silences me with a painful jab of her elbow into my ribs. "You can keep the rest of my food, just return the containers when you're done." Same reaction, same elbow, same result.

I watch as both of my tenants make their way out of my door. So now we wait.

# FIFTEEN

My expectations for achieving any results from our Hail Mary to Leo and Rebecca are virtually non-existent, so I shouldn't be distracted by thoughts of what actions they may have put into motion. My brain apparently never got that message, though, as my mind conjures up an image of Leo meeting with a lean, scar-faced man hiding behind the collar of a raincoat pulled up high late at night in a dark alley behind his diner, both men weighted down by the multitude of weapons they carry. Rebecca, on the other hand, is passing the photo around a nail salon as she gossips about whether leggings can ever be considered high fashion no matter what's showing on the runway in Milan, and whether OPI or Essie has the better palate of polish colors.

All of which would be a harmless way of passing the time if my daydreams weren't occurring in the middle of my Introduction to Crime Fiction seminar. It's a small 300-level class for bright juniors and seniors, so other than the necessity of throwing out a topic for discussion my presence is often superfluous. Today's assignment of bringing in three passages from three different authors detailing creative methods of murder is instructive as a point of reference for how writers' style affects the level of description and brutality of the crime, and a lively discussion ensued almost instantly. Unfortunately none of the passages referenced removing a bone from the forehead, which led to the wandering of my thoughts.

It's my last class of the day and Vinn has labs until late, so I stuff my backpack with papers to grade and head for the el and home. I'm no sooner through the gate and steps from the stairs than I'm intercepted by Leo as he emerges from his apartment. His doorway is partly below ground level, hidden from view by a brick barrier lining the top of his stairs, and the view from his front window is blocked by all of the herbs he has stacked there, even in winter, so I'm not sure how he always knows when I arrive. Either the gate has a squeak that only fake Cuban chefs can hear or he has some sort of sixth sense. It's spooky.

"Come," he mumbles in his usual loquacious style. Without waiting for me to respond, he turns and heads back to his place. Like the trained puppy I am, I follow. Once inside we settle in our usual spots at his table where the customary shot glasses sit waiting. He pours a generous swallow of a dark, smoky liquid from an unlabeled bottle into both glasses. I've never had the nerve to decline a drink when Leo's determined to offer one, and he's not likely to share whatever information he has until we've entered a certain level of haze. Hoping he's ready to reveal something relevant to the investigation and not priming me for an explanation as to why he has to pay rent in the form of four weeks' worth of chickpea stew, I take one, then a second and a third, for the team. My eyes are watering and my throat feels like it's been invaded by a thousand poisonous tree frogs. I like it.

"That man," he finally says. "I have name." He refills our glasses as he says this, then sits back and speaks no more. His eyes are beginning to get glassy and while it takes a lot for Leo to feel the effects of the swill he serves, I'm worried that either he or I will be unconscious before long or that he's only got the name committed to memory and that those particular brain cells will be eaten away by these frogs. Time to prompt.

"And," I begin gently, "do you want to tell me what that name is and how you got it?"

Leo looks at me like he just remembered I'm here, then fishes around in the hundred or so pockets of his army-green colored shirt. Eventually he pulls a scrap of paper out of an inside compartment and passes it across. It's not in his handwriting and grease stains threaten to block out a few of the letters, but it's still readable, or at least would be to someone who's sober. To me the words are moving around on the page, so I tuck the paper in among the bills in my wallet and hope that later I'll remember that's where I put it. No explanation of who gave him the name or under what circumstances appears to be forthcoming.

I'm just at the point where I'm wondering how I'm going to get up the stairs to my unit when there's a loud pounding at the door. Leo glances in that direction and seems to be assessing if he can make it there when it opens and a vision in pink spandex pants, oversized purple fuzzy sweater, summer sandals with three-inch heels, and white fake fur flounces into the room. I guarantee it'll be the last time Leo doesn't lock his door.

"Darlings, I'm so glad to find you both here," Rebecca begins as she nears the table. I've never understood what the word "sashay" means but I think I just witnessed it. "Malcom, doll, do me a favor and get another glass. A clean one."

If Leo feels insulted, he doesn't show it. I stumble to the cabinet holding the glasses, find an old coffee mug adorned with an emblem of a long-defunct band, and manage to get it to Rebecca without dropping it. She eyes it with distain before walking into the kitchen and replacing it with something more appropriate for a woman of her stature. She pours herself a stiff one.

"Malcom, dear, you're going to just love me forever. You know my friend Tasha, she's the one that wore that simply dreadful gown to the Harvest Ball two years ago, do you remember? Of course not, you weren't there. Anyway, she used to date the brother of that guy whose name I never remember, you know the one. Well, last summer he hired this landscaper to mow his lawn when he was recovering from that operation that he said was for prostate issues but Dawn has it on good authority it was a to help with impotence. Imagine that, Dawn's heard that it didn't exactly turn him into Don Juan."

Rebecca stops to eye her glass as if mystified as to where the contents have gone, pours herself several more fingers, then continues on. Leo's eyes are shut. "Where was I? Oh yes, the landscaper. I don't know why I mentioned him, he's not important. Oh yes, he cut down the neighbor's bush and she threw a fit and almost sued so the guy—is his name Gregory?—got a letter from a lawyer but then he bought her a tree and it was all okay after that. Well, his attorney had a client who had been arrested for assault so he knows some naughty people and one of them thinks that maybe he knows who the man in the photo is."

My head is spinning, not entirely due to the alcohol. Like Leo, after arriving at the reason for cornering me Rebecca stops short of the big reveal. It takes all of my effort to get one word out. "And?"

"And what? Oh, yes. Do you like these heels by the way? They're just too adorable to keep in a closet just because it's cold outside. I wrote it down. It's in my purse."

Rebecca proceeds to spend the next five minutes rummaging around in her purse before finally dumping out its contents on the table. It takes her another thirty seconds before she grasps a small page torn from a spiral notebook with something written on it in fluorescent pink Sharpie. I once again put it in my wallet and start to thank Rebecca but she's already pushed everything back into her purse and is heading to the door.

"Ta ta, Malcom. You can thank me later. Leo, always a pleasure."

Only when the door closes does Leo open his eyes. Like a toddler, I think he believes that if he shuts his eyes no one can see him. Thankfully Rebecca's imbibing emptied the bottle so there's nothing left when Leo attempts to top off my glass. I use that as an excuse to head in the direction of where I hope the door is. After that, everything goes blank.

"You mean to tell me that you haven't even looked at them yet?" Vinn is incredulous, her voice echoing in the nearly empty cafeteria. "How could you possibly not?"

"Would you believe me if I told you I wanted to wait until we were together?" I ask, only slightly slurring my words. Vinn's frown is all the answer I need. "Seriously, my memory is a complete blank between when I stood up to leave Leo's place and when my alarm went off this morning reminding me that it's not the weekend. We're lucky I even remember that they gave me the name. Or names." I take a nibble of this morning's obligatory muffin purchase in an effort to mask the residual taste of booze that coats my mouth. The fact that I can't distinguish if it's lemon poppyseed or pumpkin spice tells my brain that maybe it's best not to risk consuming it at all. I push it closer to Vinn, who's eaten most of it already anyway.

Vinn sits expectantly with her arms crossed. My mind is mushy enough that it takes me a few seconds to puzzle out what she's waiting for. I pull out my wallet, find the two scraps of paper hiding in among several singles, and pass one across to her. I hold the remaining piece closely in the palm of my hand, sneaking a peak before closing it inside my fist, as if I were hiding a royal flush from my opponent. Vinn is clearly not playful this morning and sighs in exasperation.

"Okay, if you want to be that way, on three. One, two."

"Hmhrephregotkj" we say in unison. At least that's what it sounded like. If she expected a harmonious reveal of the name Vinn seriously misjudged the situation. Without another word she reaches across, snatches my paper out of my hand, and lays both pieces side by side in front of her.

Despite being upside down in completely different handwriting, and the fact that I'm unable to actually read what's written there, I can tell that the two scribbles match. My sigh of relief is matched by one coming from the other side of the table.

"I guess this is worth the cost of one hangover," Vinn ventures, her mood suddenly elevated. "Nelson Crum. One spells it with a 'b,' the other without, but it's safe to assume it's the same guy. Any details on where we might find him?"

"First of all, no. And second, there's no 'we' here. It's fine if you want to do a little online surfing to gather some information on who and where he is, but we leave it to the authorities to take it from there. Agreed?"

Vinn gives me the stink eye, but she knows I'm right. Still, she doesn't waste any time opening up her laptop and typing in a quick command. Several clicks and a deepening frown later, she slams the screen down. Vinn has a habit of punishing whichever device fails to deliver the information she seeks, which explains a perpetual parade of new laptops, tablets, and phones over the course of time.

"I've got to get to class. Nothing pops up, but if both Leo and Rebecca were able to get the name from different sources, he must be in the system. Somebody's system. I'll keep looking. In the meantime, feel free to pass it on to Mendez. Who knows, Crum might be on the prowl even as we sit here."

I have class too, but a long enough gap before the next one to get the name over to Jenkins, who has more of a direct line to Mendez than I do. Despite my throbbing head, cotton mouth, and a minor case of the shakes, I feel good. All in all, we wrapped this up quickly without ever putting ourselves in harm's way and are getting a bad guy off the streets. It was almost too easy.

Jenkins isn't exactly displeased with the information I give him, but he's not doing cartwheels either. "You realize," he lectures me, not making any effort to avoid sounding condescending, "that this isn't even enough to make an arrest, much less lead to a conviction. You won't reveal who produced the man's picture but they're at best an amateur not connected to law enforcement. The photograph itself was taken by god knows who and probably posted on the Facebook page of a tourist from Des Moines, all it shows is that he was in the vicinity of the victim at a single point in time, he's only in the background behind some drunken yahoos, and it's not even in focus. Then we have two anonymous sources who magically assign the identical name to the image. For all we know they were at the same séance."

"You're forgetting the docent from the zoo who saw them arguing," I push back without conviction. Jenkins rolls his eyes. "Look, I never claimed that this was ironclad evidence and I understand it's all circumstantial. But it's more than we had twenty-four hours ago. It should at least be enough to bring him in for questioning."

Jenkins' expression softens. "Yes, it should do that. Probably. I think. I'll try to package this up to make it look a little more, um, palatable to an officer of the law and then pass it on to Mendez. Good job. Let's hope it leads to something."

The "something" we're hoping for apparently didn't happen over the weekend, which did little to calm the nerves of either Vinn or myself. Temperatures creeped up just enough for sleet to mix in with the snow and the normally temperate breeze off the lake turned into the bone-chilling, damp, howling menace the locals refer to as the "Hawk." Under most circumstances this would have been the perfect recipe for cuddling under the covers for forty-eight straight hours with the person you love, but when the nervous energy of both snuggler and snugglee makes you wonder who put a quarter in the magic fingers box, intimacy is impossible. I guess that's why we have a television, although I'm not sure I could name anything we had on.

I'm hosting office hours after classes on Monday, dealing with a tearful student who's so sorry he couldn't get his paper in on time, but his favorite grandmother died on Saturday and the grief was just too great to be able to focus on putting together five hundred words on what suspense means to him. What he doesn't know is that the faculty host an off-the-books Google doc page listing the various deaths of relatives for each student. Some are legitimate, of course, but this is the third time Grandma Willow has died in the last five semesters. I don't let on, tell him to get it to me by Wednesday, and am shushing him out the door when my cell phone sings out the theme from "Law and Order." Jenkins.

"Winters, Mendez wasn't enthusiastic at first but once he started doing a little digging he began to get on board the Nelson Crum train. Turns out the boys in vice know him. 'Crum' is an alias he hasn't used in a year or two, it's Nick Carson now. He's half a step above a street-level punk, hiring himself out to anyone who'll give him spare change for a bottle of Jack. Murder is a step up for him, but according to the men in blue not out of the question. Definitely a viable lead."

"That's great, London. So what's the next step?"

"That's why I'm calling you. To show his appreciation for the tip, Mendez is letting me come along when they pick the scumbag up. In the rear in more of an observatory role, granted, otherwise there'd be too much paperwork, but I'm still close to the action. I thought if he can do me a solid, I can do the same. If you and Vinn don't mind hiding behind a tree or something, you can see it go down."

The excitement in Jenkins' voice is palpable. As much as he resents the reputation of campus cops as something less than the real thing, the reality is he doesn't get his hands in many serious crimes, especially as the newest guy on the force. For me, and I assume Vinn, we've been involved in too many takedowns and the thrill is long gone. I get the impression, though, that our presence has been requested not for our own gratification, but so that Jenkins' big moment has an audience.

"Of course, we'd love to be there. Reach out when you know the details."

# SIXTEEN

"Remind me again why I'm here?" Vinn knows quite well that sitting this out wasn't an option if we want to keep cordial relations with Jenkins, who's on occasion shown his usefulness, but she's never quite forgiven him for what she feels was a snub the first time our paths crossed. She might have been more tolerant if we were passing time under a budding young tree listening to the birds welcoming spring to the city as a warm breeze caressed our faces rather than shivering in our down jackets with snow up to our ankles as we slowly and painfully slide into hypothermia.

"It shouldn't be long now," I respond, as much to assure myself that this outing is worthwhile as to pacify Vinn. She doesn't need to remind me that I've used the same words at least three other times over the past thirty minutes. We're trying to blend into the surroundings as we lean against a parked car sipping out of our respective Thermoses, but anyone with common sense would wonder why we weren't inside somewhere with heat.

Not that it really matters. Our perch is about halfway down a side street in Uptown, a neighborhood that's been in developers' crosshairs for decades but so far has resisted most gentrification efforts that would displace the low-income residents who make up a major percentage of the local population. While the reasoning for keeping the status quo is noble, its effects also show up in the lack of upkeep of many of the homes. Several of the two- and three-flats on this block have boarded up doors and windows and others are long past due for the same treatment. The target apartment is six buildings down on our side of the street. A few plain-clothes officers pace nearby waiting.

The plan is for two squad cars to pull up in front and another to simultaneously block off access to the alley in the rear, then to have the uniforms storm the second-floor unit from both sides at the same time. Jenkins will be riding along in one of the cars but will be positioning himself on the sidewalk in front of the home. He called his role "backup" but it sounds more like having a seat at the kiddie table while the adults get first crack at the Thanksgiving turkey. He can still say he was in on the bust, though, which is the whole point of risking frostbite as we wait on the street.

I've lost the feeling in seven of my toes when Vinn points out a squad car, sans lights and siren, moving the wrong way down this one-way street. As we stare down the block at it, another car moves past us from behind, traveling fast and silent. We're supposed to stay exactly where we are, but Vinn and I apparently have the same idea, which must come from sharing a bed.

"I need to get feeling back in my feet. What do you say we move in a little closer to the action?" She's already walking as she speaks and I follow dutifully in line. We stop two houses from where the occupants of both cars are exiting, the outlines of bullet-proof vests clearly visible, sidearms drawn. Jenkins brings up the rear similarly attired, albeit in a slightly less imposing uniform. He glances over at us once he reaches his appointed spot on the walk just outside the front gate, nodding his acknowledgment of our presence.

"He saw us and knows we're here. Can we go now?" Vinn mumbles under her breath. I swear, sometimes she's worse than a teenager. She's probably just venting because she makes no move to leave the scene.

Almost immediately, there are shouts at the door and seconds later a battering ram is produced from out of nowhere. It takes four attempts to get the door smashed open enough for the cops to push through and even then it's a tight squeeze. It had to have had some darn good locks. We're too far away to hear what's happening within until the distinctive sound of a single shot echoes through the stone façade. No sooner does it register as gunfire in my frozen brain than several more pops, overlapping and serial, break out as well. A brief pause gives me reason to think that it's all over.

I lean in to Vinn. "A little more excitement than I anticipated. At least—" I don't have time to finish my thought, as movement at the front door catches my attention. A man in short sleeves and bare feet pushes the damaged door aside with one arm as he emerges quickly. In his other hand it's impossible not to notice the long-barreled, magnum-style handgun. He jumps down the stairs in a single leap. Despite my experience, and that of my companion, we're frozen in place as we watch what develops next. It seems to be occurring in slow motion.

An astonished Jenkins fumbles as he tries to quickly retrieve his weapon, which most likely hasn't been drawn in his entire time on the force and may not even be loaded. The target ignores him and turns in our direction, running as rapidly as possible on the slippery sidewalk to where Vinn and I are positioned in such a way as to block the sidewalk. The man's arms are flailing as he attempts to keep his balance while simultaneously pumping them to maximize his speed. As a result, whether intentional or not, when he's about twenty feet away the arm holding the gun levels itself in perfect position to take aim right at us.

Vinn and I instinctively dive to our left toward the icy ground. At the same time we begin our move, a loud crack sounds in my ears. We roll onto our stomachs and brace to again scramble to safety before the second shot, but the fleeing man doesn't appear. Slowly we rise up just far enough to peek over the fence meant to keep dogs off the lawn, then stand up completely when we view the situation.

Ten feet in front of us, Jenkins stands over the prostrate body of the man from the photographs. It doesn't take more than an instant to see that he won't be rising up again and that no ambulance is necessary. A crimson stain slowly spreads over his back and begins to drip down onto the snow below. Jenkins' eyes are glassy and his expression one of shock, as if he can't process what just happened or his part in it. I'm not even sure he feels the cop come up behind him and gently pull his weapon out of his hand. As he's escorted back toward the squad car, another cop heads our way. It's comforting to know that for once we're being approached as witnesses rather than victims or suspects. Wherever they take us, it had better be warm.

"Remind me again why I'm here?" Vinn asks, although whether she's intentionally being ironic by invoking a déjà vu moment or simply speaking her mind is hard to tell. At least this time as she utters those words we're out of the elements, sitting comfortably at a high top in an Irish pub in the Avondale neighborhood that's popular with cops. I'm on my second whisky while Vinn, who normally can drink me and ten more like me under the table, is nursing her first Guinness, which barely looks touched.

"Look, I know Jenkins isn't your favorite person in the world, but the fact that we had to spend the better part of a night answering questions at the station wasn't his fault. For all we know, if he hadn't shot Crum we might not be alive to be sitting here now. Besides, this is a big deal for him and we need to be supportive."

A little more than a week has passed since Crum crumpled to the sidewalk only a few feet from where we were standing. The shooting was quickly ruled justifiable, and Jenkins had his fifteen minutes of fame as a hero campus cop who brought down a double murderer. It didn't do much to influence the way his fellow officers at UIC view the 'new kid,' probably due to a healthy dose of envy at the publicity Jenkins was receiving, but his stature did grow slightly in the eyes of the Chicago officers who had been a part of the team assigned to bring Crum in that night. Maybe not a lot, but enough that when the team and most of their shift reserved the bar for their customary celebration when a killer is taken off the streets, Jenkins was invited to join them. As before, he recognized our role in all of this, or wanted us to join him for his big moment, so he asked us to attend as well.

I wasn't thrilled about having to venture out in the snow and slush myself, but once here chose to do my best to enjoy myself. It's proving difficult, as Vinn seems unusually glum in the midst of a celebration, and her mood begins to rub off. I down the rest of my drink, decide to switch to booze-free libations, and excuse myself to go to the bar to see what my options are. When I return, Vinn's seat is vacant.

It's doubtful that she went home on her own, so she most likely took advantage of my short absence to head to the ladies' room. After several minutes, though, I begin to get edgy. I make my way to a crowd of loud men looking for Jenkins to ask if he's seen her, only to find him the center of attention as a drunken cop recounts how the baby-faced officer of the law who just gunned down a perp got carded at the door. Jenkins doesn't seem to mind the attention even if not entirely positive, but then again I see that he's way past caring about much of anything. I move on.

A few minutes later, a random glance outside to the bar's garden, as they call it, reveals a solitary figure sitting on a stone ledge among the stacks of tables and chairs piled high with snow. What looks like a pleasant place to spend a summer evening is anything but that in the middle of winter. There's a reason it's been closed for three months.

I push out the glass door and am immediately hit by a wall of cold. I retreat, retrieve my coat and gloves, and try again. Vinn is staring in the direction of nothing, eyes unfocused, her head bowed. I brush snow off a spot next to her and settle in. Not knowing what's going through her head, I can't offer appropriate words of comfort, so I settle on putting my arm around her. For several minutes, neither of us breaks the silence. It's Vinn who goes first.

"It's not right. I'm sorry, I just can't get in the mood to celebrate because I feel we're missing something. I can't put my finger on it, but it was just too, well, neat. There's a little voice in the back of my mind that tells me we need to keep going, but it doesn't tell me why. Are you satisfied that this is over?"

Now that she mentions it, a similar voice has been speaking to me, but I've just been better at ignoring it. It's an occupational hazard that in a world where nothing is as it seems, and where there's always more to a crime than meets the eye, that a seemingly open-and-shut case with a patently simple resolution is viewed with a hefty suspicion. It's possible that my desire to close it up and return to a sense of normalcy overrode my usual skeptical outlook. I tell this to Vinn, and now we're both morose.

It's getting colder and I'm just about to suggest that we go in and say our goodbyes—in his condition, Jenkins won't know we're gone—when the door opens and a commanding shadow is cast in our direction. Two steps later and I can see it's Mendez, who duplicated my mistake of not putting on a coat first, but in his case he doesn't go back. He stands in front of us, towering above.

"A bit chilly to be outside, isn't it? The party's nice and warm."

"We just needed a little time to ourselves. We'll be back in soon." I'm hoping that's enough to satisfy Mendez and send him away. Vinn doesn't give him the chance.

"Are you okay with thinking that this thing is all wrapped up?" she challenges him. "That Crum is dead so that ends the investigation? Put the case file away, move on to the next one?"

Mendez eyes her carefully. "It was him, Ma'am. We found notes in his apartment that link him to both murders, a piece of rope that matches the markings around the young lady's throat, DNA matches, blood droplets. You name it. Any one of those things would be enough to prove Crum's guilt but together there's not the slightest chance it wasn't him. He shot at cops rather than risk being caught. He was the killer."

Vinn isn't going to let it go. "I know. I'm not disputing that. But why? Don't you guys care about the 'why'? I mean, okay, there are nuts out there who kill strangers at random, but this guy chose these two, and sought them out. Why? They have absolutely nothing in common, didn't know each other, didn't know him, were both broke-ass kids with nothing to steal. What's his angle, where's the benefit? I admit, I'm a scientist, so maybe my need to make sure all the pieces fit before coming to a conclusion isn't the way the legal system works, but there's something out there that tells me that we're missing something. I can't explain his behavior and that bothers me."

Mendez stares at Vinn for a long time before moving on the other side of her, pushing snow aside, and taking a seat. He glances at the door before leaning in and speaking softly. "It bothers me too. Cops follow their gut and mine is telling me that it doesn't stop with Crum. But we have absolutely no evidence to show that it goes further. Nada, and a gut feeling isn't enough. The brass wants to close cases and this was an easy call. Crum's the killer, hands down, no indication anyone else is involved. Score one for the clearance rate."

Vinn and I both return his stare from earlier. I don't know what I expected when he moved outside to join us, but this wasn't it. He's not done talking.

"Look, for me the case is over. But if you ever want to float some ideas in my direction, I'll listen." He looks up at the bar as a burst of loud laughter carries outside. "But I wouldn't go through Jenkins from here on. Let him bask in his glory. Maybe a cop's hunch and the persistence of a scientist aren't that different. Follow your gut. It'll help me sleep at night knowing someone's doing something."

Mendez stands and in one fluid motion and a few steps, slips back into the warmth of the bar. Vinn bites her lip and a look of determination that I know so well fills her face. We follow Mendez' path, finish our drinks, and head out the door and onto a path of uncertainty in a crusade without end.

# SEVENTEEN

"No, Vinn, we have not been 'deputized,'" I insist, keeping my voice low even as I try to stress my point. Our customary spot in the cafeteria, even when busy over lunchtime, always seems to have a wide perimeter around it into which no one dares venture. There's not a soul within fifteen feet of where we're sitting. Diners are choosing to join strangers at their table instead of taking advantage of the empty tables on either side of us. If I wasn't so antisocial, I might take offense. Still, there's no sense taking the chance that someone will overhear something that'll make our lives difficult with our higher-ups. "Mendez was merely letting us know that if some brilliant insight comes to you in your sleep, you have someone who may let you bounce it off him."

"On the surface, you're right," she responds, making no effort to stay hushed. "But you know as well as I do what he wanted us to hear without saying it. He can't explicitly sanction our investigation but he's no happier with closing the book on it than I am. Or that you are, if you'd ever admit it to yourself. Yes, Crum killed those two kids. But there's more to it than that and he's not around to admit it or to bargain for his life by giving up who ordered him to do it. Maybe it was voices in his head and if that's what I—we—discover, then fine. But I need to know for sure."

I haven't admitted it to her, but Vinn doesn't need to convince me to keep looking into the killings. I already conceded that we were headed in that direction before I fell asleep last night. Even though my mind isn't that of a scientist where every puzzle needs to be solved and where the right answer isn't enough if you don't know how you got there, I've had the same nagging questions that won't let me rest either. But I need to appear that she's dragging me into this as a bargaining chip to get her to agree to some ground rules. Vinn can be impulsive and doesn't always listen to that little voice that tells her to slow down or to back away, and that behavior can be dangerous. For both of our sakes, she needs to stay within certain limits. Time to lay down the law.

"Okay, fine. I admit that there's a chance that there's more than meets the eye here. And yes, it bothers me and I'd like to keep going with it. But Vinn, we've put our lives and those of other people in the line of fire in the past when we got so passionate about bringing down the bad guy that we became reckless. If we're going to do this, we need to agree on a couple of things. Agreed?"

Vinn looks wary. "How can I agree unless you tell me what I'd be agreeing to?"

Point taken. "Right. Just a few commonsense guidelines, all right? First, that we don't represent ourselves in such a way someone would get the impression that we're cops or otherwise have authority that we don't actually have. Okay?"

Vinn compresses her lips. "Fine. Is that it?"

"A couple more. Two: That we don't involve any innocents in our investigation in any capacity where there's a chance they could get hurt. This should be a slam dunk, right?" Vinn gives me the death stare. In truth, it's not a slam dunk. It hasn't been long since we used a young freshman as bait and it put a target on her back. Granted, it ended up as an essential step to saving lives, but I've never been comfortable with how easy it was for us to take advantage of her naivete. I stare right back without blinking.

Vinn gives in first. "All right, fine. But on the condition that if it comes to that, the rule isn't ironclad. You need to agree that it would be a point for discussion."

My turn to press my lips tight. "Okay, but waiving that rule will require that we're unanimous." Vinn nods.

"One more, and this one will be hard but it's necessary.

If we get to the point where we get so consumed by finding out what happened that it affects our sleep or our health, threatens our jobs or prevents us from giving our students one hundred percent effort, interferes with our friendship slash relationship, or puts our lives in mortal danger, we back away and let it drop. Completely, never to return to it."

I see a flash of fury in Vinn's eyes but it quickly dissipates and turns to thoughtfulness. Obviously there's history behind this demand, and she's replaying events of the past before responding. She might think that this one is aimed at her, but I've been just as guilty as she has. We're both driven individuals, but as much as I want to discover the truth behind the deaths of those two young people, I want even more for Vinn and I to have the time to see if we have a future together and if so to allow us to do just that. I see concession in her features before she has the chance to speak.

"Yeah, granted. But that doesn't mean that we won't be pushing this hard, right? If either of us starts to cross a line, the other has to act as our conscience. But we can still go right up to the edge of that line."

She makes it a statement rather than a question, and it's my turn to assent by a slight nod of my head. I take the opportunity to glance around. The café has mostly cleared out, which means we need to wrap this up so that one of us isn't late for his "Crime in Film" class.

"Vinn, I need to get going. Maybe later we can discuss what our first step as freelance investigators will be."

"No need." She looks smug. "We'll start the same place we began with Rachel. We need to go talk to the parents of that boy."

The contrast between the homes of Rachel Yoder and Scott Kaufman are striking. Rachel's farmhouse was probably built before electricity made it to the Indiana countryside, and still managed without it, and you can look across the fields in any direction and not see another home. Scott lived in the basement of his parent's mid-1960's suburban ranch house, a bi-level blond brick model with attached two-car garage, its crabgrass-laden yard crammed between neighboring homes on either side. This visual reminder of how unlikely it is that the two kids had much of anything in common emphasizes the difficulty we face in establishing a connection that'll make our job of finding the mastermind behind the killings, if any.

We ease our Zipcar into the asphalt driveway but don't immediately make a move to exit. Part of our hesitancy is our reluctance to move out of the warm car into the cold, part to give us time to look over the exterior of the home, but most of it is due to the unpleasant next few minutes, where we again need to interact with a couple who are unsuccessfully trying to cope with a parent's worst nightmare. Their emotions will still be raw but they're meeting with us only because they hope that we can provide answers to the unanswerable questions that haunt them. We finally give each other a glance of resignation, open our doors in unison, and head up the walk. The door opens before my finger even leaves the doorbell.

It's the father, freshly shaved and showered and dressed neatly in pressed pants and an ironed shirt but with drooping eyelids barely open enough to reveal the reddened eyes behind. Our impending arrival may have encouraged him to put his best self forward for the first time in weeks.

"I'm Andrew Kaufman, Scott's dad," he says in a wavering voice as we shake hands. "Please come in, we can sit at the kitchen table." He leads us down a short hallway and up three steps where he motions us in the direction of an oval dinette with four chairs evenly spaced on each side. The air has a faint aroma of sour milk and fried food.

"My wife told me about your call," he goes on. We still haven't said a word. "But she couldn't face talking about it again, not yet. And we're not really sure what your purpose is or what you can do that the police haven't already done. There's certainly more that we want to know. I mean if there's someone else involved we want him caught, don't get me wrong. But at some point we have to just deal with it and try to move on. I hope you understand."

"We do, believe me," Vinn responds softly, putting her hand out and reassuringly placing it on his forearm. In similar situations Vinn has been quick to jump in first on the belief that it helps to smooth a difficult conversation with a woman's touch. I'm not so sure, especially where the woman swears like a sailor and can drink a lush under the table. "We don't want to add to your pain. The police got the killer but like us, they think there's something more here. They asked us to assist them in looking into it."

Two minutes in and she's already broken rule number one. Time for damage control. "What she means is that an investigating officer still has some concerns which we happen to share. Officially the matter is closed." Vinn gives me an evil stare, which I send right back. "We believe that the man who killed your son and the young woman was acting on behalf of someone else. If that's true, finding out who that person is could save more lives. I'm sure you share our desire to prevent that. And we promise that after today, we'll try to avoid bringing you and your wife into our investigation as much as possible."

Andrew turns his sad face from me to Vinn then back again. He takes in a deep breath and releases it in one long exhale before responding. "Yeah, I get it. But that doesn't make this any easier. Let's get this over with. Ask your questions."

"We don't have many. Can you start by giving us some general background on your son? What he was like, where he worked, what his interests were?"

"He was a good kid, never any trouble. He'd always been a fair student, not the smartest but he got decent grades. Most subjects just didn't interest him. He was, how do I put this, I guess an underachiever in school. I don't mean that negatively, just a way of explaining that he didn't see much point in a lot of the subjects and his friends were kids similar to him. We like to think our children are going to stand above the rest but that just wasn't Scott. After graduating he went to community college for two years while he was figuring out what he wanted to do. We were hoping he'd go on to a four-year college, get a degree, but he was still kind of lost even after those two years.

"So he'd been working a few different jobs, and for the last six months or so had been trying to become a professional blogger, whatever that means. He had an interest in outer space since he was around four years old but never figured out how to monetize it. So he thought he'd write about it, create some stories, that kind of thing." Andrew stares off into nowhere for a full thirty seconds. "I guess he got some followers but just didn't have enough time to build it before..."

We wait, but we can see that we're losing him. Vinn steps in. "Mr. Kaufman, thank you for that. Would you mind if we take a look at Scott's room for a little bit?"

Without a word, he stands and heads for the stairs. We follow him to the basement, but two steps from the bottom he stops, either unable or unwilling to go any further. He turns to face us. "You can go in and look, but don't take anything. Please make sure that you leave it exactly as it is right now. My wife would insist." He passes us as he walks back up. I'm not sure how long we have here, so we quickly enter the room.

My first reaction is to freeze and gawk. To say he had an interest in space was an understatement. Celestial bodies hang from the ceiling, a poster demanding rights for Pluto adorns the wall above his desk, and model spaceships cram the top of a dresser. His bedspread shows a crescent moon surrounded by stars, a touch that borders on the juvenile but brings his personality more into focus. The reminder of how young twenty-three really is saddens me.

Vinn brings me back down to earth. "Let's get to it. We may get kicked out of here if the mother returns."

We have experience searching together and without speaking move to different parts of the room. Vinn takes the desk area while I examine everything else. Out of the corner of my eye I see Vinn rapidly taking pictures and turning pages. I've just about covered everything when I hear the outside door open and close. Vinn looks up as well.

"Shit," she mutters, increasing her pace. I'm about ready to join her when I feel a file buried at the very bottom of a drawer full of sweaters. I pull it out and go to open it when I hear loud voices immediately above us. An argument, presumably about us.

I rush over to Vinn with the file. "Quick, put this in your purse." She gives me an inquisitive look. "He hid it for a reason, so his parents won't know it exists and that it's missing." No sooner does Vinn comply and put whatever she was looking at back neatly in place than we meet the mother. Fifteen seconds later, we're back in the car.

# EIGHTEEN

"I'm not sure what I expected, but this isn't it," I tell Vinn, my disappointment evident. We're back at my place and have the papers that Scott had hidden away spread out over the island in my kitchen. There are roughly sixty to seventy sheets of standard copy paper, each with sketches of some sort of structure or parts of one. A few are artist's renderings of what it would look like from different perspectives. At a glance, they could be drawings of anything from a doghouse to a castle. One thing they're not are notes detailing a secret rendezvous with an Amish teenager or a mystery man.

Vinn isn't any more thrilled with my find than I am but isn't ready to give up on them yet. "It's probably a waste of our time, but before we scroll through my phone to see if any of the pictures I took will be any help, which I doubt because I didn't have time to look at what I was photographing, let's at least try to puzzle this out. C'mon, it might even be fun. First one to guess what it is correctly gets a prize."

The lure of an unspecified prize notwithstanding, I have doubts as to the allocation of our time to puzzle out what is most likely some sort of fantasy abode of a kid yearning to escape his parents' basement, but on the other hand it's not like there's a long list of other things on our to-do list. I take a perch on one of the stools and Vinn climbs onto the one next to me.

"Let's start by sorting them into groups. It looks like he drew variations of the same areas over and over. We can make piles." Vinn is ever the organized scientist, which is why I'm letting her run this show. We take our time, and I have to admit that for a waste of time, it's a fascinating one. The young man had some talent with the pen and a good eye for color. We don't pause from our task long enough to study any one page in detail yet, though, saving that for when we're done grouping them. A few minutes of labor later and we're staring at six piles of diagrams that appear to be floor plans or a sort of poor man's blueprints, and one pile of drawings that we assume are his visions of what the structure would look like when completed.

Vinn picks up the largest stack and sets it down between us. It's a circular room with doors on two sides directly opposite each other with windows lining the entire wall area. As we finish looking at the top page, we spread the remainder out across the counter. They're all variations of the same room. In some the roof has skylights, written dimensions change, one has the footprint of a waterfall sketched in, and there's a rectangular box that moves around from one page to the next in search of the right location. Tiny, neat printing questions where to put chairs or couches and a debate about colors fills the bottom of one page. The last paper we look at is titled.

"All right, it's a reception area," I remark, reading off the paper. "Makes sense, I guess, so that box must be a desk." I reach over and grab hold of the stack of renderings, paging through it slowly. I set five documents aside. "These seem to be his efforts to bring these outlines to life."

We study them carefully. Unlike the flat outlines of the room, these are filled with color. Scott's talents in design didn't transfer well to actual drawings, but his intent seemed to be to give a sense of the finished area, not a final rendering. A few ideas were modernistic, others more cozy and warm, as if he couldn't decide which his guests would prefer. Vinn scoops up the first set of papers and I hand these to her to clip with them.

The second set of drawings, only three pages here, is of a room sharing the two doors but otherwise is much more spartan. An oval room with only a few windows, the only difference among the sketches is the location of more rectangles, which are conveniently labeled as conference tables. In the corner is a tiny scribble "cap 21." I brilliantly deduce for Vinn's benefit that this is a conference room with a capacity of 21 people. She grunts in response. I'm sure she means that as high praise. I find one drawing in the rendering stack. It shows crude outlines of people at the tables, presumably conferring as to how they can obtain bodies from someone who can draw.

The next stack has almost as many efforts as the first one. The dimensions of this room, again the familiar circle, are much larger than the other two, and several of the drawings are of rooms within the room. The general outline indicates seven units containing multiple rooms on the perimeter. Scott's drawings of a sample unit clearly indicate that these are living quarters, each with its own bathroom, bedroom, and open space that we assume is the living area. He played around a lot with the floor plan and seemed to end up favoring a circular hallway on the inside of the rooms, with an outdoor space in the very middle. His color drawings attempted to convey the openness and beauty of such a set up. One of them had been crumpled then retrieved and saved.

"I don't know," Vinn interjects before we reach for the next stack. "Reception area, conference room, and small apartments with no kitchens. Almost like a hotel for business people, but it wouldn't survive financially with only seven rooms. Unless his intent was for it to be a lot more floors of seven rooms each? But why would a kid of his age and his geeky interests have any desire to design a hotel? Doesn't make sense."

I have no answer for that and reach for the next pile. The fourth circle actually has a title on each page, saving Vinn and I the trouble of discerning that this is the dining area. Scott did us a favor and drew chairs on either side of his three circular tables indicating seven seats at each. A kitchen area was drawn in behind one wall.

"Have you noticed the patterns?" I ask Vinn, always

trying to score points with my insight. "All of the rooms have doors on two opposite sides, as if the rooms were meant to be laid out all in a row and connected by these doors. Twenty-one seats at the tables in the dining room, a capacity of twenty-one people in the conference room. Kind of an odd number, don't you think? Not twenty, or twenty-five, but twenty-one. And they're all circular, which isn't the most efficient shape in a structure. It may mean something, or it may just be something stupid a kid in his early twenties would envision."

Vinn picks up the renderings and pulls one out, placing it in front of me. "You're right about the way they're connected. But the doors don't open directly into the next room. There's a glass-lined passageway between them. Unusual choice. Okay, any guesses on the last room? Lecture hall maybe?"

There are only two drawings of this location, and it breaks the pattern by only having one doorway, with stairs etched in, so it may not be on the same level as the other rooms. The simplicity makes it difficult to ascertain its purpose. It's a large square with a circle in the middle that takes up most of the useable space. An 'x' marks the spot in the middle of the circle. There's no concept drawing to give us a clue.

We both stare at it for a good five minutes before giving up. "Show me those last few drawings," Vinn asks. I comply and line them up before us. There's a crude drawing of what looks like a swimming pool, various sketches of colorful bushes and trees, and some attempt at the exterior of the building which far from giving insight into what it's meant to be, only causes more confusion.

"Time's up, genius," Vinn says with a sigh. "What's your best guess?"

"I dunno. A retreat, maybe? Space station? What about you?"

"I was going to say a self-contained harem for a filthy rich recluse with rooms for all twenty of his concubines, but your ideas make more sense. You win the prize. You get to buy us dinner."

Weighed down by the disappointment of not finding anything useful in what we had hoped would be a treasure trove of information, we decide to postpone adding additional hurt by going out for a bite to eat before we review whatever Vinn caught by chance in her furious effort to photograph the contents of Scott's desk. The weather and our lack of wheeled transportation force us to venture close by, which is fine since Ukrainian Village offers a variety of tasty options within easy walking distance.

Without a particular destination in place, our feet choose for us as we subconsciously wander until we find ourselves at the door of the Tamale Guy. For two decades he hung around outside the bars of the city where he sold his homemade tamales out of a red plastic cooler to overserved patrons who needed a quick bite to absorb the spirits before heading home. His legendary status and the unmatched quality of his food eventually led to this small restaurant where he can let his customers, many of whom are actually sober, come to him. It's one of our favorites.

We're still defrosting when our order arrives, half of them Oaxacan-style pork and half cheese and pepper. We allow the scented steam to bring joy to our noses as we unwrap the banana leaves to get to the tamales within. Vinn waits until she takes a man-sized bite of one, not caring that the homemade salsa drips down her hands, before she breaks our silence.

"I know that we see those drawings as a dead end," she begins as she chews. "but it's curious that he obviously put a lot of thought into them and kept tinkering with variations to get it right in his eyes. And why would he keep it hidden? It's not like he was drawing naked women like other kids his age."

"I'll have you know that I never drew naked woman as a young lad," I retort, trying to sound affronted. Ogled, yes, but never drew. "Maybe he was spending all of his time on his little fantasy project when he was supposed to be looking for a job, so he didn't want his parents to find out. I really don't think it's anything, but we'll hold onto the sketches. It's not like we're going to drive back out there to give them back." To prove that at least one of us has manners, I wait until I finish speaking to take a bit of my cheese and pepper. Ambrosia.

"I guess," Vinn concedes. "It's probably my wishful thinking because I don't anticipate that I got anything that's going to be helpful. I didn't get the impression that we'll be welcome back at the Kaufman abode, so whatever we have is going to be all we get. Not a promising start."

As that dispiriting thought lingers in the air, we finish our tamales in silence before heading back to my place and what may be our last hope in finding something, anything, that'll give us the push we need.

I begin brewing tea for myself and coffee for the cretin on my couch as Vinn transfers the photos from her phone to her laptop. She waits until I join her with two steaming mugs in hand to open them so as not to be alone in her disappointment.

"There's forty-two of them," she informs me. "Let's stay positive. All we need is one."

Our vow to stay positive immediately takes a blow as the first seven pictures are so blurry that Vinn deletes them without comment. The next several are in sharp focus but are of lined paper with nothing on them. They also quickly find their way into the trash. We move on to wade through copies of online job applications, which we save in case the relevancy of his efforts to peddle sandwiches at Subway or sling burgers at Wendy's ever becomes apparent.

It's only when the images of what appear to be random doodles and notes written in haphazard fashion over a couple pages of copy paper do things begin to get interesting. Like me, it appears that Scott would jot down a phone number or name, or maybe a thought he wanted to preserve, onto whatever scrap he had handy with the idea of transferring it to a more practical location later. Also like me, his scribbles aren't always the model of perfect penmanship. In fact, some of them are downright unreadable. To aid in our deciphering, Vinn magnifies portions of a page at a time. It helps, somewhat.

Over the next hour and a half, most of it scrunching our noses as we try to make sense of his scrawls and a few heated debates about what a letter might be, I copy down about half a dozen phone numbers, a couple of addresses, a few dates, and several sets of what may be initials. Not exactly fodder for celebration, but at least we have leads to follow up on. Vinn chooses to go back over the documents alone while I start Googling the phone numbers and addresses.

Two are numbers for take-out food joints near Scott's home, another is for the Adler planetarium, and one's for the Subway where he applied for a job. Google has no information on one number, so I call it only to get the familiar recording telling me that I'm an idiot and to recheck the number. I dial again, same result. The last phone number coincides with an address that's written next to it. I ask Vinn to go back to the page it was written on where I see that Scott drew an arrow from the address and phone pairing up to a date half a page away. Here, at last, I get a tingle in my spine.

"Vinn, you have a better memory than I do. What was

the date that Rachel ate at that Lou Malnati's?"

Vinn hears the quiver in my voice and sits up straight. Her fabled memory not as good as I anticipated, she types in a few commands to bring up the scans of the receipts Rachel kept from her time in the city. She finds the right one and tells me.

I smile for the first time in days. "From his notes, it appears Scott was at the same Lou Malnati's on the same day as Rachel. Vinn, it looks like we're going out for pizza tomorrow. We have a link."

# NINETEEN

Anchored by the massive Merchandise Mart just across the river from the Loop, Chicago's River North neighborhood is crammed with luxury apartment buildings, trendy art and design galleries, hotels with tiny rooms and large prices, and a plethora of cocktail lounges and restaurants aimed at young locals with money to burn and tourists who don't know to seek out the dives away from downtown that offer better food and more authentic atmosphere without hurting the pocketbook. Typical of the décor of eateries in tourist areas, the walls of Lou Malnati's are covered with framed jerseys and other memorabilia from the local sports teams that visitors from Iowa expect as part of the true Chicago experience.

The place is virtually empty, which we should have expected on a Sunday in winter when out-of-towners have the sense to stay home and most offices in the Loop are closed. Expecting a crowd, Vinn and I had devised a game plan which would take advantage of a harried hostess and a crush of impatient diners crowding the register area. One of us would block the view while the other—meaning Vinn, who is much more proficient with computers than I am—would quickly try to access their system to see who may have made reservations on the day both Rachel and Scott were here. Time for Plan B, which we don't have. When in doubt, maybe honesty and sincerity instead of deceit and criminal behavior will win the day. There's always a first time.

"Look official," Vinn whispers to me as we're approached by the non-harried hostess, who according to his name tag is actually is a middle-aged man named Stan. Vinn isn't above using her gender to try to pry information from a male on the assumption that all men are sexist pigs just like me.

"Table for two?" Stan asks, stifling a yawn, barely able to contain his enthusiasm that he has something to do. We aim to disappoint.

"Sorry, maybe in a minute," Vinn replies. I'm not sure how she does it, but she sounds authoritative with shades of a sex kitten undertone. Using that voice, few males can resist her and I can tell that Stan is already falling under her spell. "But we're investigating a murder, two actually that we believe are related, and both victims were at your restaurant on the same day prior to their demises. We need to see the names of individuals as well as those of the groups met here on that day."

So much for honesty. Vinn's cop-speak in using a word like "demises" and her demand for the information instead of requesting it will no doubt give the impression that we're here officially. Even so, and despite her charm, Stan hesitates before responding or quickly moving into action. Time for bad cop to step in.

"Is there a problem?" I ask, doing my best to lower my voice by an octave and moving into the poor man's personal space.

"No, no, not at all," he stammers. "Let me get that for you. Give me just a minute."

As he walks away, I hear a faint giggle from my right. "Mr. Tough Guy," Vinn mocks. We wait nervously for Stan to return. I figure there's a fifty-fifty chance that he's going to bring our appeal up the chain of command. Then again it's Sunday when the bosses aren't here, and who's going to call the manager at home on a slow day for something this minor? It won't take him long to figure out that giving us what we need ruffles fewer feathers than interrupting his supervisor's Sunday brunch.

Just as that thought passes through my brain, Stan comes into view with papers in hand. "I'm sorry that took so long," he tells us nervously, as if five minutes was an eternity, "but I had to change the toner in the copier."

"That's quite alright," Vinn coos as she takes possession of the list. "And now if you don't mind we'll take that table."

People from other parts of the country assume the only pizza we eat in Chicago is deep dish, which isn't even close to true. It's a once in a while thing and the thin crust around here can be just as outstanding. Maybe not in a chain restaurant known for deep dish, but when you're only here because you can't get the list you need from an out of the way ma-and-pa treasure, you order thin crust because you can get on your way quicker. We go with spinach and garlic.

Vinn wastes no time riffling through the copies before passing them over to me. It only takes us a few minutes to see that no one by the name of Crum, Yoder, or Kaufman made reservations that day. Not definitive, but we both feel that it's more likely that it would be a group that would lure Scott and Rachel out of their neighborhoods for pizza. There are close to fifty groups that met at Lou's that day, ranging in size from six to thirty-four. Eliminating birthday parties, which we think is safe, we're down to twenty-eight. A few, such as a chamber of commerce and a needlepoint club, are unlikely but still should be checked out. After that, it gets harder because none of them seems to stand out as a strong possibility. The Midwest Witch's Conclave, a Meetup group for travelers, an adventurers' club, two singles groups, a book club, and so forth. Several group names give little clue as to what their purpose is. I groan in frustration.

"What, did you think we'd find a social gathering for victims looking to match up with their killers?" Vinn asks sarcastically. "I know, it doesn't exactly look promising. It's going to take some time to track down who runs these groups and to convince them to meet with us. And we do have to see someone in person because I doubt they take attendance, so we'll have to show them pictures of Rachel and Scott. But right now this list is the only lead we have. So buckle up, mister, and get ready for a long ride."

Crime shows on television, under pressure not to lull the viewers to sleep, show forty-four minutes of detectives shadowing their marks down dark alleys, leaving carnage in their wake during frantic car chases, and dramatic discoveries that bring everything into focus just in time to corner the bad guy before he kills again. Parts of my former job were like that. Most of it, though, involved just the kind of thing Vinn and I find ourselves doing now, which is sorting through paperwork and playing phone tag with any number of people who end up having nothing valuable to contribute, if they return calls at all.

We divided the list of groups evenly, fourteen each, while we ate our pizza on Sunday. Our method wasn't entirely random. If it was a gathering focused on something one of us actually had experience with or knew something about, or if it seemed more likely to attract one gender over the other, we took it. Vinn was given the "Survivors of Sexual Assault" group while I was forced to add "Fantasy Football Fanatics" to my list. While neither of these meetings are likely to have attracted both Rachel and Scott, when you're grasping for any sort of straw that moves you forward, you need to be thorough.

Lou's must require that the person making the reservation leave a call-back number, which saves us the trouble of tracking them down. Considering several of the names were of the "Jane Smith" variety, that's a huge time-saver. We agree, though, that it makes sense to gather at least a little background on the groups, or at least the topic, before calling so that we would appear informed. It might help us appear just a little more official and provide a basis for some initial small talk on a topic obviously dear to the target while making them more likely to open up to us. At least that's the theory.

In practice, it isn't working out that way. The one element of this drudgery that makes it somewhat more tolerable is knowing that Vinn is dealing with the same roadblocks, obstinance, and frustration that I am. When we get together to compare notes, we'll have a warm body with built-in empathy to snuggle next to on the couch. It's this thought that keeps me going when I get off one phone call with an uncomprehending or suspicious group leader that takes twenty minutes of explaining and reexplaining that all I want him to do is to look at two photographs to see if either of the people in them appear familiar, then looking at my list to see that I still have nine more calls to make just like it.

"I wish we had felt comfortable sending the pictures to them by email or phone," Vinn sighs three days later as we pull a comforter tight around us. "But we decided it's best not to leave a paper trail of evidence of what we're doing in case someone starts getting suspicious as to whether we're really cops. I never said I was, but I don't think any of them would have consented to meet with me if they didn't think I was."

"Agreed. But it's been a lot of extra work having to track some of these people down, especially without a car. Still, of the fourteen on my list, I was able to eliminate eight of them without having to meet them in person because they didn't have anyone new join them that night. One more had canceled their meeting. Of the remaining five, two of the group leaders work in the Loop and I was able to pop down between classes to see each of them. They were sure neither Rachel nor Scott were at the meeting. One of the last two agreed to meet up tomorrow. The last one hasn't returned my calls."

"My luck was pretty similar, except I was only able to scratch off six of them without having to meet. Two groups were all women, but I still wanted to make sure Rachel wasn't there. Both leaders live not that far from me so that wasn't hard. I managed to meet four of the others—a sure 'no' from all of them. We have two from my list to visit tomorrow. One in Pilsen and the other out in Forest Park. They both said they'd be home all day but to call first."

"Damn," I reply. "Mine's up in Rogers Park. Not exactly a close grouping. But at least there aren't that many."

"I guess that's the glass half-full outlook," Vinn replies. "But while we only have four to go out of the original, what, thirty something, that means that our odds of finding a group the two kids visited has dwindled down too far for comfort. If we strike out with groups we're back to tracking down individual reservations, and I just don't see that as a viable alternative. Rachel and Scott were completely different and as far as we know didn't know each other, so there had to be some topic that brought them to the same place on that day."

She's right. I had been so focused on achieving my goal of checking off each group on my list that I lost sight of our true aim, to identify the one the kids attended as a necessary step in finding out what they have in common, if they did at all, and hoping that it leads us in the direction of whoever ordered the killings. Now I realize how much rides on the answers we get tomorrow. I take about five minutes to dwell on that depressing fact, then grab Vinn's hand, throw off the comforter, and lead her off to generate our own heat.

The first two names on our list are able to tell us so quickly that neither victim had been at their meetings that we don't even get invited inside. Neither Vinn nor I detect any effort to mislead us, which at this stage is almost disappointing. A lie would have at least given us hope that we were onto something. We leave the bungalow in Forest Park with dread. One more to go and too much time to dwell on that fact before we get to our last visit for the day. There's no direct route from the west suburbs to Rogers Park, the northernmost city neighborhood along Chicago's lakefront before you get to Evanston. We spurn the expressway north to take the more scenic route along Lake Shore Drive. The silence in the car is deafening.

Rogers Park is one of the most culturally diverse neighborhoods in the city, with a broad range of incomes as well. We pull up to a courtyard building on a stretch of Jarvis Avenue that reveals all levels of upkeep, lucky to find a place to park right in front. Neither of us exits the car, stalling. Finally, with a glance of resignation from Vinn, we both open our doors and hasten to the entryway. Vinn checks the name on her phone, then pushes a button. A buzzer invites us in out of the wind.

Mavis Wilson, the organizer behind the "Exploring Hidden Gems in the City and Beyond" Meetup group, is waiting for us on the second floor landing. A strikingly attractive black woman in her thirties, she gives us a broad smile as she swings the door open. We step through but don't move to make ourselves at home, yet. This may not take long.

"Ms. Wilson," Vinn begins. "Thank you for seeing us. As I mentioned—"

"Oh yes, I remember, of course. Those two poor children. It's possible they were with us that night. If I recall, we had a good turnout for a meeting so close to the holidays. We usually have a core of the same seven or eight people every month and then the rest come only if they're interested in the topic. We have over 250 members in the group, but obviously not all of them come every time."

"How many do you think were there that night?" I ask.

"Maybe around thirty-five, forty. Most of the faces looked at least somewhat familiar, but not all. The meeting was to discuss one of what we call our annual 'cultural crawls.' This year it's to some of the more obscure museums in the city. For example, the International Museum of Surgical Science, the Maritime Museum, The Center for Intuit and Outside Art. We rent a bus and hit as many as we can in one day. We debated which ones to put on the list. Now some of the members thought that we should—"

"Um, I'm sorry to interrupt Mavis, but we don't want to take up more of your time than necessary. Can we show you the pictures?" Vinn holds them out as she speaks and Mavis pulls out a pair of glasses, holding the photos close to her eyes, examining one and then the other carefully once before going back to Rachel's picture a second time.

After a long couple of minutes, she hands them back to Vinn. The moment of truth has arrived.

"No, I'm sorry, I'm sure they weren't with us that night. I would have remembered. They look so young and I would have made an effort to make sure they were comfortable and felt welcome to the group. I'd like to help, but the answer is no."

We give our thanks and turn to leave quickly so that she doesn't see our crestfallen expressions. Neither of us speaks until we get in the car. Vinn starts it and turns the heat up high but makes no move to pull away.

"You said that you have one number that hasn't called you back. Did you find out who it belongs to?"

I pull out my list. "It's just a man's name. He reserved space for up to twenty attendees. I Googled him but nothing significant came up. I left three voice messages but he never returned them. I haven't gone as far as to use my connections to get an address. If I had known he was our last hope..."

"I know, I get it," Vinn does sound understanding. "But hold on, let me try one of my own connections." She punches buttons on her cell phone and eventually puts it to her ear. "Hello, is this Stan? This is Vinn Achison, do you remember me? Yes, that's right. I'm—it was very good, thank you. We're—it was the spinach and garlic. No, it was just the right amount. Stan, listen to me. We need you to do one more thing for us."

# TWENTY

We caught a break from Vinn's impromptu phone call to Lou Malnati's, although whether it'll result in a viable lead or an entire investigation coming to a screeching halt remains to be seen. Stan had no idea what the name of the last remaining group on our list is or what they discuss when they get together, but he was able to check his computer and let Vinn know that whoever they are, they're meeting again this Saturday. It's our good fortune that they don't rotate locations and that the next gathering is so soon, and it gives us hope that the fates may finally be shining on us. The possibility that they're merely toying with us, though, still weighs heavily on both of our minds.

The days crawl by, bringing up memories of a five-year-old Malcom wondering if Christmas will ever come. With no parent handy to constantly ask how much longer my impatience is directed toward Vinn, but if anything she's even edgier than I am. It doesn't help that the cold snap lingers, we haven't seen the sun in about five weeks, and my students' moods seem to reflect the gloom outside the classroom window. I've been consuming a lot of chamomile tea, which is supposed to help calm the nerves and help with anxiety, but its ineffectiveness to that end has only increased my angst.

Saturday inevitably does arrive, dawning dark and, what else, cold. Vinn arrives at my door just in time for lunch, something of a habit with her. I'm prepared for her and am putting the finishing touches on a steaming hot bean soup and pulling crusty bread out of the oven. With barely a hello, she settles in at her customary seat at my island.

"Smells good," she tells me as I ladle the soup into her bowl. "If you keep it coming, maybe I won't have to order pizza again tonight."

"Stan will be disappointed," I tease before getting down to business. "Have you given any thought into what approach to take tonight? Showing up at an individual's door to show a couple pictures when we've already prepared them by phone and they're expecting us is one thing. It's a little different crashing a large group's meeting uninvited. We may not exactly be welcomed."

Vinn nods as she chews. "I think we get there early before everyone shows up, see who looks receptive to greeting new faces. Introduce ourselves and basically seem reluctant to bring it up, but then reveal why we're there and ask who we should approach about passing the photos around. Make it low key, but we shouldn't limit ourselves to just the leader this time. It's possible that the kids interacted with someone else."

"Right, I agree. Casual but official. And if someone recognizes either of them, maybe hang around to see if we can determine what attracted Rachel and/or Scott to this particular meeting. Do a more extensive interview with anyone they spoke with afterward."

Plan in place, such as it is, Vinn and I move to the couch to go back through our notes on both victims, which may have been a mistake. The paucity of anything remotely linked to anyone other than Crum only reinforces our awareness as to how much is riding on what we find out in a couple of hours.

Not wanting to place our trust in the reliability of the trains, we Uber down to the meeting to make sure we can get there early. Once she learns of our destination, our driver chooses to share her vast knowledge of the pizza scene in the city along with recommendations for where we should go instead of Lou's, even offering to drop us off at one of her favorites on the west side at no additional cost. We promise to try it another time.

It's no surprise that Stan is there to greet us, whether

due to a fetish for being used by a woman with authority or a simple infatuation is impossible to tell. I sense Vinn's discomfort but whisper a reminder that this should be the last time we'll be here so maybe she should get his number. An elbow to the ribs indicates that my helpful suggestion was not well received.

Ever willing to please, Stan escorts us upstairs to the site of the meeting, which being the only room up there would have been just as easy to give us verbal directions. I'm leaning toward a crush. In the far corner, tables have been pushed together to form a square with eighteen chairs set around the perimeter. We're twenty minutes early and only two people, a middle-aged man and a woman in her late twenties, have beat us there. The woman approaches us as we head in her direction.

"Hi there, my name is Dawn! It's my job this time to greet any newcomers. You are new, aren't you? I don't remember seeing you before."

"Yes," I say. "But I'm not sure we're in the right place. Can you tell us the name of this group?"

"Oh, sure. We're the local chapter of the U.S. Raelian Movement. Some people call us the Disciples of Rael. Are we who you're looking for?"

"Um, yes?" I reply unconvincingly. "I mean, I think so. Does Amir Ibrahim belong to this group?"

"He sure does," Dawn replies. "He's kind of like the unofficial leader, I mean, he sets up the times and where we meet and starts the discussion. Rael, of course, he's the real leader."

Vinn sees me floundering and takes over. "We'd love to hear more about that, but first I'm afraid we have to confess that we're here on business. We're investigating the deaths of two young people and believe that both of them were here last month—no, don't fret, we don't suspect anyone here of anything, we've already caught the killer. We're just trying to track down their movements to try to understand the whole picture."

Vinn pulls out the photos and hands them to our hostess, who only glances at them before giving them back.

"No, sorry, but I wasn't here last time. Phil, can you come here a minute?"

Dawn explains the purpose of our presence, Vinn repeats her role and the disclaimer that we don't suspect anyone here, and Phil stares thoughtfully at the pictures before handing them back.

"Maybe. I'm not sure, but there were several visitors last month and I only met one or two. I got here late and had to leave right away at the end. Ah, here's Amir. He might be a better person to talk to."

We turn and a tall, handsome man with Arabic features is striding toward us, a folder in his hands. He smiles as he nears and holds out his hand while still in motion.

"Amir, thank you for coming. You are?"

"Malcom. This is Vinn, my colleague." I mimic Vinn's earlier speech, putting a greater emphasis on our sincere apologies for intruding on their meeting. "We don't mean to be disruptive, but would it be possible to pass these pictures around before you begin to see if anyone recognizes them?"

"Certainly, we're always happy to cooperate with the police," Amir states as he reaches for the photos. He studies them carefully. "But I can already tell you that yes, both of these people were here last month. The young man might have come once or twice before that as well. I didn't get the opportunity to speak with them, as I was busy with running the meeting and a few other details afterward. I believe Madison took them aside when we were done. If she's here tonight she's the best person to talk to."

It takes all the control I have not to shout out an excited "Yes!" in front of our little group. Vinn's eyes are wide and considerably brighter than when we first entered. We both sense a trail opening before us. Rather than corner each member as they arrive, we take chairs off to the side of the square and wait for the meeting to begin.

By 7:30, there are sixteen people in attendance not including us. Amir draws their attention as he stands. "Thank you all for coming out in this terrible weather tonight. Before we begin, these officers would like all of us to look at the photos of two young people who have met a tragic end. They were both at our last meeting, so if anyone interacted with them they'd like to have a few words with you."

As he speaks, Vinn rises and hands the pictures to the man closest to us. Amir sits as quiet murmurings accompany the passing of the photos. We watch a few faces show clear indications of recognition. When the pictures make it around the tables, Amir asks for a show of hands. Five people raise them. One woman looks in our direction.

"I talked with both of them after the meeting. If I can help in any way, I'd be happy to do so."

Amir stands again. "Thank you, Madison. I told them as much. If you want to take a few minutes now while we take care of preliminaries and order the pizzas, please do so. No olives, correct?"

Madison smiles as we move together toward a quieter spot along the far wall. She's an attractive woman of around our age, seemingly friendly and eager to please. She looks us over, evaluating, and waits for us to go first. I oblige.

"Thanks for your help. First, can you tell us what the Raelism Movement is?"

She shifts in her chair and glances back at the main group. "In short, we believe that celestial beings, far more advanced than ourselves, created humanity and have been guiding us toward the enlightenment for several millennia. Once we achieve the necessary level of peace among ourselves, they'll return." Vinn and I exchange glances, both of us thinking of Scott's interest in all things space. "But it would take too long to even fill you in on the basics. Feel free to stay for the meeting and see what you can learn, but for now please tell me what you want to know."

"We're trying to make sense of the murders of both Rachel and Scott by retracing the last days of their lives. You spoke with both of them. What did you discuss? Why were they here?"

Madison looks thoughtful, as if trying to bring back the memory. "They were both quiet, shy. It was the second meeting for the young man. He was very interested in learning all he could about the Elohim, the creators I mentioned, and kept asking about how he could be involved in preparing for their return. Frankly I think he was more focused on the mechanics of that than of following the teachings of Rael, of becoming a better person. Rachel I remember because she reminded me of myself at one point. A very shy young woman. Unlike the boy, she wanted to talk about finding peace within herself and our belief that there is no right or wrong type of sexuality. She was looking for a place to fit in, for acceptance. I was hoping she would return but obviously given what you're telling us she wasn't given the chance. Even though they didn't come together and had different goals, they seemed to pair up in the way that newcomers do in a room full of strangers."

Madison again looks over her shoulder at the group and her fidgeting increases. I can tell that our time is growing short.

"Madison, how did your conversation end? Did they give any indication as to what they were going to do?"

For the first time, she appears reluctant to share what she knows. "Rachel, I strongly urged her to join us, that we could provide the answers to what she sought. I offered to meet with her to talk further and gave her a book summarizing our beliefs. The young man, I suggested he look inward to ask what he was really looking for. I even—"

She stopped, suddenly regretful for what she was going to say. We're losing her. Vinn reaches over, puts her hand on Madison's arm, and in a soft voice says simply, "Madison, please."

The young woman makes a quick decision and leans forward, whispering so that we need to lean in as well to hear her. "I determined he would not be a good addition, but he was persistent, so I gave him an alternative. At the time I saw it as a way to shift his focus away from us, from our chapter. I shouldn't have done it and feel guilty. There's a woman who used to be a member here but she was driven by other motives, by her goal of centering attention on herself, of being an Angel. She left a while back, either to form her own group or to pursue her agenda on her own. I don't know if she ever did. I suggested he speak with her. I noticed that the girl copied down her information as well."

Madison pushes her chair back, ready to rejoin the meeting. Vinn and I both instinctively reach out in vain, leading Vinn to rise and move to intercept her. "Madison, what is the woman's name? And what do you mean, an 'angel'?"

Madison again looks over her shoulder, this time to make sure she won't be overheard. "Veronica Struthers. Now please, I need to go. We're starting."

Madison hastens back to her seat just as the pizzas arrive and assiduously avoids any further eye contact with us. Rather than move back to our own former positions, we stay put to clearly demarcate ourselves as observers rather than participants as Amir rises to start the meeting.

We sit, transfixed, as we hear an update on the status of organizing demonstrations for peace and sexual equality, a brief discussion on the latest developments in cloning and genetically modified organisms, and individual members' testimonials about what they've done in the last month to promote peace and harmony within their own lives. Amir reviews the ethical code for Raelism and a date and location are set for the initiation of two new members. As the meeting progresses, less time is spent on information relevant to our purposes and more on administrative tasks. My attention starts to wander but is immediately drawn back when my ears pick up the phrases "sensual mediation" and "cosmic orgasm."

I feel a strong tug on my sleeve and look up to see Vinn standing by my side, coat in hand. "That's enough, we're out of here," she insists. "You don't need to go to outer space for one of those."

We make our own way to the door.

# TWENTY ONE

"What was the attraction of that group that led both of our victims to it?" Vinn asks as we sit in my office the next morning. "Is it a cult? Just a bunch of kooks? And what is it about this mystery woman that was so offensive that they cast her out? Did Scott meet with her? Did both of them? And most importantly is she or someone else in the group somehow connected to Crum? We have some work ahead of us, but I'm not quite sure where to start."

I peer at her over a stack of papers from a freshman class that I should have graded last night but put off after finding myself unable to focus on the first one. I need to get them done before my early afternoon class, so while Vinn's raising questions that definitely need attention, the timing is poor. "Don't you have a lab or something you need to get to?" I grumble as I take my red pen in hand.

"Fine, I see you're being professorial for once. But before I leave you to impose angst and agony upon your students, can we at least quickly outline a course of action and divide up who does what in case we have a few minutes of free time during the day?"

I hate it when she makes sense and put my pen down. "The first step is obvious, don't you think? We need to learn all we can about this Raelism thing and only then try to connect the dots to see why the kids ended up there. What we discover will determine what we do from there. I guess it wouldn't hurt to track down that Struthers woman, but right now we're not ready to meet with her. We need to be better informed. Now scoot."

Vinn doesn't take offense. She'll do what she wants to anyway and was only asking my opinion to make me think that I have some modicum of input into how we proceed with the investigation. "Okay, I've got class anyway. Let's reconvene at my place tonight. Bring snacks, I anticipate it'll be a long night." Vinn moves to the door and winks as she says this, lending an air of suggestibility to her comment. Among her many strengths, she can be a great motivator. Now she knows I'll be on time, chips and cookies in hand.

As it turned out, I had no time between grading papers, teaching, and hosting unusually busy office hours to even begin any research, so I arrive at Vinn's door (two minutes early) as ignorant about Raelism as I was in the morning. I know Vinn's class schedule by heart and her Mondays are jammed as well, but being who she is I'm sure she still found a few minutes somewhere to run a fast Google search.

"Smells good," I say as I drop my bags of dried seaweed, cheesy jalapeno popcorn, and homemade bourbon chip cookies off in the kitchen. "What's for dinner?"

Vinn frowns. "It's supposed to be lentil stew with spiced chicken, but I'm not so sure. We may have to call Stan to have a pizza delivered."

I dip a spoon in the sauce and bring it to my mouth. Even before I swallow I know there's no pizza in the forecast tonight. It's marvelous, as I'm sure she knows. "Mmm. Did you get this recipe from Leo?"

Her reaction is swift as she hits my head with a stalk of celery but can't hide the smile from the corners of her mouth. I remove garlic bread from the oven and slice it as Vinn serves out portions of stew. We eat contentedly, comfortable in the silence. There'll be plenty of time for conversation when we sit down in front of her laptop after dinner. That time comes all too soon.

"I didn't have much time to get started today," she explains as we snuggle into position on the floor, backs against the couch. "But I can give you a few basics before we get back online. Raelism is a religion—some call it a cult—that was formed in the early seventies by a Frenchman. I don't remember his real name, but he now goes by 'Rael.' Supposedly all of humanity was created 25,000 years ago by an extraterrestrial species called the Elohim. Throughout history they've sent Elohim/human hybrids to Earth as prophets to help us harness new scientific and technological developments to bring peace to the planet. Buddha, Jesus, and Mohammed were supposedly a few of these prophets. The fortieth and final one is, no surprise, Rael.

"Once this peace is established, the Elohim will send a delegation to Earth, share their own technology, and usher in a utopia. That's about as far as I got. Pretty wild so far, though."

Vinn opens up her laptop, navigates to a site she had bookmarked earlier, and we're off and reading. "Interesting," I say. "It says here that the Elohim are not considered gods, only alien beings much more advanced than we are. They actually reject the existence of God and see their beliefs as science based." Here, Vinn can't help but cough scornfully. She clicks on a link.

"I glanced at this earlier," she tells me as she scrolls down. "Some of their beliefs are fairly progressive. Equal rights, in fact women seem to hold a higher place within the group than men, they acknowledge gender as an artificial construct and emphasize its fluidity, their goal is world peace, they discourage the use of drugs, and they feel that any behavior is acceptable as long as it doesn't harm others or science itself. They support a woman's right to choose."

Tired of being behind as we read, I fire up my own laptop. "They're also strong advocates of cloning, which makes sense because one of their fundamental tenets is that science will solve the world's problems. But despite all of these things that make some sense, there's also their belief in these beings from a planet outside our solar system with 90,000 immortal Elohim who monitor our every move. Oh, and here's some information on that 'sensual meditation.' It's purpose seems to be to telepathically send thoughts of love to the Ehohim light years away, and they believe that having sex increases intelligence, but it also looks like an excuse to have orgies."

Vinn snorts in disgust. "Leave it to you to pick up on that. Enough of the generalities, this is all interesting but it's not getting us to Rachel and Scott's connection. Dig deeper, hombre."

For several minutes there are no sounds other than the quiet tapping of keys, a grunt from one or the other of us, and the tearing of plastic as Vinn opens up a package of seaweed. Right on cue, we both break the silence and start speaking at once. Vinn tells me to go first.

I can't keep the excitement out of my voice. "Listen to this. When that magic moment finally comes and the Elohim are set to return to a new, peaceful planet, Rael wants to be ready to receive them. For years he's been working on building an embassy, even purchasing a large tract of land in Europe. He's pretty specific about the requirements and there are even plans on their website. Look."

I turn my screen so that Vinn can see. She lets out a low whistle. "Wow. Reception hall, living quarters, meeting room, all round. Now those drawings Scott produced make sense. He was designing the embassy. For whatever reason, he thought he could find a place among these people by drawing up specifications or projections that could be used to make architectural plans. Was he asked to prepare them or did he do this on his own? We have a thread to unravel, good job. Now my turn."

Vinn gathers her thoughts before she speaks. "It's not as direct a connection as what you found for Scott. We already learned that Raelism values peace, love, and togetherness, and not always in a sexual sense, Mr. Pervert. But they're also extremely structured, with an established hierarchy, a code of ethics, and rules. It may call itself a religion, and so far we haven't seen where it has its members leave society and donate all their worldly possessions to it, but religions and cults in some ways aren't that different. They foster a sense of belonging and offer a reward down the road.

"So I looked up typical traits of people who join cults. Here's a sampling: They feel neglected by their parents and want to feel good about themselves. A need to belong. Seeking a meaning in life. Low self-worth, suggestible, a follower. Sexually marginalized, which would definitely fit an Amish teen and a geeky kid. A willingness to let others make decisions for them to avoid personal responsibility. Blaming others for the results of their own actions. Sound familiar?"

Vinn jumped in to interpret what I found, now it's my turn to do the same. "So let me see if I understand where you're going with this, starting with Rachel's parents. Father is stern, strict, doesn't show positive feelings and the mother is too cowed to do so. She grew up with a set of rules she was expected to abide by. Her whole life she had been conditioned to conform. So now she's a teenager and a rebellious streak emerges, Rumspringa gives her the opportunity to emerge from her shell, but she's not ready to fully embrace her new-found independence. She's still a follower. She latches on to the other three kids, then once here finds this group—maybe while using a computer for the first time—that offers her a chance to belong but still to conform, but with a greater sense of freedom and a wild set of rules that could pull her as far away from Amish beliefs as possible."

Vinn nods as she continues to stare at the screen. "Something like that. We're making a lot of assumptions about Rachel's mindset and desires, but it makes sense. And there's more. People who join cults can be more susceptible to accepting odd or even supernatural beliefs and behaviors. I don't know how she found them, but it sounds like Raelism was just waiting for Rachel to drop in."

I close my eyes in thought while Vinn continues to click and scroll, looking for any last crumb of information before we discuss what to do with what little we have. I'm just entering that happy realm between wakefulness and sleep when a simultaneous shriek and elbow to my ribs brings me back to the land of the living. I open my eyes to see a pale and trembling Vinn pointing at her laptop screen. Assuming that she won't be verbalizing her find, I lean in to read for myself.

I don't shriek but understand why she did. Buried deep within a long summary of Raelist beliefs is a single, two-sentence paragraph that verifies that we're on the right path in the creepiest of ways. To join the movement, parties must sign a contract with a local mortician so that their "third eye," a portion of the frontal lobe, can be cut out and packed in ice before it's sent to a bank vault in Switzerland for storage and safekeeping. This process allows the member's genetic code to be telepathically transmitted to the Elohim through an earthly Guide, ensuring that they can be recreated after death on the Planet of the Eternals and retain all of their former memories.

I turn back to Vinn, who's recovered from her initial shock. "I almost missed it," she tells me. "I was seconds away from pulling the lid shut. On the one hand, this is huge. It validates our assumption that the answers we seek can be found through the Raelists."

I jump in to finish her thought. "On the other hand, it doesn't offer us any hints of the path we need to take next. It always feels good to be right. It would feel better if there were neon arrows pointing us in the direction we need to go."

With heavy sighs, we sit back and digest what we just discovered along with the popcorn we ate as we talked. The question we're both pondering is what we now do all of the facts and factoids we've uncovered. I offer my own thought.

"I'd like to talk to Scott's parents if we could, ask them about his behavior, whether he ever let something slip about what he was doing. But before we do, and I admit that I may be procrastinating approaching them again and am looking for alternatives, I think we need to talk to Veronica Struthers. Find her first, then arrange a meet."

"Yeah, I agree with the Veronica part," Vinn replies. "Not so sure about the parents. One step at a time, though. Let's see if we can get in touch with this woman and see where that leads us. She may give us all we need. I can start searching for her presence on social media right now, but you have to do something for me first."

"Yes?" I may have sounded too eager. Vinn looks disgusted.

"Down, cowboy. Not that," she says. "I need you to bring that bag of cookies over here."

# TWENTY TWO

It doesn't take long to discover that Veronica Struthers isn't shy or wary about public exposure. On the contrary, she seems to thrive in the social media spotlight and posts on her pages regularly throughout each day. Most of these entries, whether they're on Facebook, Instagram, or Twitter, include pictures of herself. She's an attractive woman in her mid-thirties whom the camera seems to love. Blond in most of the photos, she's also experimented with other colors and with bright, unusual highlights and streaking. She's always immaculately made up and dressed as if she were on the runway, without a hair out of place.

Working our way through her various sites, we observe her choosing her wardrobe for the day, eating a salad, choosing her wardrobe change in the middle of the day, petting a cute dog, and choosing her wardrobe for her evening sojourn. For any given day as long back as we cared to look, we were well informed as to every meal she ate, every drink she drank, and every thought that may have crossed her mind. She has a number of followers on each site but very little interaction with any of them. Most are probably there just to see the show.

"Let's move on to LinkedIn to see if she actually has a job," Vinn suggests as she shakes the last of the cookie crumbs out of the bag and into her mouth. "Let's see. A degree in sociology from Wesleyan, some mentions on lists of women to watch in business—none recent—a few blurbs from charities thanking her for her efforts. Ah, here we are. She lists her current job as Vice President in charge of marketing at Samson and Peabody, Ltd. Not that I would, but I've never heard of them."

"On it." I'm glad to have something to do and type in a few commands then look for the link most likely to help.

"It's a legitimate company, over a hundred million in income. Looks like they're kind of a brokerage and sales-oriented firm, not manufacturing anything themselves. Her picture is on their website along with other officers."

"All right, so we know we're dealing with an intelligent woman, perhaps ambitious, has some money. Not exactly the typical profile of a murder-for-hire solicitor, at least where the spouse isn't the target, but you never know. Now how do we make contact?"

"Before we get to that," I interject, "about what you just said. How are we going to determine if there's any connection between she and Crum? Or if she's even met Scott and Rachel? We can't exactly tell her we're investigating their deaths and show her their pictures, or ask if she knows the guy who killed them."

Vinn thinks for a minute. "With J.J. out of the picture, we don't have access or authority to get credit card records, subpoena bank accounts, or any of the usual ways that law enforcement uses to see if two people are in the same place at the same time or if money changed hands. We're going to have to be more creative. We need to get close to her, find some way to convince her that we have shared interests, spend time with her. Ultimately, create a sort of false intimacy that'll encourage her to open up, to unwittingly drop a remark or reveal something that will tell us what we need to know. We'll never be able to prove that she didn't order the killings, but if she did hopefully we'll get affirmation of that fact. After that, we see where we go and how much of a case we can turn over to Mendez."

"Vinn, I'm impressed. You've obviously thought this through more than I have. But..." I hesitate to go on, "I have to say that it still sounds like our plan is to basically fly by the seat of our pants and see what happens."

"Wouldn't be the first time," she says with a grin. "The idea is that it'll become more refined over time as we interact with her. So the second step is to find common ground, real or otherwise, that'll give us an excuse to spend a lot of our leisure time with her."

The tease. She leaves it hanging, waiting for me to ask. I do. "And the first step is?"

"We have to find her."

We both return to our laptops in a race of sorts. Contacting her at her job is a last resort, as people normally keep their work and personal lives separate and take offense when one is thrust into the other. It wouldn't get us off to a good start in creating the sort of "false intimacy" that Vinn has set as our goal. We need a home address or an email address.

Sighs of frustration emanate from the sleuth to my left as she tries to use any visual clues in the thousand or so photographs Veronica posted on social media to narrow down where she lives or what organizations she belongs to so that we can just happen to be at the same meeting as enthusiastic devotees of the cause. Rather than duplicate the effort that Vinn's better at anyway, and which isn't yielding results, I choose a different approach.

It's a different kind of social media, more of a public record, that I search. Criminal records, to be precise. I begin with general databases available to anyone with a computer and time on their hands and mix in a source I've had bookmarked for years that only someone with government credentials can access. Not for the first time, I thank the bureaucracy for its inefficiency in updating who can enter its portal.

As Vinn tires of uttering English-language profanity and switches to French, I calmly take a few notes, send documents to my inbox for printing later, and close my laptop. I guess I can't avoid looking smug, as within seconds Vinn looks over at me. "What?" is all she asks.

"Apparently our social butterfly has a past. About three years ago she was arrested for domestic abuse, fought it, and lost. Husband filed for divorce. Both her parole records and the court documents for the divorce list the same home address. If it's current, she lives in Humboldt Park not far from where we know Rachel ate lunch all those times."

"We need a hook," I mention to Vinn as we settle in for the evening at my place a few nights later. "Something to make Veronica instantly curious about us and about how we can fit into her life. For that to work, I think it's important that we just show up at her door. It's too hard to sell ourselves over the phone and too easy for her to hang up if we're perceived as a nuisance. We'll have one shot at this and need to make it count."

"I've been thinking the same thing," Vinn admits. "And it's got to be linked to Raelism, don't you agree? Other than fashion, where let's face it you are I are totally clueless"—she nods toward my tattered Montana State University sweatshirt with a cartoon bobcat on the prowl across the front— "the only thing we know that she's passionate about, or at least assume she is based on what Madison told us at that meeting, is this crazy UFO religion. Using that as our common ground gives us a better chance to bring Rachel and Scott into play. And I've got an idea."

Vinn has a mischievous twinkle in her eye that I know all too well signals that the next words out of her mouth are going to be sound absolutely insane at first but that she's convinced make perfect sense. They're the kind of thought that comes to you in the middle of the night and at that time seem like pure genius, but upon waking the next morning is revealed to be idiocy at its finest. Except she never gets to the waking up stage. Whatever she's about to say, she already knows two things: that I won't like it, and that she'll wear me down until I agree to quash my objections and just follow her lead. I brace myself.

"First," she begins, eyeing me to gauge my reaction, "I did a little more research into Raelist beliefs with the express purpose of finding some way to insert ourselves into Veronica's inner circle. You're not going to like this"—here it comes—"but it has a very female-centered ideology. I don't mean that it caters only to women, in fact there are more male members, but it reveres women to the point that it espouses that the world would be a better place if all of its leaders were female. A point on which I happen to agree.

"You know how they want to build an embassy to greet the Elohim when they return to Earth? The protocol set forth by Rael, the head honcho, is that other than himself it would be only women present to greet them. A select group. Which bring us to my first point. You're going to have to take a secondary role here, at least as it appears to Veronica. I'm certain that she would be much more receptive if I take the lead in dealing with her, not only because most women prefer dealing with other women but because of the Raelist belief system."

Vinn pauses, waiting for my inevitable and explosive reaction. I withhold it for now because I know there's more to come. "You said 'my first point.' There are more?"

She grins. "Yes, one more. Remember how Madison mentioned that Veronica needed all of the attention focused on herself, and that she wanted to be an 'Angel'? I didn't think much about her use of that term at the time, assuming she was just using it in a pejorative sense, but she may have actually been referencing something much more specific. There's a group within the Raelian Church called 'The Order of Rael's Angels.' They're the ones that will be the sole people allowed into the embassy, the only humans permitted contact with the

Elohim. Hold on, I want to make sure I get this correct."

Vinn pulls her laptop over, opens it up and finds her notes. "According to their fearless leader, only women can be Angels because men aren't feminine enough for the extremely gentle, delicate, and sensitive Elohim." She smirks and cocks an eye at me before continuing. "But it goes beyond that. The Angels would act as liasons between the Elohim and our politicians, scientists, and journalists. Not to mention that they would be the Elohim's, ah hem, 'consorts.' There's a whole tier structure for these women and each level wears different colored feathers on a necklace. The white-feathered women are the entry level and their job is to attract other women to the Raelian movement. The top two tiers, Pink and Gold, though, are supposedly handpicked by Rael for their physical beauty and would remain chaste, except when they receive instruction from him in the lovemaking skills necessary to please the Elohim."

I'm sure I'm gawking. "I'm sure Rael just loathes life at the top and being tasked with such an oppressive duty. Nice work if you can get it. Vinn, this is all fascinating and you've given me a new occupation to aspire to as Rael's understudy, but how does this fit in with what we've got to do?"

She avoids making eye contact, which is not a good sign. "I think this Angel aspect might be our way in, if Veronica aspires to be one of Rael's Angels and we can somehow convince her that we can help her dream come true. Maybe even provide a companion aspiring to do the same so that they can have intimate talks that might reveal some secrets from her recent past. Something we can use, if she ordered Crum to kill those kids."

"I still don't follow. Are you volunteering yourself to be this companion?"

Vinn snorts, not an attractive trait for an Angel. "Thanks for the complement, but no. I couldn't begin to be the girly girl that would require and I don't think you would appreciate my refraining from all sex. But I do have someone in mind, especially considering that one demographic of women has an inside track to being chosen as an Angel. Rael reserves special praise for transwomen because they actually choose to be a woman."

I'm once again speechless. She was right that I wouldn't like what she was going to 'suggest.' Vinn appears to be finding amusement in continually bringing Rebecca into our investigation and into our lives. I put on my unhappy face as Vinn mockingly covers hers with a pillow, and once again reach for the phone.

# TWENTY THREE

"I mean, really girl, an overall lightening and a few highlights, and then trim it to frame your face better. What foundation do you use? You might consider something that hides the shadows from your nose, and my goodness, those lashes!"

Vinn's level of misery is probably equal to the amount of enjoyment I'm feeling watching Rebecca give an impromptu and unsolicited evaluation of her cosmetic and hair styling preferences, or lack thereof. Physical appearance has never been a top priority for Vinn. As long as I've known her I think she's worn makeup maybe twice and she's never suffered for it. She's naturally beautiful and doesn't need any enhancement to prove it. Not that it would matter to her anyway. Making herself pretty whether through makeup or stylistic clothing simply isn't important to her. Rebecca, on the other hand, for obvious reasons, is the exact opposite. She needs as much help as she can get to cover her maleness. Given the fashion magazines I've seen littering her apartment, she's put a lot of study into it, albeit with questionable success. I'll bet she knows more about eye liner than Vinn ever will.

Before Rebecca dropped in, Vinn and I debated our approach in bringing her into our investigation. She's never been shy about putting herself in the danger zone and even appears to welcome a change of pace from her everyday routine beyond even her nightly transformation across gender lines. We're not sure that there's much risk in the role we want her to play but decided that we'd still feel better if we let it be her own decision whether to get involved. Granted the odds are stacked given that we're going to do everything we can to lead her in that direction, but it'll still help me justify her involvement later should anything unexpected happen to her.

Rebecca only lives one floor down, so we didn't have much time to come up with more than an overall concept totally lacking in specifics. On the phone I told her that Vinn needs to look her best for an opportunity she has coming up and that we could use her guidance. Ultimately the idea is for her to get so exasperated with Vinn that she'll jump at the chance to tag along and demonstrate how the advice she's giving looks on herself. She was barely past the doorstep before she began spewing "honest" but brutal opinions about Vinn's appearance, her frustration level reaching a peak much earlier than we expected. She's clearly getting under Vinn's skin. If I let this go on much longer, there may be bloodshed. I've had my fun; time to step in.

"Rebecca, before you continue it might be helpful if I explain a little better what it is we're looking for. This isn't necessarily about making the right choices for Vinn, but about transforming her into what another woman would see as the personification of beauty. That might mean turning her into something that she's not."

Rebecca looks confused and for once has nothing to say. As planned, Vinn takes over the conversation. "Mal, I don't think we can explain this without giving her the full story." She turns back to our guest. "Rebecca, you know that we were looking into the murders of those two young people and you're also aware of how that ended in a shootout and the death of their killer. What you don't know is that neither one of us is convinced that the culpability ends with him. Now we're investigating whether someone else was behind his actions, that someone gave him orders to kill them. We have a suspect but the evidence against her is flimsy, more of a hunch really. We need to get closer to her."

Rebecca's eyes widen as Vinn lays out specifics as to what led us to the Raelist group and then further on to Veronica Struthers. A broad smile forms as Vinn gets to the part about Rael's Angels and the feathered necklaces. The bait has been set. When Vinn lets slip the fact that transgendered women may have an advantage in the selection process, she's swallowed the hook.

"So," Vinn goes on, "I could use your advice on how to look, I guess the word would be 'angelic.' You can see that I don't use a lot of makeup, so I need a quick tutorial on what I need to do to convince this woman that I'm a good candidate to join her in her quest. That's the critical first step to have any chance to get close to her, which I need to do to find out if she even knew the kids before moving on to anything else that might help us."

Now clear as to the mission before her, Rebecca launches into a baffling speech that I mostly tune out, catching only key words like "mascara," "color palate," and "shading." I pay attention again when I hear the word "hopeless."

Vinn looks on the verge of tears. "I'm so sorry, Rebecca," she says as she stifles sobs, "it's just all so overwhelming and I just don't think I can do it. And it's so, so important that I get this right the first time. I won't get a second chance, I just know it. And we haven't even figured out how to get Mal at my side. He obviously can't be an Angel, but if we're right about Veronica she's a dangerous woman and I don't want to be with her all by myself. We thought about him posing as a sort of valet or servant, but he's even more hopeless about all of this than I am."

Rebecca sits up tall, hopefully not noticing the sly wink Vinn throws my way. "Girl, don't you worry your cute little head any longer. Miss Rebecca knows just what to do. I can't imagine why you didn't think of this yourselves. Shame on you, Malcom." I try my best to look abashed. "I volunteer to join you when you go see this woman. Don't take this the wrong way, but I'm a bit more accustomed to making myself just absolutely stunning. An Angel for sure."

Vinn looks up at Rebecca like she just rescued her from a deep, dark well. "Would you really? Oh, but we couldn't ask you to put yourself at any sort of risk. Although with your beauty know-how and the inside track accorded to transwomen..." She lets it hang.

Rebecca looks extremely pleased with herself but in the next instant her features take on a darker, more somber tone. "Um, about that. I mean, does it matter, well, how far, I mean..." Rebecca is clearly flustered and her usual outflow of gab stinted. Vinn and I look at each other, puzzled, but the realization suddenly hits me.

"Oh, no, Rebecca. I don't think it matters how far down the path you've gone in that regard." I'm struggling. How do I put this delicately? "I mean, we don't anticipate this getting far enough where she would actually check, um, down there."

The corner of Vinn's mouth turns up as she catches on to what Rebecca was worried about. She's no doubt suppressing a fit of giggles. Rebecca simply looks relieved.

"Well then," Vinn jumps in to lift the awkwardness and move forward, "if you really want to do this, I think we have some planning to do."

The women agree that the planning would best be done in my absence, or at least that's what Vinn professed to. They set a time and date on a weeknight, leaving Rebecca with a definite lilt in her step when she heads back downstairs to, in her words, "start clearing out Net-a-Porter." Once we hear her enter her apartment, though, Vinn's face falls.

"Mal, I don't mean this to sound cruel, and I'm as far from an expert as you can get, but I'm not sure that Rebecca is the best judge of how feminine she looks even when she goes all out. Granted, she's able to bury a lot of the masculinity under layers of Maybelline, but that doesn't get her very far along toward the beautiful end of the spectrum. She's improved a lot since I first met her, but would Veronica take one look and say 'That's an Angel if ever I saw one?'"

"I'm glad to hear you say that because now I know it isn't only me. You know there's a part of me that, let's say, appreciates a good-looking woman. Don't give me that look—when we're out together I've seen your head turn toward a particularly pretty face as she passes us by. Rebecca turns heads as well, but not for the same reason. Do you have any suggestions? The last thing I want to do is hurt her feelings by telling her that the beauty regimen she's so proud of falls short."

We sit in silence for several moments before Vinn sits up, pulls her laptop open, and begins furiously typing. It takes her a few minutes to find what she's looking for.

"Mal, slide over and look at this. A couple of years ago there was a production on campus written by theater majors as their senior thesis. I didn't see it so I don't know much about the story itself or if this was part of the plot or just pretense on the part of the students, but some of the male roles were played by women and some of the female roles by men. They didn't reveal which parts those were until the end, and I've heard that it was virtually impossible to guess. I've pulled up some pictures taken of the play."

I stare at the images on the screen, both close-ups and full-stage shots. I gently push Vinn's hands aside as I take over her keyboard, clicking back and forth on several pictures. I finally give up. "I can't tell."

"I know, right?" she replies with satisfaction. "I cheated before I called you over and looked at the cast list. We can ignore the women playing men. There are three male students who took on the roles of woman. This one here, and that one are two of them." As she speaks, Vinn uses the cursor to identify the two actors. I'm astonished.

"Even now that you've told me, I'm not sure I believe you. They're not only passable, they're beaut—"

"Beautiful, yes. Faces that both you and I would rudely stare at on the street. And the student who designed the makeup for the entire cast should still be on campus this year. I know because I recognize the name. She was in my freshman biology class three years ago, so unless she left school, she'd be a senior this year."

I take a minute to consider the possibilities and one potential roadblock stands out. I address Vinn but am talking it out to myself as well. "Let's assume this student is still at UIC, that we can find her, and that she's got both time and interest in helping us out. And that Rebecca isn't too great a challenge. She's not as fresh-faced as a twenty-year-old but that doesn't mean we could convince her to submit to it. She's proud of her own shall we say, skills with brushes."

"I've thought of that too. We follow the same plan as tonight, which worked so well. You heard how critical she was of my meager efforts at beautifying myself."—I think that stung more than Vinn cares to admit— "We can say that I've made arrangements for myself, and as long as I'm going to do it Rebecca might as well come along as well. I don't know any woman who would say no to a free makeover. If that doesn't work, we'll appeal to her love of espionage and tell her it's her disguise."

Vinn's enthusiasm is growing the more she thinks this through. My guess is that she includes herself in the category of women who will jump at a free makeover. Free, because I have a feeling that I'll be paying for it. I've learned to follow Vinn's leads in areas in which I have no experience and do so again here.

Vinn uses her position as a tenured professor to access the admission's office student records and finds the student's email address, which may or may not have been legal. She types up a quick note telling the young woman what we need but not the truth about why, offers some of my hard-earned pay, and asks what she needs in advance to plan the transformations. Once she pushes 'send' we glance at the time. We've done all we can for tonight. Operation Build an Angel is underway.

# TWENTY FOUR

"She's actually extremely enthusiastic about the idea," Vinn tells me as we sit in the café before classes. Today's treat that I'll never get to taste, which doesn't break my heart, is a simple English muffin with the jam that comes in those little single-serve plastic containers. It's irritating to contribute to a landfill for a couple teaspoons of tasteless flavored spread, so I take comfort in my tea. Today I've splurged on a rare Japanese Sencha sourced from an ancient tea grower I once met in my travels through the countryside. I'm not usually a fan of floral, and prefer Chinese leaves to those of Japan, but this is subtle and heavenly.

I realize I've zoned out as I savor my drink and pick Vinn back up in mid-sentence. "...a project of sorts that she may even get credit for. Kind of a side-by-side study of the different challenges of applying make-up to a woman and to a man." Vinn frowns. "I'm not sure I appreciate being labeled as a 'challenge' and having to endure being photographed every step of the way so that my 'transformation,' as she calls it, can be shared with another faculty member, isn't something I would do unless I had to. But it's probably the only way we could have convinced Rebecca to go along even though she did seem excited at the prospect of being the center of attention."

Vinn's prediction that Rebecca would gladly undergo a free makeover was not only accurate, it was an understatement as to the exuberance with which the proposal was met. It was all Vinn could do to convince Rebecca that she had to wait until the timing was right, which for now is open-ended. We need to coordinate the makeovers so that they occur immediately prior to our "accidental" encounter with Veronica, whenever that may be. Considering that Heather Chapman, our magician with the brushes, said that she would need at least four hours, maybe longer, imposes an unexpected obstacle in our already difficult task of finding an ideal situation in which to arrange the encounter. Heather is aware that we may end up pulling her from a class last-minute and Rebecca doesn't seem bothered by the prospect of leaving work on a moment's notice. It also made convincing her that for Heather's purposes she'd need to show up as Ted a little easier, although Vinn now has three of Rebecca's dresses hanging in her office to bring with her whenever it's time.

"I've instructed Rebecca to study up on Raelism and sent her some useful links," I say as we gather our trash and prepare to head off to class. "The threat of leaving her behind seemed pretty effective in encouraging her to do her home-work. I guess all that's left now is to find the right opportunity to run into this woman, get the timing right on the make-overs, convince her to bring us into her inner circle, lure her into complacency so that she'll tell you guys something that'll connect her to Crum or at least the two victims—whatever that may be—and then build a case strong enough to bring to Mendoza so that the cops reopen the matter while still main-taining your fake relationship. Piece of cake."

Vinn looks glum as she wraps up the remainder of her muffin to finish later. "When you put it that way, I don't know what I've been worried about."

Over the next several days after our conversation in the café, each of us devote any free few minutes of time to perus-ing Veronica's posts on Facebook, analyzing the pictures she put up on Instagram, and mining every word of every sentence she wrote on social media for any hint of where she would be at a given time, preferably in the afternoon to give Heather time for the dual transformations. For someone who likes to be noticed, even adored, she's remarkably guarded about the types of personal information that would allow any of her followers to interact with her outside the distance of the internet. Our frustration level is rising by the hour.

"I have noticed one thing that may prove helpful," I tell Vinn over the phone as I lie propped up in bed late one night, my laptop open to one of Veronica's pages. "In a number of her selfies taken on different days and in different locations, she's either holding a hot drink container or has one sitting nearby. There's the same logo on the cup each time. Not easy to make out, as it's either partially covered by her fingers or too far away for a good look, but it may be a favorite stop for her. Sending some of the better pictures now."

I expect a few minutes of silence as I wait for Vinn to view the photos, but she surprises me with a near immediate response. "You're lucky not everyone is as averse to coffee as you are. That's clearly the logo for Dark Matter Coffee. They're near the top of the list of any local aficionado of roasted beans. Their main shop is on Western near Chicago."

I'm elated. "Wonderful! Then Veronica must stop by there on a regular basis and we can bump into her there."

"Not so fast, Mr. Tea Leaves. They have more than one location, and other coffee shops in the area, especially around Humboldt Park, use their coffee and have cups with the same or a similar Dark Matter logo. We can't be sure which one she frequents."

I'm deflated. "Okay, a minor setback. But that still gives me an idea. Let me make a call and I'll see you tomorrow."

"Yeah, she told me about the makeover and that she was involved in some sort of 'mysterious intrigue.' Her words, not mine. You know Rebecca, when it comes to drawing attention to herself she can't keep quiet, but she's still careful not to reveal details. And I knew better than to probe."

I still have Chuck's number in my phone from a prior

adventure when we used he and a team of assorted acquaintances of Rebecca on a tailing job. Chuck is half a head taller and a third weightier than me but proved to be exceptional at remaining invisible while conducting surveillance. Our common love of fine tea also proves he's trustworthy and a true gentleman.

"I appreciate it, thanks," I respond. "This should be simple for you. We just need to determine a reliable daily routine for someone who would have no reason to suspect that she's being observed. We think she goes to the same coffee shop on a regular basis. We'd like to know which one and when, hopefully around the same time each day. There's more Dragon Pearl Jasmine in it for you."

I can sense him grinning through the phone. "Still have some saved from the last time. You'll have to expand your bribery repertoire. Text me her address and picture. I'll get back to you in a week or so."

It was eight days, a period in which Vinn asked me about progress eight times, Heather emailed Vinn four times and called twice more, and Rebecca called, emailed, or sent texts on 114 different occasions, give or take a few. Sitting idle has always been the hardest part of any investigation, but being the point man for the impatience of three others made the time crawl at glacial speed. I've rarely been happier to receive any phone call in my life.

"After all that, she does go to the main Dark Matter shop on Western." Vinn stopped by unannounced just as I was plating a spinach-lentil casserole and pulling dinner rolls out of the oven. I push my plate across the island and go to grab another. "Not every day, but five of the seven—she usually skips Wednesdays and Sundays. And at almost the exact same time each day. That's the good news. Bad news is that it's at 10:00 in the morning."

Vinn's fork stops midway to her mouth. "Shit," she mutters. "I guess we don't have much choice. And getting up early isn't the worst of it. There's no guarantee that she'll be there and we might have to repeat it."

"On the bright side," I cheerily respond, playing Mr. Optimistic, "at least you'll be able to wake up with some outstanding coffee."

Vinn did not see the bright side. We eat the rest of our dinner in silence.

# TWENTY FIVE

Neither Rebecca nor Heather are any more enthusiastic about the early start time than Vinn was, with Rebecca loudly and at great length complaining that interfering with her beauty sleep would more than offset any benefit of a semi-professional makeover. Much of her bluster is just for show, as she wouldn't be left out of the chance to play a role in our investigation even if it means making a few personal sacrifices. We agree to take a chance on the upcoming Saturday, on the one hand to avoid all of us having to miss work or class and also on the assumption that Veronica would be less likely to have a conflict that would interfere with her routine. Once that's decided, Heather notes that on a typical Friday night she often doesn't even get to bed by the time she'll have to start working her magic.

With a date set and everyone equally unhappy, we turn our attention to what kind of scenario we'll play out if we actually luck out and end up at the coffee shop at the same time Veronica is there. Vinn and I bounce ideas off of each other both in person and by text throughout the week, but nothing shines through that doesn't immediately scream "contrived" to the extent that alarm bells would immediately sound in our target's mind. By the time Friday night rolls around, I'm getting nervous. We have one shot at an "accidental" encounter and we have to make it count.

"Actually," Vinn begins as she dries the dishes I hand to her after rinsing them off, "this morning I thought of an approach that may work. I've turned it over in my head all day and then discussed it with Rebecca. She thinks it has a chance as well."

I'm momentarily stunned that Vinn bypassed me to run it by Rebecca first. "Would you like to share this revelation with your partner in crime?" I ask with only a hint of annoyance in my voice.

"No, not really," she answers without any indication that she's teasing. "Rebecca and I agree. Based on everything that we've read up on Raelism and in particular the whole concept of Angels, men take on a totally subservient role in preparing for the return of the Elohim. Like it or not, you're going to have to appear to be in the background on this, at least when we first meet Veronica. Besides, I don't trust your acting skills. No offense. I think it'll work better if you're genuinely surprised by what we do to attract her attention."

Admittedly the first images that flash through my mind as to actions likely to attract attention aren't healthy ones, which work to distract me from what should have been my response of being totally offended at being left behind. By the time I recover and plot a witty and face-saving retort, Vinn's moved on to other things.

"What do you say we watch a movie and then get to sleep early?" she asks as we move toward the couch. "We're due on campus at 5:00 tomorrow morning and don't want to be late. I have a feeling Heather will need every minute of her four hours to create two creatures of incomparable beauty."

Immediately a caustic remark comes to mind that could redeem my male pride. I swallow it and reach for the remote.

There's no good way to rouse a loved one at 4:00 a.m. The gentle approach is too passive to be effective. Dumping a bucket of ice water on her head too extreme, or so I've been told. So too, as I discover, is throwing off the covers in the middle of winter in a drafty bedroom. At least the effort to cast a creative and biting string of unique expletives my way has the desired effect of waking Vinn up. Sort of.

No sooner do we emerge bleary-eyed into the kitchen seeking caffeine than a pounding at the door compounds our misery. A hazy shouting of my name eventually lets the synapses in my brain conclude that there's a live person behind the knocking and that she wants to come inside. I look at my watch. Still too early for Rebecca, but...

"Well, it took long enough. Don't you know it's fourteen degrees out there? And of course it's snowing on our big day. Will that make it harder to get an Uber? Do you think this woman we're supposed to meet will be scared off by the snow? Where exactly are we going anyway? Wouldn't it have been easier to do it here? Do you have my dresses? What is that you're doing? Do you really think you have time for tea?"

Not getting the desired reaction from me, Rebecca turns to Vinn and immediately turns two shades paler upon seeing her angry face, which she must practice in a mirror. I've been the recipient of it on more than one occasion and it still rattles me. Rebecca retreats to the living room, sits down in a chair, but immediately stands up again and begins pacing.

"Rebecca, relax." My voice is hoarse. "I rented a Zipcar yesterday and it's parked right out front. We're meeting Heather in the theater department's stage area. And I can't imagine that traffic will be too bad. We have a few minutes."

The alarm from the coffee maker sounds, perhaps the only sound that would prompt Vinn to move off of her chair. As she chugs one cup and pours the rest into a Thermos, I do the same with my tea. Thus fortified, we find our shoes, make sure the right and left match, then grab our coats. Vinn retrieves a garment bag from the bedroom and I grab a bag of Ann Sather cinnamon rolls for the two beauty queens to eat on the way.

Heather's waiting for us just inside the back door of the campus theater, her puffy features a clear indication that she didn't alter her usual Friday night routine. Kids. She appraises my two companions as they enter the building with the practiced eye of an artist. I take it as a positive sign that she doesn't throw up her arms screaming and make a dash out the door. Instead she leads us down the hall, through one set of doors that brings us somewhere behind the stage, and to a door marked "Dressing Room 1."

The women enter but I stop just outside the room. "Well, good luck Heather. Ladies, I'll see you in four hours." I barely turn away before a torrent of venom hits me in the back.

"Where do you think you're going? Back to bed?" It's Vinn, but all three sets of eyes are focused on me. And yes, sleep was the plan. "Not a chance, buster. We're in this together. Sit down and pay attention. You might learn something. Maybe you can help with the pictures."

I stifle a groan that might justifiably come across as a form of protest, take an empty chair at the far end of the room but still aligned with those of Vinn and Rebecca, and try to prop my eyes open. We're stationed in front of a long mirror with vanity lights positioned along its entire perimeter. Heather pulls a portable light out of a gym bag and fiddles with it until it hits Vinn's face just right, then attaches a utility belt with every pocket crammed full of brushes around her waist. Only now do I notice that the counter at which we're sitting is covered with at least fifty more different brushes of varying shapes and sizes and countless pencils, jars, tubes, and other accessories. I've observed women put on makeup before but couldn't begin to guess what most of this is.

Heather takes a color wheel out of her pocket and spends several minutes evaluating as she places different shades next to Vinn's cheeks. She then dabs a small amount of foundation on one cheek, a different one on the other. Once she makes her decision, her speed increases. I only half pay attention as powders fill the air, tubes are opened and shut, small curses are uttered as a decision gets reconsidered, and slow progress is made. At some point Rebecca leans in to get a closer look at the proceedings, blocking my view, and giving me the opportunity to close my eyes for just a second.

"Well, what do you think?" I startle myself awake to see Vinn's chair turned my way to grant me a full frontal view. I move closer, shoulder to shoulder with Rebecca. "It's amazing. It hardly even looks like you." Both statements are true, but that doesn't mean I like it. Vinn has such a natural beauty that toying with it is like adding mascara to the Mona Lisa. On the other hand, the effort shows and I'm sure most women would be impressed by that fact alone. I look at my watch as Vinn and Rebecca change seats. Only an hour and ten minutes. Heather left plenty of time for Rebecca.

This time I actually am intrigued by the process. For our benefit, and perhaps for that of Rebecca as well, Heather keeps up a running commentary as she works. To save time, Vinn helps with the photography.

"For her, we have to be concerned first with making sure no stubble shows through. We start with a paint stick for fuller coverage that'll last before moving on to foundation and then we add translucent powder to make sure it all stays where it should." Rebecca starts to protest as Heather moves to her eyebrows but calms when she's assured that no plucking will occur. Her brows are reshaped by using wax to hide portions of them.

"There are eighteen different structural components between the male and female faces and we need to address them all to be most effective. I use bronzer to slim the forehead down, reduce the width of the nose, give the illusion of a sharper cheek bone and to soften the jaw." Heather quiets as her efforts intensify, leaving it to Vinn and I to just follow along. She takes a lot of time before stepping away and nodding to herself. She then mentions something about plumping the lips and a few other details. I check the time and am astonished that it's after 8:30.

Heather caps a tube of lip gloss, turns Rebecca in her chair to view her creation from every angle, then exhales deeply. "Lady and gentleman, I present Rebecca."

I realize then that I was so focused on the minutia that I never took time to examine the overall effect. As Rebecca's face comes into full view, my jaw drops. Even knowing what really lies below her waist, I can't convince myself that I'm looking at a man. She's not what I would call pretty, but is definitely striking in a good way. And definitely attractive. It says something about Heather's skills that I simply can't look away.

Rebecca has avoided looking into the mirror this entire time, remarkable restraint for her, but now Heather swings her to present her first look at the results. A small gasp fills the room. While we watch, Rebecca leans into the mirror, then steps further back, twisting to look at first one side and then the other. Without saying a word, she gathers a startled Heather in a close embrace. A few awkward moments later, it's Heather that speaks.

"Rebecca, don't you dare start crying and ruin your makeup."

With that, Rebecca releases Heather from her death grip. All three women look in my direction but I'm slow on the uptake. Vinn pulls me up out of the chair. "Time for you to wait outside, Mal. The ladies need to get dressed."

# TWENTY SIX

The aroma of coffee as we enter Dark Matter is almost in itself enough to pump my veins full of caffeine. A quick glance at the menu posted high on the wall confirms that they take their beans seriously enough here that they totally ignore tea drinkers. I designate myself as the table-saver, as seating is limited, and give Vinn cash for her own cup of fuel along with a croissant for myself. After looking at the bill she compresses her lips and vigorously tilts her head in Rebecca's direction. Sighing, I pull another five out of my wallet and hand it over.

Just as it looks like we'll have to settle for a spot against the wall to lean, an exasperated mother with a pair of screaming toddlers stands to vacate one of the few tables. Ever helpful, I hand her the hat one of them dropped on the floor while in the same motion sliding my coat off onto the chair the child just left, eliciting a glare from the twenty-something who'd been eyeing the table. I throw my most disarming smile her way to no avail. A Prince Charming I'm not.

Rebecca arrives soon after followed close behind by Vinn, who slides a plate with a large pastry across the table in my direction. I eye her suspiciously.

"Do they really sell croissants with a bite out of them?" I ask innocently.

"Mmphhmh," she mutters before turning her head to swallow. "I guess the baker tastes some of them for quality control purposes. If you're afraid of germs, I'll tear off that half and eat it for you." Getting no response, she quickly changes the subject. "Are you sure you don't want something to drink? I ordered a Red Eye, a house blend with espresso." She takes a drink and closes her eyes in rapture. "Marvelous. Rebecca, how's yours?"

"Heavenly, thank you. I got the latte and might need another." She sips hers through a coffee stirrer that doubles as a straw so as not to "mess up the lips."

I check the time on my phone. 9:51. We've been up for almost six hours. "Well, make them last. If it becomes necessary I might have to break down and order one myself. We still have almost ten minutes and may have to stay here for at least another half hour after that if she doesn't show on time."

Vinn and Rebecca fall into casual conversation about their morning makeovers while I stare out the window willing Veronica to appear in my field of vision. The snow has stopped, but the swirling wind continues to carry flakes in intricate patterns, limiting visibility. With every shadow that passes the shop I tense until I realize I need a distraction. I reach down to tear off a piece of my croissant, only to notice most of it is gone.

I look up to say something to Vinn but am immediately put on alert when I see both she and Rebecca staring over my shoulder to a point near the shop's entrance. Rebecca tilts her head and squints her eyes before nudging Vinn. They send a silent signal between them, simultaneously drawing deep breaths. I begin to slowly turn around before I feel a sharp kick to my shin. "Don't look. Keep your eyes on us."

"Like hell!" Vinn says loudly, startling me and most of the other customers, who are still half a cup away from emerging from their morning haze. "It'll be me. I'm the one who's putting together the reception. I'm the one figuring out the embassy. If anyone deserves to be in the lead to greet the Elohim, it's me."

"Nonsense," Rebecca replies at an equal volume to make sure it carries to the line for coffee. "Who's the one Rael said would make a magnificent Angel? And I have the feather to prove it!"

"You bought that feather yourself! And he didn't use the word 'magnificent.' I believe the term he used was 'fine.' Not the same thing. Besides, to be a consort for the Elohim they'll want a genuine—"

The sound of the slap Rebecca applies to Vinn's cheek resounds through the shop and the entire room falls eerily silent until I hear a low but feminine voice behind me.

"I'm sorry, but I couldn't help but overhear." A small chuckle. "I think everyone here overheard. Do you mind if I join you?"

Vinn and Rebecca gaze up past me at the source of the voice, glance at each other, then look back again. Vinn finally lowers her eyes to look directly into mine. "Mal, would you be a darling please and give up your seat for this lovely woman?"

I push away from the table and move off to the side to find a place against the wall after all, not far from my friend who wanted our table. She turns away. I focus on tuning out all background noise and place my concentration on the con-versation among the three women.

"I apologize," I hear Vinn begin. "We didn't mean to disturb you. I'm Vinn and this is Rebecca. We're involved in a kind of a project that's extremely important to both of us and don't always see eye to eye. We should've known better than to be so loud about it though. We're sorry, right Rebecca?"

Rebecca says something too softly for me to hear, appar-ently trying to bring her voice more into the feminine range, something she has yet to master. In response Veronica stares at her for two long, uncomfortable minutes, eventually reaching across the table and running her hand across Rebecca's cheek, lifting her head gently by her chin, and deftly pinching her painted lips.

"Fascinating," she says, then speaks no more for another moment after she turns to Vinn, silently evaluating. "I'm sorry if this seems rude. I heard you mention the Elohim, who happen to be a passion of mine. It sounds like we may be on similar paths. I too am making plans for the arrival of the Elohim and am an ardent follower of Rael. I once spent time with him in France, where he also anointed me an Angel. And I too have a feather. A gold one." It may be my imagination, but she appears to say this with a tone of condescension as she looks upon the faces across the table. "My name is Veronica."

She extends her hand across the table and Vinn and Rebecca take it in turn, Rebecca wincing briefly when Veronica squeezes in a test of supremacy. Veronica can't seem to break her gaze away from Rebecca. She finally turns her head to acknowledge my presence if not my ability to speak for myself. "And who it this?"

Vinn steps in. "That's Mal, my, um, assistant. We have him working on certain details involving the embassy, subject to our approval of course, and doing whatever else we ask him to do."

Veronica runs her eyes up and down my height, gives a slight "hmmph," and turns back to the women. "I used to have my own boy for similar reasons until he became..." she pauses, looking for the right word, "disagreeable." A chill runs down my spine as I picture the crime scene pictures of Scott.

"Perhaps we can work together, share what we've done," Vinn suggests, bringing us to the key moment we've been leading up to. Everything rides on this.

"Perhaps," Veronica responds coolly. "I have my own associate, a would-be Angel. A pretty little thing, maybe too much so. I'm not sure that we need to step outside our circle at this point, but she hasn't passed my tests yet, which are quite demanding. So we will see." She turns to address Rebecca directly. "Why don't you give me your number, dearie, just in case." No offer is made to give her own number. Rebecca scrambles to find a scrap of paper and pen in her purse, which like any other woman has three times more junk in it than the laws of physics should allow. Eventually she passes her number over to Veronica, who starts to rise.

"I must say it's been interesting. Perhaps we'll meet again." Instead of walking straight to the door, she first circles around the table and, from behind, leans down as she rests her hand on Rebecca's shoulder, leaning down to plant a firm kiss on the top of her head. Without another word and without looking back, she strides to the door and exits.

"I need to get this makeup off," Vinn says.

"I need a drink," Rebecca says.

"I need a nap," I say.

With those words of wisdom, we follow Veronica's path to the door.

"I'm not sure what else we could have done," I say in a meager attempt to pacify Vinn as well as to convince myself of what I doubt is true, "or what we should be doing now. Veronica could easily have given us her phone number if she were open to our following up on getting together but all she did was take Rebecca's number. I think it's pretty clear the message there was 'don't call me, I'll call you if and only if I determine it's in my best interest.' It's only been four days and I'm sure like us she's busy with other things. And it's not like she feels the urgency in the same way that we do."

We're once again lounging on my couch after classes. In our informal debriefing after Saturday's strange encounter with Veronica, all three of us felt that we'd at least opened up a strong possibility of further dialogue regarding a joint enterprise with her. She appeared especially intrigued by Rebecca, who has mixed feelings about the special attention she received. On the one hand, her ego demands that she lord over us ordinary folk and embraces any suggestion that she was a glowing beacon of beauty that morning, but a small voice in her head also suggests that being singled out by a woman who may have ordered two murders as easily as she ordered her cappuccino might not be such a good thing. At the time, we all felt that we planted a seed and needed to give it a little time to germinate.

Which turns out to be easier said than done. With each passing day and no little sprout peeking through the surface of the soil, our patience is wearing thin. The issue isn't that we're up against any sort of hard deadline but the fact that neither Vinn nor I excel at doing nothing. We've got everything riding on getting close to Veronica and at this stage there's no Plan B.

"It wouldn't be so bad if we had other possible suspects or evidential trails to follow," she replies, frustration evident. "But we don't. We have her number. How soon is too soon to call her?"

I frown. "I'm not sure that's a good idea at any point. She intentionally kept it from us and it's not listed. Her first reaction wouldn't be joy at hearing our voices but questions as to how we got her number. She would either begin to suspect something or, at the very least, label us as creepy stalkers. Like it or not, that's not an option. We can consider sending Rebecca back to the coffee shop on Saturday by herself, but I'm not sure that's a good idea so soon."

"Yeah, I know." I may have calmed Vinn down but it doesn't sound like I've cheered her up. "We could also consider doing something regarding the embassy that becomes public so that Veronica can't help but notice us. Some sort of stunt that would force her hand in taking the initiative to reach back out to us. What that would be and how we can go public while still hiding what we're doing from our colleagues at school, though, is problematic. If word starts to spread on campus it's only a matter of time before our use of students in a murder investigation becomes known, and that could mean kissing goodbye to our jobs."

"At least we obtained some insight into why she may have killed Rachel, if in fact she did. It sounds like she has very specific requirements as to the woman who will accompany her to meet the Elohim, including that she be barely pretty enough to be an Angel but not so attractive as to outshine herself. Rachel's wholesome farm girl looks may have been perceived as a threat to overshadow Rebecca, or she may have failed some other part of these tests she alluded to."

Without any brilliant ideas springing to either of our minds as to what to do next, and with my last words planting the uncomfortable idea that Vinn and Rebecca may be under more of a threat than we want to admit, we lapse into an uncomfortable silence, snuggling closer to at least share our impotence together. Just when the warmth of our intimacy begins to bring on a sort of drowsy comfort, my cell phone intrudes with my default ringtone for people I don't know. My phone is on the island in the kitchen, which means I'd have to get out from under our blanket to reach it. I let it go.

Thirty seconds later, it sounds again. This time Vinn nudges me and pulls the cover around her, exposing me to the drafts of my apartment and signaling that maybe I should find out what this person wants. I reluctantly move toward the kitchen and pick it up. The voice is familiar after all.

"Winters, this is Officer Mendoza. Are you alone? Oh, all right. Well she'll want to hear this as well."

"Hold on, Officer. Let me put you on speaker." Vinn throws me a quizzical look and I simply shrug my shoulders as I flop back down next to her and push a button. I tell Mendoza to go ahead.

"Look, sorry to intrude this evening. I don't know what you've been doing as far as your off-the-record investigation, whether you've made any progress, or if you're even still involved. But things are popping here and we may be taking another look at those two kids ourselves. About two hours ago a body was pulled out of the lagoon in Humboldt Park. A transwoman. Strangled before she went in. And guess what."

I close my eyes in anticipation, knowing what he's going to say and wishing I could close my ears as well. Vinn grips my forearm tightly. She knows as well. "Go ahead, Officer, say it."

"Yep. She was missing a chunk of bone from her forehead. We have another victim."

There's nothing to add to that other than to acknowledge it happened and to say our goodbyes. Vinn and I look at each other, startled. There's nothing that comes to mind to say to each other either. Just as we're both looking for ways to break our silence, a loud pounding at my door does it for us. It's quickly followed by the sound of Rebecca urging me to open it right away.

I open it only a crack with the intention of asking her to some back in a little bit, but don't get the words out before she pushes by me and poses dramatically in front of Vinn.

"Darlings, I have just the most precious news and I know you'll be super-duper thrilled," she begins excitedly. "I just got a call from guess who? Yes, Veronica. She was like, 'Rebecca, how have you been? I just adored meeting you,' and stuff like that. You know, girl talk. Anyway, she wants to get together again! She said that after meeting me, her little associate just didn't make the grade anymore and had to be cut loose. Isn't that the most wonderful news?"

Vinn and I only gawk, the implications of what we just heard weighing heavily on us both. Rebecca waits impatiently for us to be super-duper thrilled, a look of befuddlement spreading across her face as she begins to suspect that all is not well in detective land. I ask her to take a seat as my mind struggles to find the right words to gently shatter her world.

# TWENTY SEVEN

Mendez' eyes are busily scanning my apartment from the moment he enters, evaluating every nook and inspecting every cranny, judging where my drugs are hidden, finding the most likely places to stash a weapon, and noting where traces of blood would be found despite my best efforts to wash it away. The fact that I'm not a suspect for any crime that he's aware of is irrelevant, it's habit. I don't take offense. I do the same thing.

"I didn't want you to come to the station," he explains as I lead him to a seat. "As far as the brass are concerned those other two murders are solved, cases closed, which technically is correct. There's no question that Crum killed those two kids. And that's as far as they want to go. No sense making more work for ourselves. This new body was found in another district, so as they see it it's not our problem. They don't consider the bone thing as enough to connect this killing with the earlier two, especially since the first killer is dead."

"But you know better," I offer. Vinn sits beside me while Rebecca lounges nearly catatonic in the far corner of the room. Her condition isn't just due to our spoiling her coup at being the one called by Veronica with our news of a third body. She's still trying to come to grips with the now almost certain reality that her new bff, who kissed her on the top of her head, is behind three murders. It's a lot to deal with.

"There's nothing else that links them," Mendez replies weakly, "but yeah. I've been on the job longer than I care to think about and not once before have I seen or heard about a body with a bone removed from the forehead post-mortem. Now three within a couple of months? Yeah, I'd say they're connected. I'm hoping you can tell me how."

We knew this was coming. This isn't Mendez' case and he didn't venture over here after his shift to interview witnesses or just to say hello. He's one of those cops who doesn't give a damn about clearance rates or toeing the official line. At least on this particular matter, he's losing sleep and wants to connect all of the dots, or have someone else do the connecting, no matter how. Right now, he sees Vinn and I as the "how."

I need to choose my words carefully. "Before I say more, I need to issue a disclaimer. We don't have hard evidence of anything. If we brought what we think we know into your station we'd be ridiculed and quickly shown the door. I need your understanding on this."

Mendez accommodates me with the slightest of movement of his head. Nevertheless, he leans forward with a new intensity as if I were about to give him definitive proof of who shot JFK.

"We haven't given up on this, in fact we may have just shared coffee with the mastermind behind all three. At that time, she was merely a possibility. This third killing makes her a probability. We all agree."

"'She'?" Mendez mutters, "Shit. Go on."

"Not much to go on with. We're not ready to share details. Let me just say we believe the common tie between Scott and Rachel runs through a religious group, maybe even a cult. But we're short on facts like what their interests were, what their involvement was, how deep into it they were, and why they were killed."

"In other words, you don't have shit. You're following a hunch and that's about it." Mendez sighs as he sees the answer in our eyes. "That's all right. From where I'm sitting, it's more that we've got. And there's nothing wrong with following your gut. A lot of cases get solved that way."

"If it makes you feel any better," Vinn intervenes. "We're pretty sure we're on the right track and could make it more than a hunch if this third victim is who we think it is. Any chance of getting the file on her?"

Mendez shakes his head sadly. "No can do. As I said, not our case. Too many problems for yours truly if word gets out that I'm sticking my hands in where they don't belong. I wish I could help, but sorry."

He rises to go, his mission unfulfilled. "Promise me one thing, though. If this woman you're focused on is the real deal, she's obviously dangerous. Don't be stupid. Three people who got close to her didn't see her for who she is and ended up dead. When you get to the point that you can provide something connecting her that's more than guesswork, get out of there and give me a ring. Then I'll see what I can do to make it official."

He doesn't wait for us to pinky swear and heads to the door, shoulders slumped as if the weight of the world is on them. It's a feeling that the rest of us in the room share. The slamming of the door behind him acts as an explanation point on our despair.

Rebecca is being stubborn and there are two problems with her attitude. First, despite a couple of previous instances where she's shown she can step up in dicey situations, she's basically a suit-and-tie worker with no background in the darker world that both Vinn and I have. Second, the point she's making is absolutely correct.

"It's me, myself, and I that this Veronica creature wants to meet," she repeats for the third time. "You saw her. She couldn't take her eyes off of me and kissed me. Not either of you—Malcom, she barely acknowledged that you exist—but me. And if this poor thing they pulled out of the water really was her assistant, it confirms that she has a special interest in trans women. If we're going to pull this off, it starts with me. Besides, you're the ones that brought me into this to begin with."

"That's true," I acknowledge, "but the situation has changed. It was one thing when our theory was that she had Crum do her dirty work. With him gone, we assumed that the danger level of checking her out in person was minimal. And we were never positive that she was involved in their deaths anyway. That may have just changed. I vote that before we make any decisions or have any further contact with Veronica, we look into this latest victim like we did for Scott and Rachel and see if we can establish a connection between them."

I expected push back from Rebecca, but it's Vinn who responds. "I'm afraid you don't have my vote, Mal. We no longer have the luxury of time. Before today, we didn't have any reason to suspect that there would be any more violence. We could take our time in wedging our way into Veronica's inner circle. But that's no longer the case. Who's to say some other young thing won't take this helper's place and meet the same fate? It could be weeks before we'd be able to bribe someone to get a look at the murder book and then break into the victim's home and track down receipts or calendar notations to link her to Raelism. And there's apparently an assistant's job open for someone new right now that won't be there if we wait. I share your qualms about placing Rebecca in that role, but at least she'd be aware of the danger, unlike the others. And we'll be right behind her. Hopefully, I'll actually be at her side."

I know when to concede defeat but that doesn't mean I have to admit it. "Okay, just for the moment let's assume that we let Rebecca return her call." Rebecca opens her mouth to say something but I hold up my hand to silence her. "That is not the same thing as turning her loose and allowing her to make her own decisions. If we let her call Veronica, then what? Two days ago we were just shooting in the dark hoping that Veronica would slip up or open up to connect herself to the two kids. While we still need that to happen, now we also need to prepare ourselves on the assumption that she's guilty so that when an opportunity opens to prove that, we jump on it."

"Right," Vinn says. "So let's talk this out. Rebecca's correct that she's our strongest way in because Veronica has some inexplicable attraction to her. No question that whatever path we choose begins with Rebecca returning her call and setting up another meeting. It's safe to assume that this is our big chance to ingratiate ourselves, but to what end? What's her purpose in 'joining forces,' so to speak? What does she need us for? And Rebecca," Vinn turns to face her, "when you talk to her, it's non-negotiable that this is a package deal. At a minimum I need to be with you, and preferably Mal as well."

"No 'preferably' about it," I interject. "It's not safe for me to be on the sidelines. It's all of us or none of us. I understand that I don't qualify to be an Angel, but I need to be present in some capacity. This woman is probably more dangerous than we ever suspected. Think about it. Why take the bones from her victims? She decides they don't fit into her plans, has them killed, but still has some twisted compassion where she prepares them to visit the afterlife with the Elohim? Or maybe it's a cold-hearted calculation to get on the radar of these aliens? Whatever the case, that alone shows this woman is psychotic."

"I have a thought that addresses all of your concerns," Rebecca says quickly to get a word in before Vinn and I continue our dual colloquy. "The pretext we used in our argument in the coffee shop was which one of us would greet the Elohim when they visit, right? That's what caught her attention and brought her to our table. And she mentioned a project she was working on, which based on Scott's drawings was probably the embassy. Vinn, you told her that Mal was working on details regarding the same thing. So our mutual goal, or at least what we sell to her, is to work together to plan and build the embassy and to lure the Elohim here. Vinn, you and I do whatever work is suitable for Angels, and Mal will be around to put our ideas about the embassy into form."

Vinn and I stare at Rebecca. She may be more than a semi-pretty face after all and I make a mental note to stop underestimating her. I notice that Vinn is bursting to contribute. She's sexy when her brain is working at a genius level. She doesn't disappoint.

"Thank you, Rebecca," she says excitedly. "You've given me an idea. It's going to take a lot of work and involve the help of the UIC theater department, our IT connections, and who knows what else. It's wild but might give us just what we need. Mal, can you get some paper and pencils?"

We gather close as Vinn starts sketching on a long sheet of parchment paper I retrieved from the kitchen and spread out over the coffee table, speaking rapidly as ideas spill from her mouth more slowly than her brain generates them. Over the course of the next few minutes, her plan begins to take shape. "Wild" doesn't begin to describe it.

# TWENTY EIGHT

"Is this really necessary?" Rebecca bitches as Vinn fits the transmitter inside the cup of her bra. "It's uncomfortable and ruins my figure."

"Believe me, you'll get used to it and won't even know it's there after a while," Vinn soothes her. "And it doesn't show at all, you look gorgeous as always. If it makes you feel any better, I have one as well." What she doesn't say is that Vinn's is hidden inside her purse and that "gorgeous" may be a bit of an exaggeration. Rebecca did her own makeup this morning, doing her best to imitate Heather's miracles, but it falls a little short. We can only hope that the impression she made upon Veronica at the first meeting carries over despite a marked diminishment in her femininity.

"And yes, it's necessary," I add as I turn around just in time to see Rebecca finish adjusting her dress to cover the offending object. "We agreed that it'll just be the two of you at this meeting, but given what we suspect about Veronica I need to be nearby and listening to every word in case things go south. We don't know if she'll be okay with Vinn tagging along or if she'll want to speak to you separately. To be safe, we're fitting both of you with wires.

"Remember, don't push the conversation at this point. Let Veronica think that she's the leader in this dynamic. Your main objective today is to sell her on the idea that working together is to her benefit. We think she wants to use you in some way to prepare for the coming of the Elohim and our whole plan depends on that. But if she takes another direction, go with it. Don't force that on her, not yet. The last thing we need is for her to decide that we don't have a common goal."

Vinn gives me a side glance, her lips compressed. She

can tell that my nerves are in overdrive and she's right there with me. Our confidence level would be higher if it were just the two of us. Rebecca's a wild card whose instincts we haven't learned to trust and who we know we can't control. She may be necessary to our success but that doesn't mean that we want her there.

"Rebecca, do you have the notebook?" Vinn asks, the barely perceptible waiver in her voice her own tell as to her state of mind.

Rebecca rolls her eyes as she pulls the cloth-bound, deep blue notebook from the depths of her purse. "For the fifth time, yes. And before you ask, I reviewed everything again this morning. I know it as well as I'm going to."

We were up late into the night filling its pages. A pricey "idea book" we paid to have shipped overnight, its sections broken down into project pages, task checklists, blank pages for sketches, and the like, it's meant to give the impression that Rebecca takes her role as planner for the coming of the Elohim seriously. The fact that it contains any number of facts about the Elohim and Rael's specifications for the embassy also allow it to act as Rebecca's cheat sheet. We had her write in it with several different pens and even added a coffee stain to give the impression that she's been at this for quite some time.

"Time to test the mics," I announce as I slip on my shoes and grab my coat. "Give me a minute to get to the car." I don't have any doubts as to the functionality of the equipment, which Uncle Sam, or a variation thereof, paid for a few years back. I conveniently forgot to return it when I went my own way. Vinn and I tested it earlier this morning between rooms, but it's good practice to make sure it works in conditions closer to what we'll find in the field this afternoon.

The skies are overcast but the temperature has risen to

the tolerable range, meaning that my face doesn't freeze instantly upon leaving the warmth of my apartment. Our Zipcar is half a block away parked between a fire hydrant and a dumpster. I slide into the driver's seat and fire up the receiver.

Rebecca's voice instantly fills the car. "… so mister 'do it my way or the demons of hell will be released.' Right? I mean, c'mon, I'm just as. . ." I switch it off before hearing Vinn's response then change frequencies to Vinn's transmitter.

"I mean, who wears orange and gray? Is it Halloween in the 80s? And that hair! That's why I. . ." I could wait all day for Vinn to get a word in, and I'm sure she's being cautious knowing I may be listening, so I'm just going to assume that if I can hear Rebecca, I'll be able to hear Vinn.

Reentering my home, I turn a sour look in Rebecca's direction but am still able to discern Vinn's smirk as I do so. Rebecca is totally oblivious and has moved on to the use of pets as a fashion accessory. I decide to "do it my way" and take control.

"Everything checks out. Are you both ready? Time to hit the road."

The Pan Artesanal Café' is an unassuming but apparently popular storefront spot on Fullerton Avenue nestled in the heart of Humboldt Park along a strip of Hispanic groceries, beauty salons, and dollar stores. Luck is with us as I find a parking spot in front of a realty office in the next building to the east. We're five minutes early.

"Good luck," I tell my companions, trying my best to infuse my voice with a tone of confidence that I don't feel. Being left behind is an unfamiliar and unwelcome feeling, like a coach helplessly watching his players attempt to execute the game plan while standing on the sidelines.

"Thanks," Vinn mutters as she opens the door, letting in a cold blast of winter air. She pauses, puzzled, expecting Rebecca to be at her side but the diva remains in the car, waiting. After a moment Vinn catches on and steps back to open the back door for her, allowing Rebecca to exit. I see her features tighten. Rebecca's lucky we're all on the same side or whatever Vinn had to suppress would not have been pretty.

The women are barely on their way before I flip on the receiver, at first just catching the sound of the wind and nearby traffic. Within a few seconds I watch them disappear inside the café's front door and the outside noise is replaced with a cacophony of voices and the scraping of chairs. I listen with envy as Rebecca orders a mango, ham, avocado, and jalapeno sandwich. Vinn settles for a raspberry turnover and a coffee. Seconds later my attention is diverted as a familiar figure approaches from the west, her ankle-length, fashionable coat flapping in the breeze. It's all I can do not to follow her in.

A minute passes, then two. The only words passing between Vinn and Rebecca are a brief "she's here." Mentally, I imagine Veronica's progress as she approaches the counter, places her order, then waits impatiently for it to be filled. By now she should have it in hand and is scanning the room, recognizing Vinn and Rebecca with a forced smile, and is walking over. Three, two, one...

"Good morning." My timing is right on the dot, but there's no one here to gloat to. "It's so good to see you again. Only the two of you today?"

"I told Mal to wait for us in the car," Vinn responds casually. "I thought it best if it were only us women today." It may just be me, but there seems to be a bit of a superior tone in her voice, as if giving me orders were an everyday thing. Perhaps a good approach given who she's talking with, as long as she doesn't make it a habit outside this context. A discussion for later.

"Very wise." Veronica seems pleased with the decision

to leave me out. "I'm glad you were able to meet up on such short notice. I thought we could talk about what your interest is in Raelism, what you're working on at the moment, and determine if it makes sense to join together if we're at similar points in our journeys. How long have you been followers?"

"I've been, how should I put it, 'intrigued' for several years, but didn't start serious involvement until about a year ago when Rebecca and I discovered our mutual interest," Vinn replies, following our script. Our hope is to have her do most of the talking. "She introduced me to a small group of devotees, but eventually our interests diverged. The rest of them were content with holding meetings and having discussions, which is fine as far as it goes, but the two of us wanted to push further."

"In what way?"

"We think it's important to be ready. It would be catastrophic if the Elohim choose to visit and we're not properly prepared to greet them. We need to be forward thinking, which means having a physical space built to certain specifications that will be pleasing to them. The last thing we want is for them to be dissatisfied with our preparations and decide to wait another hundred years to try again."

"It's more than that." Rebecca interrupts, which immediately puts my teeth on edge. "Even if the embassy is everything that they expect and meets their every need and desire, it's just as crucial that the right people are there to greet them. That's why Vinn and I have been stressing the importance of living life to the standards of Rael's Angels, of being pure in body and spirit. We want to be there to meet the Elohim when they come. The rest of the group thought we were prima donnas, they didn't understand. That's when we went off on our own, just the two of us." I didn't realize I was holding my breath as she spoke and only now release it. Not part of the plan, but not bad.

"I see," Veronica says. "I don't believe we were a part of the same group, but I followed a similar path and was asked to leave. Ignorance is simply ugly and I was happy to exit. I believe I'm more than qualified to lead others in the right direction. I've been a convert for many years and spent time with Rael himself in France. I believe I informed you before that I was gifted the feather of an Angel. A legitimate one."

I cringe at the dig, which implies that Rebecca and Vinn can't truly lay claim to Angel status. Vinn will let it roll without a reaction, as she's not only a professional but has no desire to be labeled as a sex kitten. Rebecca, on the other hand, is probably seething. Vinn must sense the need for a distraction.

"We've been making plans. Rebecca, why don't you show Veronica what we've done so far?" Bless her.

I hear the opening of a latch and a rustling, which presumably is Rebecca searching the cavernous depths of her Louis Vuitton knock-off for the notebook. Her voice is next. "You see, we've been..."

"Let me take a look at that," Veronica intrudes. I envision her establishing her alpha credentials by snatching the notebook out of Rebecca's hands. Moments of excruciating silence are only broken by an occasional "hmm mmm" from Veronica.

"Interesting," she finally says. "I didn't expect that you would have progressed so far. Your sketches are admirable but flawed. I have some that a former associate prepared for me but they also have issues." Bingo. My heart leaps into my throat, but my excitement is tempered by the remote chance that she could be referring to someone other than Scott. "Perhaps we should compare and between the two sets come up with a final version. Have you considered a location?"

"Of course. In fact we already have one," Rebecca blabs, eliciting a choice word that I may have said out loud.

"But," Vinn quickly jumps in, "we've obviously kept it under wraps. We don't want word to get around about what we're doing and draw attention to ourselves. Not even our former group has a clue." Nice try, but too late.

"Well," it's back to Veronica, "there's no time like the present. Let's retreat to my place and I'll show you what I have. It's just around the corner, not far. We can walk."

As the sound of chairs being pushed back fills the car, I begin to panic. The signal won't carry far, especially with brick buildings in between us. I'm debating whether to follow behind them with the car when the group emerges. Vinn glances in my direction and almost imperceptibly shakes her head. Like it or not, I have to stay put. I hear movement through the receiver for a few minutes after they turn the corner, then nothing. My fellow investigators who I swore to protect are now heading into the lair of a probable murderer with only Vinn's savvy and defensive skills to protect them. I pray they don't need them and if they do, that it's enough.

Each minute is an eternity. I leave the receiver turned on in what I know is a futile act but my only reward is static. Our notes with Veronica's address are back in my apartment and on Vinn's laptop and I waste twenty minutes trying to mimic Vinn's success in tracking it down on my phone but fail miserably. At the one hour mark I decide that if they don't return in fifteen minutes I'll call Vinn's cell. I begin my vigil, watching each second blink by on the dashboard clock. My nerves fray just a little bit more with each flash.

With only three minutes and forty-eight seconds until my deadline, the static begins to take on some sort of pattern, eventually forming the words "...on our...soon." Seconds later the pair rounds the corner, Rebecca gesturing wildly with her arms while Vinn gives me a forced smile and a small wave with her left hand. My relief is palpable and my nerves relax, making me realize how badly I need to find a bathroom.

"Sorry, Mal," Vinn apologizes unnecessarily as she folds herself into the front seat, ignoring Rebecca's expectation to have the rear door opened for her. "We couldn't take the chance. There's no plausible explanation for your following us, or at the very least it would raise suspicions. Could you hear anything?"

"Not after you left the café," I begin, but any further explanation is drowned by the entry of an insulted and disheveled body into the back seat.

"How was I to know she expected to see it?" Rebecca exclaims loudly. "I mean, we didn't anticipate that and I was improvising. I don't know what the big deal is."

I cast a puzzled glance Vinn's way and she shrugs her shoulders. "We can go into detail back at your place, but to re-cap, all we did that entire time was listen to Veronica lecture us on her expectations for the embassy, which are pretty specific by the way. Rebecca took notes. Do you want the good news or the bad news first?"

"Surprise me."

"Okay, the good news, and it's very good, is that the plans she showed us were photocopies of the drawings we found in Scott's room. She also railed about what she per-ceived as their defects and the intractable stubbornness of the 'architect' she had prepare them and how she had to fire him when he wouldn't bend to her will. She didn't say it in so many words, but I got the impression that Scott was forced upon Veronica so he had two strikes against him from the start. You want my guess?  Scott and Rachel approached Veronica together. She's interested in Rachel but the kids present themselves as a package deal. Anyway, we thus have a connection between she and Scott. Nothing to link her to Rachel specifically other than theory, but we have a start. And furthermore, on the good news front, she wants to work together to plan and build the embassy."

"That's huge!" I exclaim, and I mean it. "That's what we needed. Mission accomplished." My elation quickly deflates when I notice Vinn's expression and sense the tension in the back seat. "Okay, how bad can the bad news be?"

"Nearly as bad as the good news was good, I'm afraid," Vinn sighs. She looks to her left, causing Rebecca to shrink away from her glare. "I assume you heard Rebecca say that we have a location for the embassy already. I tried to downplay that and move on to other things right away and thought I had finessed the subject. Unfortunately, in her apartment Veronica insisted on visiting the site. She was adamant in needing to give her approval. We're not going to be able to talk her out of it."

My head starts to throb while I silently count to ten before responding. "All right." I look directly back at Rebecca. "Rebecca, I'm sure you didn't mean to put us in this position. You were caught up in the moment. We'll work it out. Somehow. For right now, let's get back to my place where we can get some tea and you can fill me in on your alone time with Veronica."

I pull on my seat belt. "And then we have to shop for a field."

# TWENTY NINE

Despite our near immersion in the world of the extra-terrestrial, our paychecks demand that we devote at least a portion of our time to our teaching duties, and there were papers to grade, labs to review, and lesson plans to prepare. Vinn and I agreed that Sunday would be best spent catching up on those more mundane matters, she in her place and me in mine. That would also give us an excuse to isolate ourselves from Rebecca, who isn't in our good graces at the moment.

I find my mind wandering to visions of aliens, occasional flashes of memory of Scott's sketches, and the problem of finding an acceptable open space that could plausibly serve as the location for an embassy for beings from another solar system. It doesn't take long to realize that I need help in focusing on the stacks of essays piled around my living room. I head to the kitchen and have to dig deep into my stash of teas to find what I'm looking for, a sealed bag of Rhodiola Root I picked up in the mountains of the Yunnan province several years back. Simultaneously both sweet and bitter, it's not one of my favorites, but it supposedly has the benefit of increasing concentration and stimulating the brain. It'll definitely be put to the test today.

Early-semester papers from the freshman classes take substantial time to grade both in terms of the number of "suggestions" as to ways to improve and in finding various delicate verbiage to say "this is really awful." The improvement in the upper classes' submissions helps me fly through them faster and restores my faith in future generations, so that by the time my stomach tells me I've worked through dinnertime, I'm red-penciling my final essay. Some of the better efforts are from my "History of Science Fiction and Fantasy" course, which gives me an idea.

I no sooner tuck the bundles of paper into my briefcase than my cell phone chirps, letting me know that Vinn is calling. I'm happy for the diversion.

"Have you been able to get anything done today?" she intones before I even have a chance to say "hello." "Hard to believe, but even preparing a discussion on the problems of applying quantum theory to the notion of gravity hasn't been holding my attention." With anyone else I would think they were being facetious. Vinn is serious. I know not to suggest Rhodiola tea to a science-minded coffee drinker.

"Just finishing up," I tell her. "But I know what you're saying. It's been difficult to focus. I think we need to prepare a 'to-do' list to keep us on task."

"There is something satisfying about being able to check items off of a list," I can hear Vinn smiling through the phone. "Give it some thought, cowboy. Your office, 8:00. See you then." She hangs up without a goodbye. Customary niceties aren't her thing, at least with me. I grab a pad of paper and pencil, throw leftover black bean and andouille sausage stew into the microwave, reheat my tea, and settle down for an evening of focusing my thoughts out toward the stars.

"I think some of the initial groundwork can be done separately, but then we'll come together when it comes to actually putting anything into action or making important decisions," I tell Vinn as she settles into one of my student chairs.

"Sounds good," she replies. "Let's proceed chronologically. I'd love to push it further down the list, but to keep Veronica on the hook we're going to need to show her our chosen location for the embassy. Which means we need to actually choose it. I think that needs to be a top priority."

"Like it or not, I agree. I can take that. I'll come up with some options and then run them by you. And yes—" I anticipate Vinn's next words "—I know that Rael set certain standards for it, which we can assume Veronica will know and require." I check my notes which I took from a website devoted exclusively to plans for an Elohim embassy. Yes, that really exists. "A minimum of four square kilometers with room for the embassy and a swimming pool at least 1,000 meters from an outside wall. In a pleasant country with a warm climate, which let's hope she'll concede that summer in the Midwest will have to suffice if she wants it nearby, airspace above not subject to military surveillance, and in a neutral location which 'has been granted rights of extraterritoriality and diplomatic immunity.' Some of that will require a little creativity and some flexibility on her part. I have an idea for that which I'm not ready to share."

Vinn gives me a quizzical look. "All right, run with it, at least for now. While you're working on that, we need to get some plans drawn up. You think the requirements for the land are specific and a little bit out there? Listen to this: The structure needs to be 'approximately' 132 meters long by 49 meters wide. Maximum two stories, with a terrace on top with a landing pad. Entrances and exits on the north and south sides only. Seven living quarters with private bathrooms, dining room and conference room with a minimum capacity of twenty-one, specifications for foliage, soft and feminine decorating touches, etcetera, etcetera. No wonder Scott couldn't satisfy Veronica. If he exercised any independence and inserted his own aesthetic, which apparently he did, she'd freak out."

Vinn looks up from her notes before continuing. "Anyway, UIC has a college of Architecture, Design, and the Arts. I don't know the dean, but I've been around campus a lot longer than you have, and, ahem, have a slightly more creditable reputation, so I'll reach out to see if we can grab a few students for a special project."

"That leaves the hardest one, which maybe we need to work on together from the start." I pause, hoping Vinn will jump in and overrule me, taking this on herself as well. No such luck. "We're going to need some real expertise here if we're going to create a believable visit from beings from outer space. As you know, it all depends on convincing Veronica that it's real. Hopefully she'll be willing to suspend her disbelief to a certain extent, but we can't count on that."

"I know," Vinn says with a sigh of resignation. "And if we had unlimited time and a big budget, we'd be okay. But we have to work with what we have. I say we start by meeting again with Malika. This isn't going to fall exactly within the IT parameters, but it's a start and she seems like she's pretty intelligent. Worst case, she can tell us who we need to talk to or send us off in the right direction. UIC does offer a degree in Theater Design, Production, and Technology which may be of some use. And maybe we'll need to bring in someone from computer science. Might as well get the whole darn school involved."

Except that she didn't say "darn." Just hearing the obstacles we face out loud is enough to make anyone curse. A quick glance at the clock shows it's time to get to my first class of the day, my "History of Science Fiction and Fantasy" course. Which means it's also time to put the first element of our plan into action.

My comments on the students' papers were not received with raves or a general feeling of glee, but these are juniors and seniors, some of whom have been in my classes before, and they accept that there's room for improvement. Still, I sense an overall sense of gloom. Time to bring a little cheer to the atmosphere and assist Vinn and I at the same time.

"Class, I can tell you put a lot of effort into your papers, and for those of you who want to try to raise your grade you can rework them and submit them again by next time. But I think you could also use a change of pace. On your way out, please take one of the sheets here on my desk. It gives a general description of an alien being. Delve into the most imaginative depths of your mind and create drawings of this extraterrestrial creature. Note that there are some requirements, such as rather than frightening, they have to be as beautiful as you can imagine them to be. It's all set forth in the assignment. You're graded on effort, not artistic ability. Due on Friday."

With that, I dismiss the class a few minutes early. Excited murmurs run rampant as they exit and glance at the sheet as they leave. Bless my geeks. They're going to make our job a lot easier and maybe without their knowing it, help catch a bad guy.

# THIRTY

"She wants to see it this weekend," I tell Vinn as she returns to the table after fetching a coffee cup from Manuel. This morning dawned unexpectedly frigid, so to change things up a bit from my usual tea and to provide some much-needed sweet and decadent inner warmth, I whipped up a batch of hot chocolate before leaving for work. No powder for this guy, I just can't do it any longer. It only takes a few more minutes than the store-bought mix, but combining 54% bittersweet chocolate pieces with premium cocoa powder, milk, heavy cream, and a dash of quality vanilla will spoil anyone for life. Vinn never shares my tea but insisted on splitting my cocoa. I thought the cherry croissant she brought back with her was payment for my thoughtfulness, but I was wrong. It never leaves her side of the table.

"See what?" she inquires, clearly distracted as she lets the steam from her cup assault her senses. "Oh, wait, you mean the location for the embassy? That soon? What did Rebecca tell her?"

She correctly assumes that Veronica only communicates with Rebecca and would never lower herself to reach out directly to the hired help. "Do you have to ask? Of course she said yes. Anything to keep her new bff happy. At first I was irritated with her, but frankly it's probably for the best. We've got to keep Veronica on our leash and we definitely don't want to let her thoughts wander to finding someone other than ourselves to partner up with. The body count is already high enough."

"So what are you going to do?" she asks sincerely, whether concerned about the task that lies ahead for me or the success of our operation I'd rather not know.

"Time for some serious research online, then I guess a few field trips. Literally. To reward Rebecca for her initiative, I'll insist that she come along when I visit the sites in person. Besides, we wouldn't want her to be seeing the location for the first time along with Veronica—it's got to look like she's been there before. And since it gets dark so early these days, considering our work schedules we'll most likely have to drive to see them on Saturday morning. I'll tell Rebecca to schedule our meeting with Veronica for mid-afternoon."

"Good luck with that," Vinn says with a frown. "While you're playing Marco Polo and exploring new lands, I'll set up an appointment with the dean of the Design department to go over in person what we need from a couple of select students and put some specs together for the embassy's interior that I'll send to him in advance. We've already exchanged a couple of emails and he gave me the name of a star junior architecture major who could draw up some professional quality plans. If he's interested. I'm meeting Chad in my office at 4:00 today if you want to drop in."

"Absolutely, I'll be there. It'll give me a break from my search for a location, although I may even be done by then. I mean, how long will it take to find a thousand square acres of park land for an extraterrestrial meeting ground in the middle of a wooded area with at least a thousand feet of clearance to build a surrounding privacy wall while leaving room for a swimming pool? Of course, it might take a few extra minutes to get a certificate of extraterritorial and diplomatic immunity."

"That's the spirit," Vinn chuckles as she stands to leave. "Do you want the rest of this?" She pushes a tissue with a few pastry flakes and a smear of jam across the table in my direction. I gratefully accept the gift and wait until she's out of sight to crumple it up and discard it in the trash.

I have another hour before my freshman composition class, what Vinn pejoratively calls "Discourse for Dummies," so I retreat to my office to begin looking for a suitable location. Before I can get to my door, my boss Stuart intercepts me in the hallway. I've learned not to make any assumptions about his intentions based on his expression because his face seems to have been frozen in a permanent sneer ever since he hired me.

"Mr. Winters, how nice to run into you. I'm so sorry that I haven't had the opportunity to sit in on one of your classes yet this semester. I would have especially enjoyed the class where you assign drawings of space people as homework. Don't look surprised, I have my sources. Is this institution teaching cartooning now? Perhaps I missed that in the course book."

I'm not the least bit surprised that he spies on my classes, although it's doubtful that he has a mole among my students. Sitting right outside the classroom door with a drinking glass to his ear is more his style. My subconscious has apparently been expecting this, as a response immediately comes to mind.

"Stuart, no need to be alarmed. I'm sure you're keenly aware that when it comes to the problematization paradigm of students' dialectic approach to disputatious engagements, where iatrogenic paths are often the result of idiopathic homogeneity, professorial divagation toward the inapposite, here in the form of a demiurge, can lead to originative solutions. Don't you agree?"

I speak so sincerely that while a portion of Stuart's brain is screaming that whatever I just said—which I could never repeat if he asked—is pure babble, it's just barely possible that I'm referencing some academic journal article or a current trend in education, and to call me on it could set him up to appear unprofessionally ignorant. Twice he opens his mouth to reply and twice he closes it just as quickly. Rather than risk a bruise to his reputation, or at least his own perception of it, he sullenly slinks away in the direction of his office.

The apparent success of using obfuscation as a weapon against an inquisitive mind suddenly produces in my own brain a possible solution to our goal of forcing Veronica to follow our lead instead of acting like the alpha dog. I make a mental note to bring it up in this afternoon's meeting with the architectural student, then make my way to my office to immerse myself in the mundane world of real estate.

I have a prejudice against anyone named Chad. My brain immediately conjures up a white, privileged male in a striped tennis sweater with clear skin and slicked back hair and a condescending attitude toward anyone who can't trace their ancestors back to the Mayflower. It's a bit of a welcome shock, then, to enter Vinn's office to find her chatting with a black, tattooed goth complete with mini-Mohawk and nose ring. I can't say the look was totally successful, but I give him credit for trying. He's probably been rebelling against the name he was saddled with his whole life.

"Mal, this is Chad Barrow, Chad, Professor Winters. We were just going over a few preliminaries, such as his experience and his thoughts on his ability to undertake this project. He seems confident he can do it."

I lower myself into the chair next to Chad, who turns slightly to face me. "I tested out of the 100- and 200-level classes and finished all of the studio classes my sophomore year. I'm taking my last two required courses this semester, the rest are electives and some independent study. It's all a bit tedious, actually. That's why Professor Achison's email about a reception hall for aliens intrigues me, but I need to know more before I commit."

His manner of speaking sounds more like a Chad, which coming out of a mouth with multiple studs on its tongue is jarring and will take some getting used to. "It's a bit more complicated than a reception hall. I'm not sure what Professor Achison has told you about the project, but we're working outside of our roles here at the University to try to take a very evil person off the streets and perhaps to save a few lives." I make a decision not to mention our loose affiliation with the Chicago police. "We really aren't authorized to tell you more. Let me just say that the drawings are a critical part of our plan and we need someone both highly skilled and creative who's willing to step outside the norms in preparing something epic."

Chad's eyes give him away. He's hooked but trying to keep it cool. Time to reel him in. "This may seem contradictory, but the specs we emailed to you are non-negotiable and you need to follow them to the letter, but outside of that let your imagination soar. For example, there needs to be a fence 1,000 feet from the structure, but no description is given of what kind of fence or any limitations. The building has to be two floors, at least in part, with a landing pad for a spaceship of unknown size, but there are no specific requirements for what the roof of the second floor or the pad need to look like.

"The number of rooms and minimum capacity are set and the various sections of the embassy have to be round with a passageway in between, but why not design them like nothing someone has seen before, something that an alien may find appealing?" I can't believe I uttered those words. "The exterior can be your vision, draw in some foliage where you think it should be, even specify the types of bushes or flowers."

Vinn finds it necessary to step in. "Now keep in mind that while we're giving you a lot of leeway and hope you let your imagination run with it, we still have to sell this to a woman in her 30s who may have issues if it's too avant garde."

Time to introduce my brilliant idea. "To that point, how are you on techno-speak? I've found that overwhelming someone with jargon and unfamiliar references encourages them to pretend to understand so as not to appear ignorant and to be hesitant to question what they don't comprehend for the same reason. Fill your drawings with labels and notes that no lay person will grasp—make up some nonsensical babble if you want. It'll help us sell whatever you come up with."

Vinn nods in approval at my brilliance. I think. "We need renderings of the exterior as it would appear to someone standing at its side as well as top view outlines of the various rooms. You can specify materials, suggested locations for beds and tables, but don't offer opinions on colors or any interior design decisions. We'll have someone else for that."

Chad's swagger seems to have taken a small hit while he tries to process all of the information we've thrown at him. I wonder if we've lost him or if he's just over-whelmed. Vinn must be thinking along the same lines.

"One more thing," she adds quickly before Chad can run screaming from her office. "I've already spoken to your independent study supervisor. She said that this can count as your mid-term project."

Chad immediately sits up straight in his chair. "Awe-some. I didn't have any ideas for that yet and this might even be fun. To include everything that you mentioned, in addition to following the specifications from that website you sent to me, I figure I could have something pretty spectacular back to you in about a month, in time for mid-terms. How does that sound?"

Vinn and I exchange a look, neither of us wanting to be the one to break the bad news. I finally lose the battle of wills.

"We might need to settle for something only mildly spectacular, Chad. We need your preliminaries by a week from today and the final versions by next Friday. That gives you ten days. Remember, someone's life may depend on it."

Now I really wish it was Vinn who had jumped in. I hate making a grown man cry.

# THIRTY ONE

"You'd be surprised at how difficult it was not to take a peek at these," I tell Vinn, holding up a manilla folder containing twenty-three different sketches of aliens as imagined by my students. We decided to unseal them with Rebecca present so as not to have any predetermined favorites when she first sees them. Somehow this morphed into an unveiling party late Friday night in Leo's apartment. Sort of like an alcohol-infused gender reveal party only with little green men and women.

"I guess you have a little geek in you after all," she replies with a smile. "I've been looking forward to this all week. Maybe we'll be the next Spielberg, albeit with an audience of one."

We decide to snub our noses at Mother Nature and risk the trip down two and a half flights without coats, running into Rebecca while descending the stairs. She, of course, didn't pass up the chance to wear her new blue faux-fur wrap despite facing only about five seconds of exposure to the cold. Leo is waiting for us at the door.

We settle into our usual seats, where mismatched glasses await us. For any visit to Leo's, protocol requires pleasure before business, so I set the packet of drawings at my feet while our host pours generous portions of some sort of clear liquid out of an unmarked bottle into our glasses.

"Cachaca," is all he says. I don't know what that is, but the one guarantee is that it will be strong and sneakily drinkable, so that no one here will remember the time passing between the first sip and when the walls of the room begin to sway.

Before we can taste, Rebecca raises her glass in a toast. "To the Elohim, may they live long and prosper." Vinn's nose scrunches at the reference, but whatever her views of old television shows are, they don't prevent her from downing a healthy gulp of the booze. Not to be outdone, despite being fully aware that Vinn can outdrink me without even trying, I take a good-sized swallow myself. Smooth, slightly sweet, and extremely fruity, I can see where it'll be easy to consume copious amounts as if it were juice. Better get down to business right away, or our choice of an alien persona will end up a cross between the Michelin man and the neighborhood bag lady.

I pull the stack of artwork out of the folder and clear my throat. "Before we begin, I should clarify that as tempting as it will be, we're not here to choose our favorite design, or the best drawn, or the cutest. The winner will be the one that adheres most closely to how Rael described them from when he supposedly was invited onto their spaceship." Leo is rolling his eyes. I should probably avoid mentioning Rael's contention that he was offered sex with six robot women while on board. "It should also have some sort of mythical irresistibility where you just can't take your eyes off of them. We need Veronica to be instantly drawn to them to the extent that a voice from deep inside of her tells her that this is how she pictured them all along."

"That's asking an awful lot from a stupid picture," Rebecca mutters. She's right, but she still didn't have to say it.

"I'll tell you what I told my students," I continue. "All we know is that the Elohim are slightly shorter than humans but look somewhat similar because eons ago we supposedly were made in their image. They're a pale green with almond-shaped eyes. They're ten times more feminine than the most feminine human, however that translates. Oh, and on their planet they don't wear clothes." Snickers all around. We're apparently back in middle school. "Raelians are prohibited from painting or sketching the Elohim, so we don't have any visual clues to follow. That may work to our advantage, though, because it means that Veronica can't look for flaws in our design."

Everyone moves closer in as I raise the first sketch, holding it off to my left side so that I can get a look myself. Before that happens, Vinn lets out a giggle and Leo snorts, not good signs. Now I can see why. This student apparently was either raised on cartoons or didn't take the assignment seriously, as the resemblance to Papa Smurf is impossible not to see. I can only imagine Veronica's reaction if we put that image before her. The next one shows some effort, but a mixture of a bird of prey and a dragon isn't even close to what we're looking for. The third one is a total disaster.

My heart sinks with each passing sketch, while the Cachaca begins to loosen the judges' tongues and the criticism flows freely. I'm the last one to get a glimpse of the pages, but the immediate hoots of derision as I drop each prior sheet to the floor have been accurate foretellings of my own opinion seconds later. Then, around the sixteenth or seventeenth drawing, total silence. Warily I lean forward to take a look for myself and can see why. The artist captured precisely the image that we couldn't adequately put into words and that we only now, upon looking at the alien being before us, know is precisely what we were hoping to capture. Slight but commanding, an inexplicable aura of femininity, and just the right shade of green. Everyone seems mesmerized.

"Put that one aside," Vinn finally says softly to murmurs of assent.

We quickly page through the remaining drawings. One gives us pause, but a side-by-side comparison quickly dispels this would-be competitor for the crown. A student named Lori just got extra credit. It's too bad I can't tell her how her winning image will be used.

Relief washes over me as I carefully place the stack of papers back into the folder. Vinn winks at me, the corners of her mouth raised. Leo simply refills our glasses. I notice that the bottle is now empty.

Vinn is quick to cast a pall over my moment of happiness. "Of course we still need to find the voice for this creature from outer space," she reminds me. "I don't think there's any question it should be female."

"Then it has to be me," Rebecca jumps in before the echo of Vinn's last words leave the air.

"Rebecca, it can't be you," I interject before she can list the eleven reasons she's perfect for the role. "You haven't been with us when we've talked out how this will go down. You and Vinn will be with Veronica as she tours the embassy and when she meets the Elohim. You can't be two places at once."

She seems mollified given that she has a starring and more critical role. "You could use one of your students."

Vinn and I simultaneously begin to speak. I let Vinn take the lead. "No, we can't. We don't mind using them backstage and away from the action. But we won't let a student get within miles when this thing goes down. Can't risk it. Not only for legal reasons and the fact we'd both lose our jobs if the administration ever found out. Neither Mal nor I will allow it."

That isn't quite true but is the story Vinn and I agreed to in advance. We fall quiet as we brood, having solved one problem only to stumble onto the next one. After a few minutes, Vinn sits up straight with a look of resolution and I follow her eyes as she casts them upon Leo. She turns to me with a broad, bright smile and I know the die is cast despite the reservations I'd expressed before we headed downstairs.

"The accent is sexy and the technology exists to make it feminine and even sultry if that's what we want. And that way we keep it in the family."

Rebecca twists her head back and forth between us, puzzled, before finally catching on. "You have got to be kidding me," she tells us. Now we're all staring at Leo, who looks up with bloodshot eyes to meet our gazes.

"What?" is all he says. We tell him.

Morning comes whether I want it to or not, complete with fuzzy mouth and fuzzier head. For one brief moment I can't remember what possible motivation I had to set the alarm for 7:00 a.m. on a Saturday before the sound of Rebecca whistling in the unit below reminds me that we need to go look at properties before the afternoon meeting with Veronica. Vinn rebuffs my suggestion that she make me pancakes while I get ready by turning over and pulling the covers over her head.

I force down a couple handfuls of cashews and the remnants of a chocolate bar I find in the back of my freezer while I brew some pu'er tea, which an ancient "barefoot doctor" in rural China, essentially a folk healer, once swore to me could be used as a remedy for hangovers. He also suggested consuming ginger, so I quickly peel a toe's worth of ginger root with a spoon and throw it in the mix. It may taste awful, but if it clears my head it'll be worth it.

I'm just pouring my steaming cure into a vacuum-insulated container that promises to keep it hot for twelve hours when a gentle knock at my door is accompanied by a not-so-gentle "Malcom, get your butt out here!" I grab my coat, check to make sure I have my keys, and peek in at my slumbering companion before heading for the door.

We find the Zipcar I'd arranged and drive toward the Kennedy Expressway. "I narrowed our options down to two forest preserves," I tell Rebecca once we're on the southbound entrance ramp. "Ultimately it'll be my decision as to which one we use but I want you to use this morning to become familiar with the final choice. I don't want Veronica to have any reason to suspect that you're seeing the site for the embassy for the first time when we bring her there. Take pictures and study them then be prepared to present arguments for why it's an ideal spot on which to build. You'll need to be passionate and remember, as far as she's concerned, we already bought the land so we're committed to it."

Our first stop is Kickapoo Woods on the far south side, which I chose mainly because of the large field primarily used to fly model airplanes. Despite my best efforts I was unable to find an aerial view of the preserve, but from reconstructing various photographs I believe a patch of woods abut the field. A nearby stream running through the parkland hopefully adds a scenic touch.

Traffic is moderate despite the early hour but by pushing the speed limit and some creative weaving, we make it to the entrance in just under thirty minutes. My initial impression is one of extreme disappointment. The density of trees is much less than I had hoped, and as we drive deeper in nothing jumps out as anything special. It's nice, but not in a way that would make it seem like an ideal landing spot for our alien friends. Once we find the open space, it becomes immediately clear how exposed it is to the rest of the park and worse, the woods are further away than I had anticipated. The final piece of bad news is that the field already has a few families wandering it. If that's the case at this time of day, it'll be even worse this afternoon. There must not be a whole lot to do in the middle of winter in this part of the city.

Rebecca senses and shares my disappointment. "Not much sense in getting out to take photos, is there?" she murmurs softly. "Let's hope the other one is better."

The "other one" is Deer Grove East, which has from

the beginning been my top contender. My plan was to see my second choice first, leaving us more time to become familiar with my anticipated winner if it turns out that way. Now, though, having badly misjudged the qualifications of Kickapoo Woods, my confidence that Deer Grove will even meet our minimum requirements is shaken. It's become an all eggs in one basket scenario, which makes me very, very nervous.

It's an hour's drive back up north to suburban Palatine, a ride made much longer by the urgency of assuring it's a location we can use and by Rebecca's decision to sing show tunes along the way. I attempt to ignore both by trying to recall what I know about this particular forest preserve.

Part of Deer Grove was the first land purchased by the Cook County Forest Preserve District over a hundred years ago, and it increased in size when O'Hare Airport's expansion required the destruction of hundreds of acres of wetlands. To gain approval for the expansion, funds were secured to replace those wetlands in various preserves, of which Deer Grove was one. Today it measures around 2,000 acres and intense efforts to recreate wetlands, woodlands, and native prairies has made it one of the area's most successful and beautiful recreations of how this part of the state looked before people moved in. Despite the lure of trails for hiking and biking, a camping area, and picnic pavilions, there are still large areas reserved for nature to do its thing. It's one of those spots that I have my eye on.

As we ease through the entrance to a mangled medley of tunes from "Wicked," my hopes immediately rise. For one, it appears deserted. Apparently no one sees a windy, gloomy fifteen-degree day as the ideal time to picnic or ride a bike. It's also absolutely captivating in its raw, natural beauty. Even Rebecca sits up and quiets down, staring out the window. I slow to a crawl, then find the small parking lot in a remote area of the park that I was seeking.

"Ready?" I ask as we both zip up our coats and put on our gloves. I pull on a wool hat with ear flaps, while Rebecca opts for a pair of oversized, fluffy green earmuffs. She nods and we simultaneously exit. Our path through the woods sits immediately in front of the car and we hustle toward it in an effort to use the trees to break the cold breeze. After less than two minutes we emerge onto an ocean of prairie grass, still stunning in its brown and red shades of winter. We walk in the direction of a distant tree line, stopping after a hundred yards or so as a frozen pond emerges off to our right. To the left, all we see is prairie.

"Bingo," Rebecca whispers as she fumbles attempting to take her phone out of her pocket with her mittened hands. We slowly turn in unison as she clicks away, then move further toward the far side before moving closer to the pond to allow her to get as many pictures as possible. It's not long, though, where one look at her reddened features combined with the loss of feeling in my lips forces us to abandon the prairie and head back to the car. As soon as we slam the doors behind us, I start it and flip the heat switch up to its highest position. I keep the car in park as I wait to thaw out.

"I have to say I was concerned after that first dud," Rebecca says helpfully. "Malcom, you did good. Whatever that special something is that you were looking for, it's here. Now, can we get moving? I'd like time to touch up my face and get a bite to eat before we pick Veronica up and it's getting late."

She's right, we need to hustle. I put the car into reverse to the dulcet sounds of "Send in the Clowns." I can only hope that's not commentary.

# THIRTY TWO

We're back in plenty of time to warm up, grab a leisurely lunch, and get mentally prepared for our most critical meeting with Veronica to date, Rebecca's whining that two hours is hardly enough time to freshen up and become her most radiant self notwithstanding. I call Vinn to bring her up to speed and briefly describe the chosen location, which she can then look up online in case Veronica has questions that Rebecca can't answer. I also tell her my idea for our site visit this afternoon.

"That would definitely solve a few problems," she admits, "but she's not going to like it. Who's insisting on it, Rebecca or me?"

"You are because you put up the funds to purchase the land. Rebecca will be reluctantly going along because it was a condition of your investment. Sorry to make you the hard ass, but I can't trust Rebecca to stand firm in the face of Veronica's fawning admiration."

"Won't be the first time I'm made out to be the bitchy one," Vinn sighs. "Part of me wishes I could go with you because waiting to hear how it turns out will kill me, but part of me is glad not to have to be in the same car as that woman or to have to trek through the snow in this weather. You have to promise to call me the minute you're alone."

"Will do," I say but Vinn has already hung up. I guess she's getting in character as the impolite member of the Vinn-Rebecca duo.

Greeting Rebecca at her door, I have to admit that she used her time well and learned a trick or two from her makeover with Heather. She may not stand up to an examination in close quarters, but for a venture outside where the focus is on the landscape rather than her features, it'll be more than enough. I do silently question her choice of a skirt and heels but know better than to argue utilitarian fashion with a diva.

It's a short drive from our place to Veronica's home but long enough for Rebecca to grow increasingly nervous, as indicated by her hand wringing and lip chewing. I don't know if it's having to spend time making nice with a murderer that's setting her off or doubts about whether she chose the right color of eye shadow. I decide I'd rather not know and leave her to her angst.

We find a parking spot half a block away, eight minutes early. Time to spring the twist on Rebecca. Hopefully the timing is right to give her the necessary time to prepare without sufficient time for panic to set in.

"Rebecca, one thing before we go. I'm sure you've thought about the issue of driving Veronica past the sign indicating we're entering a forest preserve owned by the county. She's not stupid and would immediately know that there's no way that we could have purchased a parcel of park land. To address that, and to prevent her from visiting the site on her own, our story is that Vinn put up the money to buy this plot and that her condition in doing so is that no one outside of the three of us is to know its exact location. You're very sorry to have to ask her to do this, but you have to insist that she wear a blindfold from the time she gets into the car until we're into the wooded area, and then the same thing in reverse. She'll balk, but it's non-negotiable even if she threatens to pull out of the partnership. Be understanding but firm, use your charm, and deflect any anger onto Vinn. Any problem with that?"

I expect a total meltdown, but Rebecca surprises me. Now that we're minutes away from today's crucial encounter, she has her game face on below the multiple layers of foundation. She nods determinedly. "Makes sense. Yes, I can do that."

She adds nothing else but opens the door and looks back at me. "Ready?"

"Why would I agree to that? If we're really in this together, there are no secrets between us. Absolutely not!" Rebecca waited until we got into the car together to drop the blindfold requirement on Veronica. Her reaction is pretty much as anticipated. I tense waiting for Rebecca to respond. She doesn't hesitate.

"Not my rule, sorry sweetie," she says in her best nonchalant tone, not rising to the bait of Veronica's fury. "I keep my promises and trust is essential if any relationship is to work. Vinn and I have known each other and worked together toward our goal for years; we just met you a few weeks ago. While I have no doubt that we'll be doing great things together, she's the cautious one. She made this a condition of her financial outlay long before we met you. It's not permanent, but I have to insist at least for now. I'm sorry, but if you need time to think this over we can reschedule for another day."

I'm impressed. Bold move being the first one to suggest that maybe this won't work out and that Veronica needs to consider if she wants to go back to pursuing the embassy on her own. Both women are sitting in the rear seats. I see the conflict racing through Veronica's mind as she struggles with the unfamiliar concept of giving in.

Rebecca doesn't wait for an answer to dangle a carrot. "If it makes any difference, our architect has promised to have plans ready for us by next weekend. We're ready to proceed with or without you, but would much rather have the benefit of your guidance and experience. Daylight's dwindling, darling."

I know before the words come out of her mouth what Veronica's answer will be. She's invested too much into her goal and her setback with Scott and her inability to find an associate who meets her standards have to be weighing on her mind. The prospect of starting over is one factor, but if she really is our murderer there must also be somewhere inside of her a reluctance to keep killing anyone who doesn't work out.

"All right, at least for today. We'll talk about any future trips." Checkmate. I keep my exhale of relief hidden as I start up the car and hand a blindfold to Rebecca, who passes it on to Veronica with a cheery "See how pretty!" as if no cross words had passed between them.

I'm sure it's totally unnecessary, but I make a few extra turns and go past the expressway so as to enter it by turning left instead of right just to prevent any chance that Veronica will be successful if she's trying to map out the general area in which the field is located. I also move the car's clock ahead by fourteen minutes.

Traffic is heavy on a Saturday afternoon, so it takes us well over an hour to reach the vicinity of the forest preserve. That actually works to our benefit, as we want Veronica to think that the location is further away from the city and suburbs than it actually is, and also the late afternoon shadows of winter will prevent her from an overly critical review of the more distant edges of the plot. After exiting the expressway I again drive around for several extra minutes before entering the park.

It's not surprising given the dreary winter weather and lateness of the day that we're again the only car parked in the lot near the field, but it's still a welcome sight. I nod to Rebecca and she gives me a thumb's up.

"Just a few steps with the blindfold, Veronica, dear, then we'll free your eyes. Malcom will help guide you but be careful as you walk."

Veronica's grim expression tells me what she thinks of her captive status, but she silently allows me to gently take her by the elbow and lead her into the woods. As soon as we're out of sight of the parking lot, Rebecca gives her the all clear to remove the blindfold. At this moment, all she sees is forest on all sides and a frozen mud path leading forward. She shakes her arm loose from my hold and storms ahead.

Moments after we reach the clearing, Rebecca forces us to halt. "Oh, and no pictures please. There'll be plenty of time for that." Totally improvised but a good thought. The last thing we need is for Veronica to use photo recognition software to trace the location.

No response from our companion, but her mouth opens slightly as she slowly makes her way into the grass, head swerving in all directions. Rebecca keeps to her right while I fall back a few steps but still within earshot. For at least ten minutes, there's nothing to hear as the women walk to the center of the field, Veronica continuing to turn to gaze to each side.

She finally breaks the silence. "It'll do. Yes, this may be all right." Faint praise, but the gleam in her eyes tells of a more excited reception. "Have you done all of the measurements? Soil testing? Do you have the necessary concessions?"

Rebecca looks back at me for help. "Yes, yes, and we'll have them soon," I respond. Damn. I forgot about my plans to create something to show that we have governmental agreement not to interfere with an alien landing. Hopefully Rebecca's memory is short as well. "And the architect has been here with his equipment," I lie. "He had to wear a blindfold as well."

A sharp, stinging wind suddenly blows in from the northwest, bringing an additional but welcome chill to the air. I watch as Veronica zips her jacket up the extra half inch to her chin and pulls her gloves tighter. She won't want to be standing around much longer, which is perfect. A few flurries hasten her decision not to linger. She says something to Rebecca that I don't catch and they hook arms as they walk briskly past me back in the direction of the car. As they pass I catch Rebecca's eyes and pantomime putting a mask on. She nods.

As we enter the woods separating field from asphalt, Rebecca asks Veronica to don her mask and this time there are no complaints. I again guide her to the car, hold the door open for each woman, then quickly get started home.

The chatter in the rear is animated and highly encouraging as Veronica suggests various placements within the field and how to enhance what she calls an "already magical" setting to maximize the impact of the first view by the Elohim. She asks for details about the plans, which Rebecca skillfully deflects as having to wait to see what the architect produces. The time passes more quickly on the way back and I have to remember to reset the dashboard clock as we near Humboldt Park.

I double park in front of Veronica's building, not wanting to encourage an invitation to carry on the conversation in her place if I were to pull into a space. The new best friends give each other an awkward backseat hug before Veronica departs, promising to call to set up a time to review the architectural drawings. Rebecca seems to deflate as Veronica disappears from view.

"Well, that went well," she says in an unusual display of understatement. "Home, James."

I bite back an appropriate if profane retort, make a mental note to discuss an attitude adjustment later, and point the car in the direction of home.

"Sounds like it couldn't have gone better." Vinn's voice through the phone sounds relieved. "While you were escorting a dangerous killer around town, I kept busy by baking zucchini bread, creating a playlist meant to relax me, and fooling around with a few game theoretic metaphysic equations. Oh, and I checked in with our architect student. We're meeting him Friday morning before classes. Monday evening we have an appointment with our student interior designer, our IT wizard, and a teacher from the theater department. I told them you'd cook us dinner."

This time I hang up without saying goodbye. It had been such a good day.

# THIRTY THREE

I don't own a dining room table. During my years of working in the shadows all over the world, my only "friends" came in the form of work associates who also survived by keeping out of the public eye, so it's not like we got together for dinner over a Thanksgiving turkey. Even now, out of the game for a few years, I prefer to keep my inner circle small and rarely share meals with more people than will fit at the island in my kitchen. Tonight's total of six requires menu planning which allows for balancing plates on laps in the living room with a minimum of spillage.

Along with the customary charcuterie platter of unique meats and cheeses and some fancy olives, an offering Rebecca snubs her nose at as "so terribly cliché, darling" before filling a plate with it and claiming her favorite chair, I chose to go with a variety of finger foods. The main requirements were that they're easy to eat, will cause little damage if dropped, and which allowed me to do most of the prep work on Sunday. I'm showing off my multi-tasking skills by simultaneously plating fava bean and radish bruschetta and prosciutto-wrapped arugula while slapping Vinn's hands away from the mushroom tarts when there's a knock at the door.

"I'll get it," Vinn reluctantly agrees, missing out on her opportunity to raid the food while I'm distracted with guests.

The first face through the door is a familiar one, our IT wizard Malika, resplendent in a fuchsia hijab covered with spiders, followed close behind by another student I don't know. Vinn has a short conversation with her while taking her coat before introducing her to me as Sally Carpenter, an interior and industrial design double major referred to us by one of her professors, whom apparently Vinn sought out. They need no encouragement to take plates and begin grazing. I recruit Rebecca to take drink orders while I pull crab puffs out of the oven.

Small talk and introductions are well underway when the second wave arrives. Expecting only a member of the faculty from the theater department, I'm surprised when three bodies enter together. I discreetly pull two more plates from a cabinet so that the unexpected guests would think I had planned for them all along.

"Hi, I'm Flynn Forsyth, from the arts department," the first one in projects with a flair fitting of his position. "I hope you don't mind, but I brought along one of my students who I think could be quite helpful in this endeavor. Please say hello to Blaire Brooke, a star in the making in set design and technology."

Brooke, to her credit, flushes even redder than her frozen cheeks and slinks away to grab a plate. I eye the flamboyant theater teacher, trying to get a sense as to whether we can trust him to keep our plans to himself or whether he doubles as one of Stuart's spies. He passed Vinn's furtive background check, but I know she's also evaluating him even more closely than I am.

"This is Thomas Mayfield," Flynn continues, dashing my hopes for an alliteration trifecta, "from Mad Imagination FX Studio. He sometimes acts as an advisor on our student productions. Based on what you told me about what you're looking for, I reached out to him for some preliminary guidance. He insisted on coming himself."

Mayfield is a tall, slender man in his early 30s, and looks like he could blend into the background of any room he occupies. Nothing about him screams "mad imagination," but as he walks over to me with a warm smile and extends his hand, there's an instant likeability attached to him. "I'm sorry to show up uninvited," he says, "but this is something that intrigues me and if you don't mind, I'd like to sit in and maybe even get involved."

"Not at all," I reply, returning his smile. "Grab a plate and a drink. We're just getting started."

Vinn brings out a few extra folding chairs so that everyone has a seat. They all quiet and look at me expectantly as I pull over a bar stool. All three students have gathered in a group together on the couch. Vinn and I have had an ongoing discussion about how much to reveal and ultimately decided to open up completely. It wouldn't be fair to draw someone into a potentially volatile situation without disclosure.

"Thank you all for coming. I know we've been vague both about why you're here and exactly what it is we hope to get from you. I'm going to explain that now. If at any time you feel like you don't want to be involved for reasons you'll see shortly, we understand. By the way, students," I address them specifically, "we've arranged for each of you to get independent study credit if you do choose to participate." Yes, it's an obvious and intentional bribe.

"Professor Achison, Rebecca in the corner there, and I have for the last several months been investigating the murders of two...no, I'm sorry, three...young people here in Chicago with the knowledge and tacit approval of the main police officer in charge, but not with the consent of the department itself. The actual killer of two of the victims died himself during an attempt to arrest him. Our target is a woman whom we believe ordered the first two deaths and may have committed the third herself. You will not, and I repeat not, be exposed to her and your existence will not be revealed to her. That being said, if you feel like the danger element is too much for you, which we understand, you are free to leave now."

Contrary to any interest in leaving, I have five sets of eyes glued on me as if I were about to reveal the secret of life. "All right, fine. If you change your mind at any time, simply let one of us know. I won't go into any more detail on the deaths themselves or the victims. What you do need to know is that they were all involved to a certain extent with a religious cult that goes by the name of Raelism. Our target is a dedicated believer in it herself, and that's how we intend to induce her confession and to set up her capture. Each of you will have a role in making that happen."

They may not know they're doing it, but each student has straightened up and moved closer to the edge of their seats. Rebecca gets up to refill her plate and her cup, but no one else moves a muscle.

"Now this is where it gets a bit weird and why we need imaginative and creative minds involved. I could spend an hour just describing the basics of Raelism, but if you want to know more you can look it up yourselves. The relevant belief, in short, is that humans on Earth were created by beings from outer space called the Elohim, that they're monitoring our progress in establishing worldwide peace, and that they will return one day. The head of this religion has specified that an embassy must be built to receive them. That's where we intend to corner our target, but what we'll be doing there with her is still a work in progress.

"Each of you has a different role in bringing this embassy to life. We already have an architectural student working on renderings. Sally, we'll put you in touch with him in order to coordinate. He's doing the outline of the structure but you'll need to bring it to life with design touches. We've prepared a cheat sheet for you listing certain aspects of your design that must be followed. Anything above and beyond is up to you.

"Malika and Blaire, I assume we'll need both computer and theater technology working together for this, and I profess enough ignorance that I won't be much help in guiding you. I'm sure Professor Forsyth will be able to point you in the right direction. Your mission is twofold. One is to build the reception area for the embassy. Obviously, given time constraints, all we need is something that through the magic of theater gives the impression of something it's not. But it has to be convincing. The other task is to produce realistic aliens." Malika can't help but scream a little "yes" and pump her fist, while Blaire's mouth drops open and her eyes light up. I pull out the winning design.

"I'm afraid you won't have free reign on the design. Here's what it needs to look like, although in bringing it to life you can infuse it with characteristics in line with what the Raelists believe. Same for the reception area—there are certain necessary elements. You get a cheat sheet as well. It will need to be realistic, free in its movement, and you'll have to arrange so that someone off stage can speak through it. I'm thinking something like a hologram. You know, a Star Wars Princess Leah kind of thing."

"You don't want a hologram," Mayfield interjects. "Technology has progressed beyond that. I'm thinking volumetric display. Essentially it involves manipulating nearly invisible specks present in the air with lasers to produce a 3D image that you can view from all sides. This is cutting edge and still experimental. I'd love a chance to try it out and the students would be doing something few people in the country have done. Would look great on the resume. Might be a few expenses, but I'll donate my time just for the chance to try it out."

I knew I liked him. "All right, but we have a tight schedule and can't afford to fall behind. Make sure you have a backup plan if this volume whatever doesn't work. That's all we have time for tonight, although stick around to finish eating and you can ask Vinn or I any questions you have. We'll set up individual meetings for this week. Sally, you and Chad, our architect, will be meeting with me. Malika and Brooke, Professor Achison is our scientist and her brain is wired more for what you're doing. Okay? Great, team. Let's catch a killer."

The excited buzz in the room belies what are sure to be high levels of frustration down the road once confronted with deadlines, failed experiments, and the limitations imposed by Rael's requirements, but I wasn't going to play the role of Debbie Downer just yet. Plenty of time for that. Both Vinn and I get pulled aside with requests for more details, information which we planned to give in our individual meetings but are happy to dispense now. We each schedule appointments with our students over the next few days.

As with most gatherings, people begin to exit when the food runs out and tonight is no exception. Even Rebecca bails on us, probably to avoid sharing dish duties. Tom Mayfield hangs back, however, and starts helping Vinn and I carry plates into the kitchen.

"I don't know how you got yourself tied up in a murder inquiry," he tells us, "and maybe it's best that you don't share that information with me. But I want you to know that I'll be proud to be a part of this, successful or not. If it fails, it won't be for lack of effort on my part. But you know, I had a chance to exchange a few ideas with those two students I'll be working with. Their instructor may be a total zero—an impression confirmed over several productions—but based on previous interactions I can guarantee you that tonight will be the extent of his involvement. The kids themselves are super bright, smarter than me even. I think it'll be me supporting them more than the other way around. We'll get this done, at least on our end."

The implication is clear: the tech side will do their job. It'll be up to us to get Veronica inside whatever illusion they create and to ensnare her when we do. They'll build a better mousetrap, but can we provide tasty bait and trigger the hammer? Mayfield clearly feels that the weak link in our plan is us. If asked, Vinn and I would almost certainly agree.

# THIRTY FOUR

I meet twice with Sally during the week and am pleased to find that her energy directed toward the project hasn't diminished. The first meeting involved bouncing ideas back and forth, mostly her ideas off of me, as I professed my ignorance as to color matching and what constitutes subtle feminine design. By our next meeting two days later, she'd obtained preliminary floor plans and sketches from Chad and had covered them with proposed wall colors and notes on possible furnishings, artwork, and what she called "celestial feng shui." She's already past the point where I can provide any meaningful guidance, so we agree that we don't need to schedule another get-together until she needs my final approval.

Vinn held one marathon meeting with Malika and Brooke and seems pleased with the direction they're headed, although at this stage all of their ideas are theoretical and need to be designed and/or tested. The two students are on their own for sourcing materials and planning the actual buildout of the reception area, within reason and subject to Vinn's oversight, but are coordinating with Mayfield on the projection of an alien being. He's called me three times to excitedly reveal his progress on finding the materials he needs and his insights into how to bring the aliens to life, and to repeat several times how thrilling it is to get the chance to work on this cutting-edge technology. I try to share his enthusiasm, but each time was lost the minute he began to explain the details behind the science. I hold firmly to the belief that the more complicated something is the greater the chance something will go awry, which also dampens my spirits. He and the students will be experimenting with initial prototypes in person over the weekend. I politely decline his invitation to be present.

By Friday afternoon, between the demands of the classroom and the feeling of having my head explode when overloaded with design and technological information I can't begin to comprehend, I'm mentally drained. I drag myself to Vinn's office for our 4:00 meeting with Chad to review his renderings. He's running late, probably frantically adding last-second details before turning in his assignment. He is a student, after all.

We use the opportunity to look ahead toward a detail that we've been putting off discussing. "Obviously we're not going to actually build this thing in a forest preserve, or even build most of it at all," Vinn summarizes cautiously. "So our goal is to present detailed plans to Veronica, get her all excited while simultaneously boosting her trust in us, then somehow transport her to the interior of the reception area where we get her to confess her misdeeds to the Elohim. So far so good, except where are we building the reception area and how do we get her inside without her knowing that she's not in the middle of that field?"

"Mayfield has volunteered room in his studio, which he says is the size of several warehouses," I assure her. "I'm still working on the rest of it. We may be able to use the blindfold again, so it's the transition from car to reception room that needs some ideas. We have time."

Vinn scrunches up her nose and doesn't appear to be satisfied with my reassurance that we'll work out the details before we need them. She's right in her doubts, as my apparent confidence is mostly bluster. Before she can challenge me, though, we're interrupted by a knock at the door.

A harried Chad stumbles into the room with a sheaf of large sheets of paper tucked under one arm and another bundle in his opposite hand. He drops them at his feet as he plops himself into the chair next to me. "I'm sorry I'm late," he tells us breathlessly, "I had a few additions I thought of just before I left."

"It's all right, Chad," Vinn says. "We appreciate that you've been working under a very tight deadline. Take a minute to compose yourself, then show us what you've got."

Chad draws several deep breaths then picks up his papers, spending several minutes arranging them in some sort of order. We wait semi-patiently until he finally spreads a large sheet over Vinn's desk.

"This is the scale drawing of the entire structure," he tells us before looking directly at me. "And I've written in a bunch of lingo like you asked. It doesn't always make a lot of sense, so hopefully she won't try to research what I wrote. You can see that I followed what you told me I had to do, but also added in some details like foliage, plumbing and electric notes, suggestions for placement of furnishings, etc."

His voice takes on a tone of pride as he speaks, with good reason. The floor plan before us is spectacular. It's precise, neat, and has the look of a truly professional job. We both complement him, leading him to relax his shoulders and actually smile as he lays down the next sheet.

"This is a sketch of the roof as seen from above. You can see the landing pad, stairway, and some skylights." He gives us a few minutes to admire his work and then accelerates his presentation. "I didn't have time to do every room, but Sally told me she needed a separate floor plan for the reception area. That's this one here. Then here are my drawings of my concept for what the exterior would look like. I had fun with that and like the result. I wish you were building it for real."

His drawings show a classically beautiful structure, with the various rooms connected by glass-paneled passageways. The borders are crammed with notes referencing height, options for materials, and more. He's exceeded all of my expectations.

"Chad, I'm floored," I tell him. "This is beyond what I thought we'd be getting. We can't thank you enough. Do you have copies?"

He nods and looks at me like I'm an idiot. "Of course, both paper and electronic. If you need more copies or want me to make changes, just let me know."

"This will be enough for now, thank you Chad," Vinn assures him. "Your advisor's confidence in you was justified and I'll let him know right away that you earned your credit and aced your midterm. I may need to ask you some technical questions about all of this after I've looked it over. And Sally may consult with you again. Then at some point when all of this is over, we'll let you know how your work was received."

Chad hovers, basking in the praise and perhaps waiting to see if more was forthcoming, but soon simply gives a slight bow and makes a hasty exit. Vinn and I continue to look through his drawings.

"Wow," she finally says. "If this is the quality of work we can expect from the other students, I'll sleep better at night. Now, let's talk about our meetup with Veronica tomorrow."

The microphones are back in place, hidden in an intimate place on Vinn mainly for the fun of planting hers there, but for Rebecca it replaced one of the gems in her left earring. This time I won't need to worry about background noise of the bakery or having the women travel out of range, as I'm parked one house down from Veronica's building. A parkway tree conveniently sits between myself and any windows that she could gaze out of to see me fiddling with the sound levels or taking notes.

My level of concern about the two women meeting a possible killer outside of my presence has diminished both due to my proximity to them this time and because of Veronica's apparent commitment to the team approach in preparing for the arrival of the Elohim. She should realize the necessity of keeping Vinn and Rebecca alive if for no other reason than use of the field, which she won't be able to find on her own. Still, my palms are sweating as my companions vacate the car with Vinn carrying Chad's plans and Sally's enhancements in a poster tube we picked up cheap at a local art supply store. I flip on the receiver.

Veronica's voice comes through loud and clear. "Rebecca, how wonderful to see you today. You look simply smashing in that ensemble. Oh, and hello to you, um, um..."

"Vinn." I can almost hear her counting to ten in her head in order to let the moment pass without punching Veronica in the mouth.

"Darling, you are simply looking divine yourself," Rebecca jumps in. We agreed that under the circumstances she would take the lead in interacting with Veronica, another reason that Vinn is grumpy. "As promised, we brought the plans and as I texted you, they're to die for." In reality, Rebecca hasn't seen them yet. "But maybe I could get a coffee first?"

"Of course, I'll put some on. Then you have to show me. No chit chat today, I'm too excited to see what you've come up with." It dawns on me only now that this may have been the pivotal moment that brought on Scott's demise. Veronica was unhappy with his concepts for what the embassy should look like and his pride in defending them was one of the last things he ever did. Rather than simply let him walk away, Rebecca arranged to have him killed. Theoretical or not, my formerly low anxiety level shoots through the roof.

I sense the tension through the microphones as well, as the brief small talk seems forced on both ends. Vinn and I were beyond impressed with Chad's and Sally's work but will it pass whatever tests the psychopathic cultist will impose? A few minutes later the java must be ready, as a general move-ment and the sound of the tube being opened filter through the speaker.

"Vinn, dear, will you be so kind as to tell Veronica what we're looking at." Smart move, thank you Rebecca.

"First let me say that nothing here is set in stone, but we've put a lot of thought into this and like where it is," Vinn remarks. "And it follows Rael's guidelines precisely, as you can see from the architect's notations. Obviously, this is the out-line for the ground floor of the entire embassy."

Over the next hour, Vinn keeps a running commen-tary on what they're looking at, more for my benefit than for Veronica's. Rebecca provides gushing comments aimed at influencing Veronica's opinion. Veronica shows herself to be remarkably astute when it comes to evaluating architectural renderings and asks pointed questions, which Vinn answers with apparent ease reflecting her hours of preparation and quizzing of Chad. A few sharper exchanges show that Veron-ica is not totally on board, or at least raises objections as her way of maintaining control. When they finally get to Sally's renderings, though, all three women have very few quibbles and even the strictest critic in the room manages to tone down any negativity and admit that her decorative touches are right on point. My relief is palpable. That should mean we hooked her.

"No, I'm afraid we're not ready to share them yet," I hear Vinn say in apparent response to Veronica's request for copies. "You've made your initial opinions clear and we can make some refinements to show you for the next time, but we can't risk that you would take the fruit of months of our labors for yourself. That may sound harsh, but we need to build more trust."

"I see." I can hear the chill in Veronica's voice, but she

recovers to pretend that all is well. "I do understand. I wrongfully placed too much trust too early once myself and it didn't end well. But let's hope we reach that point quite soon."

"Why don't we consider your suggestions, put those we agree with into a new set of plans, and reconvene next week?" Vinn asks semi-sincerely.

"Oh, I believe I'll be occupied for a little bit. Perhaps the weekend after that. I do want to finalize these soon, but there is a little time. We still need to get the locals and feds to grant interstellar immunity to the Elohim and there are a thousand other details to work on. I think if all goes well we should be able to break ground in the spring of next year."

The silent reaction to Veronica's timetable in her apartment is broken by my own startled gasp in the car. A year just to start on the embassy? Over 365 days coddling a killer? We don't even have a complete Plan A and it's already time to create a Plan B.

# THIRTY FIVE

"We've got to find a way to accelerate her timetable," says Mr. Obvious as he pours two glasses of wine. "Any ideas?" We were quiet in the car after the meeting with Veronica and once home Rebecca peeled off into her apartment without comment. We hadn't set a deadline for staging the Elohim's visit but our minds were focused on a vague point maybe a month away depending on how quickly the tech aspect of our plan came through.

"Nothing specific," Vinn sighs as she reaches for her glass. "But from what little we know about Veronica she can be stubborn and won't be pushed into something until she's ready. We'll have to instigate an event that forces the issue."

"Right. As much as she's enamored of Rebecca, I don't think even she has the power to persuade Veronica to move faster. It has to be someone more powerful, more influential. There's no earthly way we can do it ourselves."

"Then it has to be something out of this world," Vinn says with an animated edge in her voice. I love it when she gets this look in her eyes as if she's solved an unsolvable physics problem that's plagued scientists for decades. "What if she's summoned by the Elohim? They have a message to convey and have chosen her as their messenger?"

I catch her excitement and jump in. "That would play directly into her ego, that she's somehow special. The self-appointed gold-feathered Angel. But we wouldn't want the Elohim to reveal what the actual message is right away—they'll want to reveal it once a suitable location for their visit is prepared. That way she'll be beyond anxious to find out what they want to tell her and will be begging us to get the embassy, or at least the reception area, ready as quickly as possible."

"Exactly. Which provides us cover as well, since there's no way that we could build an entire embassy in a short period of time. She wouldn't believe us if we told her we'd done it, no matter how much she'd imagined it happening in her wildest dreams."

"That's it!" I think I startled Vinn. "In her dreams. We'll have the Elohim come to her in a dream when she's not fully awake and won't be in any condition to analyze what's appearing before her. And the Elohim messenger won't need to be as advanced as what we'll need later on."

Vinn gives me a sardonic smile. "Since the venue for this dream would be her bedroom, I assume you're anticipating a little breaking and entering to add to our list of felonies?"

I grin back. "It was put on our list already, if you recall. Several times. So we've had the practice and I'm not worried about that. What we do need to work on is a script. But first, let's give our resident special effects expert a call."

"Absolutely, that's easy," Mayfield tells us over speakerphone. "Since you don't require a lot of definition for the image all we'll need is a simple projection and a speaker. But that means you'll need to have the equipment installed in her place." We don't respond and it doesn't take him long to catch on. "Better that you don't tell me. The kids have a prototype for the alien that we can use for now. If you give me three or four days, I'll have something for you."

"That'll work," I tell him. "We'll come by your place when it's ready and you can give us a demo along with installation instructions."

"That gives us a little time to put a short speech together," Vinn thinks out loud after I hang up. "And I guess we should have Leo record it since he'll be the voice of the

Elohim when they come down for the actual visit. Better get that voice changer right away. And start putting aside our bail money."

Leo's emotional spectrum, at least on the surface, ranges from indifferent to passive. It's no surprise, then, that he greets our request for a recording session with a shrug of the shoulders and a grunt. We give him a copy of the speech on the remote chance that he'll actually practice it a few times before it's showtime and tell him that we'll be back in a couple of hours.

Upon our return, I'm more than a little concerned to see a bottle of dark liquid on the table with a portion of its contents half filling a glass sitting at Leo's customary spot. A small serving of liquid courage would be fine before his acting debut but I know better than to ask how much he's had. I'm not sure a drunken emissary from beyond our solar system will be the most convincing enticement to luring Veronica into our trap.

Vinn attempts to coach Leo in certain inflections while I set up the equipment but gets little reaction. When you think about it, there's no treatise on the elocution of aliens, so trying to convince him that there's a right way to speak might not be that big a deal. All we really need is for his voice to be clear and understandable to a sleepy consciousness. I signal that I'm ready to go, hand Leo the microphone, and Vinn holds the script in front of him so as not to have any rustling of papers on the recording.

Leo clears his throat several times. "Veronica, awake. Listen closely. We have chosen you to convey a message to your fellow citizens of the planet Earth." I nod encouragement as he speaks slowly and deliberately. "But know this. When the time comes, you must provide proof of your worthiness to act as our messenger. You must show us that you are a true follower of the Elohim. We will come again one more time to notify you of the time of our visit. Be prepared to receive us in the manner we have foretold."

I hold up my finger to indicate a few seconds of silence then relax. To my ears he nailed it, but Vinn thought he stumbled over the word "Elohim." We have Leo repeat the speech two more times until she's satisfied. It's only then that I notice that the glass I'd seen earlier is empty and the level of the liquid in the bottle is a fraction of what it was when we entered.

We thank Leo, politely decline his offer to help finish off the mystery hootch, and tell him that we'll need him again for a brief recording once we set a date for the visit. With that we head back upstairs to run it through the machine to make him sound feminine. Hopefully there are enough dials and filters to get the job done.

"It's virtually idiot-proof," Mayfield tells us, indicating that he knows me better than I thought. "Because you're doing this surreptitiously, I chose the tiniest projection device I could find. See, it's barely larger than a pin head. But that's also going to affect the quality of the image, so make sure you do this at night where the darkness will help hide the defects. It'll also make it unnecessary to show mouth movements. You said you already have the speaker, so let me just show you how this works."

We're in a small studio that would approximate the size of a bedroom. Mayfield gives us a quick tutorial on placement and reminds us that the lens has to be free of impediments. He stands on a chair to place it in a small gap between the ceiling and the molding that encircles the room. In his hand is a small device resembling a television controller.

"Like I said, very simple. You can turn it on remotely, just remember to turn it back off when you're done if you want to use it more than once. The battery doesn't hold a charge for long. When you're ready for the image to project, simply press this button. Okay, can you get the lights?"

Vinn flips the lights off. Mayfield does the honors himself, apparently not trusting me to press a button correctly. Within a second an eerie green image begins to form, hovering in the air above us. It's a crude representation of the chosen likeness of the Elohim that we passed on to the students. It's not entirely lifelike, but for a dream it's convincing enough. As I stare at it, it appears to move.

"That's an illusion, it's actually your eyes that are doing the moving," Mayfield informs us. "But it does add to the authenticity, don't you think?" He cuts the connection and the lights come back up.

"Great job, thank you," I tell him as he retrieves the projection device, storing it in a small ring box. "It'll work for now. Do you think you can have the 3D image workable within a couple of weeks?"

"It'll be tight, but yes," he assures us. "Unless something unforeseen arises."

What are the odds? We take our new toy and depart.

I have Chuck confirm that Veronica still adheres to the same working hours both on Monday and Tuesday and that she leaves for her job as usual on Wednesday. I cancel a class and Vinn skips a lab so that we can make it to her apartment by 4:00 Wednesday afternoon, which will give us two hours to install the projector and microphone before she returns. We should only need about fifteen minutes.

Difficulty in finding an Uber and an unexpected traffic jam resulting from an accident on the Kennedy delay our arrival, so that we don't get there until after 4:30. Still plenty of time. Vinn can't conceal her excitement that she gets to finally try out her new lock picks in the field as part of an actual investigation. They must suit her, as we're inside Veronica's condo in less than thirty seconds.

We're careful to avoid touching any of the clutter as we head straight for the master bedroom, although on the way I peek into the second bedroom just to make sure it doesn't look used. The bed there is made and it's piled with boxes, so the likelihood that Veronica sleeps anywhere but the larger bedroom is remote. I catch up to Vinn, who's already placing the stepladder we brought directly opposite of where the pillows rest on the bed.

"I think here is good," she states, clearly not looking for my own opinion and leaving no question who's in charge of the installation. She takes a small hammer and a nail with almost the exact same circumference as the projection device and taps a hole into the drywall. "Hand it here," she demands. I wonder if she knows how sexy she is when she takes control. I pass the box up to her waiting hand.

She pushes the device into the hole, making sure it rests flush, and assures me that even when looking right at it it's not easy to see. "It looks like a speck of dirt or dust," she says. As she climbs down we begin debating where to place the speaker, the two most obvious spots being somewhere on the ceiling fan above the bed and the back of the headboard.

We've no sooner agreed on the fan than we both freeze at the sound of a key entering the lock. Vinn instantly folds the ladder up and slides it under the bed and is right behind me as we dive into the clothes closet, resetting the doors to partially closed once we're settled. Vinn is pressing herself up against one side and I on the other. The closet is about eight feet wide, extending roughly a foot past the doors on each end. It's into those one-foot sections we're each trying to squeeze, our knees up past our chins and our heads leaning on the back wall behind the hanging dresses, blouses, and business suits.

To prevent myself from panicking and to remain as quiet as possible, I'm utilizing a breathing technique similar to what pregnant women learn prior to giving birth. It's also supposed to have a calming effect but I feel little of that now as I hear movement signaling that someone, presumably the murderous target of our toils, has entered the room. She's happily humming to herself, but that mood could instantly change if she finds two intruders in her home.

A shadow blocks the light entering the closet as a pair of high heels is placed on the floor. Veronica then moves away and her footsteps fade as she leaves the room. A clanging of pans and the sound of ice dropping into a glass is exactly what I didn't want to hear, as it indicates that she's unwinding with a drink after work and is setting the stage to begin making dinner.

I slowly pull my phone from my side pants pocket, verify that it's on silent, and hold it close to my face so that Vinn can see what I'm doing. I type out a text: "Help. Trapped in Veronica's closet. Call and ask her to dinner." I pray Ted isn't in a meeting and can transition to Rebecca in record time.

Within seconds I hear the sound of a cell phone ringing in the unit and a muffled voice speaking intermittently. The call lasts about a minute, but my inability to distinguish the actual words being spoken leave me in the dark as to whether my plea was effective or not. I move in slow motion to pass my phone to Vinn so that she can read my message and she nods in acknowledgment. No text follows from Rebecca. She may not be sure if it's safe to send one to me.

Time passes and my legs start to cramp. Finally, in what may have been anywhere between an hour and twice that, Veronica enters the room, still singing to herself. The doors to the closet are flung wide followed by the sound of hangers sliding across the wooden bar on which they hang. I try to make myself smaller.

Veronica's indecisiveness as to what to wear is causing me to sweat, which as the droplets start to descend my face are causing my nose to itch. The dresses brushing against my shoulder are suddenly pressed harder as their owner pushes them to the side for better access to something else. After five or more agonizing minutes, the doors of the closet are closed, shutting out all but a sliver of light. The darkness has never been more welcome.

My mind begins to imagine what Veronica is doing as a way of timing her departure so that I can let my now painful muscles know that their time to stretch out is near. Makeup first, then dressing, then changing her mind three times about which dress she selected to wear, then hair. Clearly an inexact science, but this time just when I thought she should be checking the temperature to determine which coat to wear, her footsteps leave the room and ten seconds later we hear the closing of the front door.

I look at my phone and I assume Vinn is doing the same. We'll wait ten minutes in case Veronica forgot something, then get our job done as quickly as we can. In the meantime, I send a text to Rebecca to let me know when Veronica shows up wherever they're meeting so that we know it's safe to leave. I also remind her not to go anywhere with her where they'll be alone.

Vinn and I move at the same time, bumping heads as we exit the closet. Without a word we both climb onto the bed, where I lift her up so that she can stick the speaker to the top of one of the fan blades, as close to the housing for the motor as possible. We're counting that no one will be using the fan in the middle of winter.

We take care to smooth out the wrinkles on the bed's comforter and stand still listening, waiting for Rebecca's text but with one foot ready to propel us back into the closet. When my phone finally chimes, we both let out a huge sigh and head for the door. It's just swinging shut when Vinn lets out something that sounds like "gawk!" and catches it. She retreats into the bedroom and reemerges, red-faced, with the stepladder. We probably have time to test the equipment, but we've tempted fate enough for today.

We head for home.

# THIRTY SIX

"She's actually a very entertaining conversationalist, and a nice woman," Rebecca tells us that night. "If you ignore the murder part."

She's sitting at my kitchen island munching on some toffee left over from Christmas that I found in the back of my freezer. Vinn went straight home after our misadventure to deal with the aftershocks of stress on her own and to prepare outlines for labs she has to monitor tomorrow afternoon. I'd left a note on Rebecca's door to meet me upstairs as soon as she got back from dinner. I wasn't able to relax until I knew she was okay.

"Just don't get lulled into complacency," I warn her. "Did she talk at all about the embassy?"

Rebecca nods as she tries to find a way to delicately dislodge caramel from between her teeth. "She's committed to taking our time to make sure everything is perfect, down to the color of the flowers in the reception area. Understand that she's been planning this in her head for years so she has firm ideas on how certain things should be."

"You need to remember that there's a good chance she killed three people when they were too pretty, didn't meet her standards, or had ideas that diverged from her own. That's why it's so important to give her cause to drop her demands for perfection in return for a commitment to speed. I just hope that our ruse gives her the necessary jolt. Were you able to find out if she retains any ties to mainstream Raelists?" The success of our plan may depend on Veronica's unwillingness or inability to use a resource available to Raelists in Switzerland.

"Sorry, no," Rebecca responds, causing my heart to fall. "If it helps, I did direct the conversation to sleep habits. Told her that I often had trouble falling asleep no matter what time I went to bed. She took the bait and of course lectured me on the proper way to assure that I would get the rest I need. She used herself as the perfect example and told me she goes to bed precisely at 11:00 every night and wakes up at 6:30."

I'm startled that Rebecca foresaw the usefulness of that information and I could kiss her, except the garish wine-colored lipstick she chose to apply today holds me back. So verbal praise it is. "That helps a lot, thank you Rebecca. Ideally we'd like to have the Elohim wake her from a sound sleep so that she's too groggy to evaluate the vision appearing before her or to doubt its authenticity. Knowing her bedtime helps."

The deepest phase of sleep occurs roughly an hour after first falling asleep and only lasts between twenty and forty minutes. That's our target time, so now we're looking at just after midnight to project the image. The problem is that it's also the period where it's most difficult to wake someone up and the risk is that we'll be performing our little alien visitation for a soundly unconscious audience. Vinn and I considered putting in a motion detector but eventually rejected the idea as too unreliable, as it could simply pick up Veronica turning over in her sleep. I'm beginning to regret that decision.

Once Rebecca departs, I text Vinn to pass on her piece of intelligence then email Chad and Blaire asking if they can meet me during my office hours tomorrow. Once the special effects part of the team is ready, we'll need a reception area to receive the equipment for installation. The hour is growing late and all this talk of sleep has my mind focused on my own bed. I like to keep my mind happy and quickly slip between the covers.

"I thought this was all for show. I didn't know you actually intended to build it." Chad is having a hard time processing the task ahead of us. "And to do it in such a short period of time? I mean, just getting the supplies could take months. And to break ground when it's all frozen? That's crazy talk."

"We're not building it, Chad, and there's no "breaking ground" here, at least not literally. We just need a temporary, smaller version of the inside of the reception area. And it only has to look real. Basically our own movie set. Convincing but fake." I still see doubt in his eyes. "All I really need from you is a materials list for a scale version and to oversee its construction. The studio will supply the labor and it'll be put inside a large sound stage."

Blaire feels ignored and steps in to make sure that I'm aware that she shares Chad's angst. "What about me? I mean, I have classes you know."

"And if you recall, you're getting credit for this. Consider this your final exam, like a term paper. Once you've completed this task, you're done with it for the semester. And yes, Blaire, your job is the same as Chad's. Just let me know what you need me to source so that the decorating and design matches what you've already provided to us. Then you can go by once it's set up to make sure it's been done correctly and to make last-minute tweaks."

As we discuss timing and assorted other details, I can see the concern start to diminish as it's replaced by an excited anticipation of seeing their visions come to life. By the time they leave my office, they're ready to pull an all-nighter to get me the lists I've requested. Now it's me that begins to worry about pulling this off in time. As Blaire said, I've got classes. And I don't get academic credit for my participation in the creation of this B-movie trap. For me, it's strictly personal.

As far as Veronica is concerned, her partnership with Vinn and, mostly, Rebecca is now established and any urgency she once felt about finding a path to move forward with her dream embassy has dissipated. She's relying on our side to continue with tweaking the plans while she plays queen bee, sitting back while her drones do all of the work then stepping in with a critical eye and an authoritative voice to push us in the right direction. To her, we have a year to get it right before construction begins. Thankfully this means that she saw no need for another meeting over the weekend, leaving us to soldier forward on our own.

And we are busy, just not in the way that she believes. Far from studying and revising the plans that were presented to her according to her direction, our activity is centered on preparing the faux reception area according to our need to build an effective trap as quickly as possible. There are too many moving parts for Vinn and I to manage while still teaching and holding onto our daytime jobs and our sanity. We agreed over dinner on Sunday that we needed help. Against my better judgment and to Vinn's amusement, we reached out to Leo.

Technically Leo has a job as well as the proprietor of The Kuban Kabana, his restaurant on the near South Side, but his claim that he's in witness protection due to his unsuccessful attempt to assassinate Fidel Castro and the facts that he has no apparent culinary talent, few if any customers, and never seems to actually spend any time there has convinced me that the diner is a cover of some sort. All of which means that we felt no guilt asking for his assistance on the assumption that he has the time.

The real question is whether he has sufficient willingness to devote to the cause and the ability to bring all of the disparate elements together. He agreed to help, or at least we believed so from the six or so words he uttered when Vinn and I dropped by with piles of plans and a list of names and assignments. He's hard to read and the ever-present open bottle on his kitchen table offers no clue as to whether he's sober or catatonically inebriated. It's possible that by the next morning he had no memory of us even being there.

We're about to find out. Earlier today I sent out a group email setting up a meeting among all of the participants in this folly for 6:00 p.m. tonight, twenty minutes from now. Unsure if the email address on The Kuban Kabana's website is legitimate, I also left a note on Leo's door with the details. I haven't seen him nor sensed his presence since we first requested his assistance.

"You do realize that any deadlines we're up against are totally self-imposed, don't you?" Vinn asks as we Uber down toward Mayfield's studio in a rusty Volkswagen Passat with a lingering odor of fried fish. "If Veronica truly is our killer, the sooner the better as far as getting her off the streets, but if tonight is a total fiasco that doesn't mean our plans are dead. We just retool and push everything back a little."

I appreciate her trying to make me feel better, but the underlying implication in her assurances is that our meeting tonight will, in fact, be a disaster, so her words aren't having the desired effect. I don't think they're even helping Vinn's own mood. Nevertheless, I reach out, grab her hand, and give it a squeeze.

Mayfield greets us just inside the main door, which he locks behind us. "Everyone else is already here," he tells us, "They all arrived a few hours ago to make sure everything's ready for you."

We walk nearly the length of a football field to get to the area where our small group of fantasy makers is gathered. I'm gratified to see Leo among them, although the blood-stained apron hanging from around his neck is a bit disconcerting.

"He's been a godsend," Mayfield whispers as we near. "Was able to get everyone on the same page. Mostly."

I nod an acknowledgment to Leo before joining Vinn in greeting the students, all of whom appear full of nervous energy. It only occurs to me now that they've been under tremendous pressure themselves and have a lot riding on our evaluation. Mayfield steps forward to act as spokesperson for the group.

"We'll be bringing you in from a different direction for the actual event, and we need to discuss that at some point soon. For now our focus has been on the room itself. We'll go inside in a minute, but be aware that this is like a rough sketch that still needs to be filled in."

Mayfield leads us to a nondescript door that could just as easily lead to an office or a custodian's closet. The students hover close behind us as he swings the door open.

Far from an office or closet, Vinn and I step into a magnificent rendering of Chad and Blaire's bland sketches and notations. Larger than I expected, it must measure at least twenty-five feet across and nearly twice as long. A high ceiling features glass skylights with a star-filled sky beyond them. My expression must betray my confusion.

"It's not real," Blaire explains in response to my unasked question. "A theater trick. It looks deep, like you're seeing the real sky. But we can change it to daylight or a forest or whatever. Leo said you plan to do this at night, so we'll have it match whatever the sky looks like at the time. Clouds if you need them."

Chad doesn't want to be left out. "The interior walls here simulate what was specified in the drawings. She wanted windows, so just in case she looks out of one of them I have some bricks indicating a wall and a few fake bushes out there. Beyond that it'll just be pitch black. There's another wall about three feet past the windows that she won't see."

Vinn and I wander the room, examining the furnishings, which at this stage are sparse. Sally is quick to jump in. "I didn't have time to finish the decorating. We'll have a reception desk up here, some seating over here, and a few tables. Of course I'll have artwork on the walls and fresh flowers every-where. You'll have to give me a few day's notice for those."

Mayfield gestures to Malika, who up until now has been quiet. "The projection will come from overhead behind the desk. There'll be a very slight trail behind the image but it won't be visible to the naked eye. The voice will be coming out of speakers that are placed all around the room. There's eighteen of them, so the sound seems to come at you from all directions. Pretty cool and otherworldly. Leo will be in an adjacent room doing the talking. He'll also be able to hear what's going on in here in case he needs to improvise."

God forbid, I think to myself. "I have to say, this is an impressive start," I tell the group. "But you know what I'm going to ask. How is the alien coming?"

Mayfield grins. "We thought you'd never ask. Malika and I have been polishing up the technical aspect of that and Blaire has been helping make it more lifelike, more theatrical so to speak. Keep in mind that this is relatively recent technology, and completely new to us. We're not quite there yet but we'll get there."

At some unseen signal, the rest of the crew retreats to near the door, leaving Vinn and I to ourselves, joined shortly by Leo. The lights dim and for a moment nothing happens, then slowly a greenish figure begins to emerge in front of us, hovering in the air before settling down to our level about five feet away. It's clearly the alien from the winning drawing although slightly out of focus. Vinn walks to one side while I circle in the other direction. As promised, we're rewarded with a full 360-degree vision of the creature: front, side, and rear. As we make our way back, I'm startled to hear a voice coming out of nowhere and everywhere.

"Well, what do you think? This is Casper speaking."

I smile. Far from being Casper the Ghost, I recognize Malika's voice.

"It's incredible, I'm so impressed," I tell them as the lights come back up to full brightness. Vinn says the same. "You've done so much in so short a time. Not to act as the spoiler, but how long to get the alien sharper and the room 100% ready to go?"

"At least a week," Mayfield responds as the students nod in agreement. "Ten days would be better."

I look to Vinn, who shrugs her shoulders. We can work with that. "Deal," I say. "While you're doing that, we'll plant the seed. It's time for Casper to make his first appearance."

# THIRTY SEVEN

We consider asking Malika to be with us when we initiate the appearance of the Elohim into Veronica's bedroom just in case there are any technical snafus. Reluctantly we eventually veto the idea. It would be difficult to explain away the appearance of impropriety of having a female student in the company of a male professor after midnight for a secret activity having no direct connection to school. Beyond that, we'll be miles away from the actual event and won't have any idea if it's working or a total screw-up. Since all we're going to be doing is pressing a couple of buttons, we also discourage Rebecca from coming by, although we do warn her that if all goes well she may be getting a frantic call from Veronica.

It's midnight on the dot as Vinn and I sit close together on my couch with two small electronic devices in our hands. With a total lack of dramatic flair, I push the sole button on mine, resisting the urge to turn my television on with the remote at exactly the same time to see Vinn's reaction. We silently count to twenty to make sure the image has time to form above Veronica's bed, then Vinn presses the button first on her contraption before doing the same on a recorder linked to it by a cord. Leo's prerecorded message, as filtered to make it sound both alien and feminine, plays softly on our end, but should be loud enough to wake the dead across town. As soon as he reaches the end of the speech, we both push our buttons a second time to turn them off. We don't want the image to hover long enough for Veronica to recover from her shock and ask questions.

"Okay, another hour to kill. Think it went through?" I ask Vinn. At the last minute we decided to send a second message at 1:00 a.m. to hedge our bets. It's possible that Veronica slept through the first one or woke up halfway through or was just too groggy to assimilate the message. If she saw it at all, we can bet that she'll be lying awake when we send the follow-up.

"No clue," Vinn shrugs. "My cell phone doesn't work half the time I need it to, so it's hard to put my trust in a fancier contraption like this. And even if it did, we don't know how Veronica will respond. The not knowing is going to kill me."

The tension of not knowing must not bother Vinn too much, as she soon falls asleep still gripping the controller for the sound. I let her snooze, wait impatiently until the appointed hour, check to make sure the recorder is set for the second message, then push all of the buttons myself, gently pressing on Vinn's thumb so that she can later say she participated. I carry her off to the bedroom, where there are only ghosts of a different kind.

"Are you sure?" I ask Rebecca for the fourth time. Her patience with me is growing thin.

"Don't you think I would remember if Veronica called me? Give me some credit, Malcom. How do we know the setup even worked?"

"We don't," I admit glumly. "All right, we'll try again tonight. If nothing happens, it looks like we'll have to get someone in there and run a test. And maybe install a camera somewhere. It'll be fine."

I hang up the phone and head off for my 1:00 class. I wish I really believed that everything would be fine. My mind is far from today's lecture on the proper use of punctuation. Normally I would revel in the classic missing comma example of "Let's eat Grandma," but today I'm already anticipating and dreading another break-in. Our prior time in the closet is not a fond memory, so I couldn't care less what happens to Grandma. I can't help but smile a little, though, when my brain tells me "It's time to screw Veronica," which shows that sometimes an absent comma is exactly the right thing.

There was a time in the not-so-distant past where staying up seventy-two hours straight on a stakeout was no big deal, so the struggle to stay awake long enough to repeat last night's button-pushing extravaganza, this time without Vinn, is a sad commentary on the domestication of my lifestyle over the past couple of years. I manage to finish the job and remember stumbling in the direction of my bed but after that it's a complete blank.

Which explains why the music playing in my pitch-dark bedroom in the middle of the night does little to raise me to a conscious state but instead intrudes into a dream in which aliens are dancing on my ceiling playing an early 70's pop tune on futuristic instruments. Only when they start pounding loudly on my door do I realize that maybe I'm should wake up, get out of bed, and see what they want.

As I open the door a frigid blast of air enters along with a blur in a yellow satin nightgown and fuzzy bunny slippers. Any remnants of the idea that I'm still dreaming disappear as somewhere deep down inside of me I seem to hold the idea that aliens with the capability of visiting Earth are advanced enough to have a better sense of fashion. The blur gradually takes the shape of a familiar face, which without makeup is enough to shock me into wakefulness.

"Malcom, Malcom, Malcom! She called!" Rebecca is rattling a mile a minute. "I mean, whatever you did this time, it worked! She couldn't wait until morning to tell me."

You could have waited a few hours to tell me I think as I shuffle to the kitchen to make some tea. I have a favorite tea for most situations, but a middle of the night visit from a crossdressing businessman to discuss alien life forms that visited a murderer isn't one I anticipated. Earl Gray it is.

Rebecca takes a seat at the island. "Veronica said that

she had been a bit tipsy after an evening out last night so she wasn't sure what she was seeing or if it was real, and she only had a vague memory of a green light in the morning. It was on her mind all day though, so when it happened again she woke up fast. She couldn't go back to sleep afterward as her mind started racing so fast that everything in her brain was a giant jumble.

"At first her main thought was pride that the Elohim had chosen her to whom to convey a message. Then panic set in. She needs to prove that she's worthy—how does she do that? And when will they be visiting? Next year or next week? Will we be able to have the embassy ready? What should she wear?" Rebecca smiles. "I understand that last one. I've been thinking about that for weeks already. Anyway, congratulations, Malcom. So now what?"

I pour two cups and Rebecca, not normally a fan of tea, pulls hers over. I have to turn my head to avoid seeing her scoop spoonful after spoonful of sugar into it. "Now we need to help direct her thoughts to the answers we want her to come up with herself. Set up a meeting with her for this weekend. In the meantime we'll have Casper choose a date based on when our students can have everything ready. We have her frazzled and with a short enough time frame she'll have no choice but to agree to some drastic shortcuts. Then it's show time."

Rebecca drains the rest of her tea and rises. "It won't be easy to get her to wait, but I'll get something set up for Saturday. Probably early. And Malcom," she looks back as she reaches the door, "try to look at least a little more presentable."

I slam the door behind her.

Rebecca was right when she predicted Veronica would want to meet as early as humanly possible on Saturday morning. As we discussed, Rebecca insisted to her that it would be a good opportunity to go out for breakfast, which allows us to skip the hidden microphone ordeal and give me a place at the table without violating the sacred space of Veronica's apartment. After my late nights this week, I'm not thrilled with having to get out of bed early on the weekend so that we can be at the restaurant by 7:30, although it's an improvement over Veronica's original proposal of 6:00.

Feed is a small, quirky southern-style shack on the outskirts of Humboldt Park that covers every breakfast item in thick layers of chicken gravy and has supersized bottles of hot sauce on each table. We arrive ten minutes early and I'm surprised to see Veronica already seated waiting for us. Naturally she's at a table with only three seats, so after placing our orders at the counter we join her with myself, always the odd one out, pulling a chair up to the end. Veronica shoots me the same kind of look she would give to something odorous she spotted on the bottom of her shoe.

She doesn't even let us get settled before starting in, directing her words only to the two women. "I mean, it's a great honor, of course," she begins, "and certainly is a reflection of my devotion for such a lengthy period of time. But then the Elohim asked me to be prepared to prove my worthiness of an appointment as their worldly messenger. Doesn't the fact that they chose me at all mean I've already passed their test? That I meet their standards?"

"You've certainly proven yourself more than any of us ever could or they wouldn't have taken this first step," Vinn assures her. "Think of it as having aced the entrance exam, but now you have to take it a step further and confirm their faith in you with a face-to-face meeting. I wouldn't worry about it."

"I guess that makes sense. And let me be clear that I'm not worried about my worthiness," Veronica assures us, the familiar haughtiness returning. "It's just that I've never had cause to prove it before. It's been obvious to anyone with half a brain. So I'm at a loss as to what they're looking for."

"Maybe the feather?" Rebecca suggests. "It shows a level of status granted to you by Rael himself.

Veronica considers it but ends up frowning. "No, as rare as that is, it doesn't distinguish me from several other women."

"I agree with Rebecca that it should be something tangible," Vinn tells her. "I had a friend once who always wore a certain necklace with a charm in it when she went to church. It was kind of like her personal talisman. She swore it made her feel more spiritual, closer to God."

"Hmm." Veronica looks thoughtful. "That does give me an idea. I may have just the thing. Now, next on the agenda..." she pauses as food is delivered to the table. I don't remember what I ordered but hope it's somewhere under the sea of gravy on my plate. "The embassy. We need to move up our timetable and get construction started immediately."

"That's why I let Malcom tag along today," Vinn says. If I didn't know her so well, I wouldn't have picked up on the slight upturn at the corners of her mouth. All three sets of eyes turn to me.

"We can pull a crew and some supplies together, certainly. But the entire embassy? Even under the most ideal conditions we're looking at six to nine months just to get a basic structure in place."

"Well that's disappointing Malcom." Rebecca sounds churlish. "But Veronica, darling, when did they say they would be coming down with their message?"

"They didn't. It could be a month, maybe five or six. They must know that we aren't yet prepared so I'm hopeful they will give us some time."

"Perhaps," Vinn offers, "we should work from the

inside out and start with the reception area so that it'll be the first part completed. If the Elohim are only coming briefly to deliver a message, we won't necessarily need the bedrooms or conference rooms. Best to have one area ready and have it done extremely well than to have three or four rooms in various stages of construction."

"Brilliant!" Rebecca intones. "I totally agree. What do you think, Veronica dear? "

"I see what you're saying, but if we're going to go rogue on the plans, the room has to be absolutely perfect." For the first time since we sat down, she looks in my direction. I'm still hunting for my food and am beginning to think I ordered a pool of gravy.

"Can do," I tell her in my most enthusiastic manner. "Complete with helipad."

"We'll make certain of it," Vinn assures Veronica. "Malcom here will be a very busy boy."

Veronica mutters something under her breath that I don't hear but causes Vinn to smirk. After a few minutes of answering questions about her encounter with the green being, Veronica has had enough of the hired help and with a quick peck on the cheek to Rebecca, hastens out the door.

"That went well," Vinn smiles as she stabs the last piece of Rebecca's omelet with her fork. "We couldn't have scripted it any better. Now, what do you say we talk to Leo about making a short recording for us. Veronica's estimated timetable is about to be shot to hell."

# THIRTY EIGHT

Knowing Rebecca would ignore my plea not to call me if she heard from Veronica in the early morning hours, I silenced my phone after sending the Elohim messenger on one more late-night visit and was able to sleep through the multiple texts and email notifications waiting for me when I awoke this morning. I'm gratified to see that Rebecca had the foresight to record Veronica's frantic 1:30 a.m. call and that she forwarded it to Vinn and I.

"That's only nine days away!" I hear Veronica's voice shriek. "Nine days! We can't be ready that quickly! I'm putting this on you and your cohorts, Rebecca. We need something incredible put together before they come."

I dress for work as I listen to Rebecca follow our instructions and assure her that while we won't be able to do everything we want to, our team will work around the clock to construct a reception area that will be both welcoming and aesthetically pleasing to our visitors. Eventually Veronica settles down and steers the conversation to wardrobe and perfume selections, which even Rebecca chooses to deflect and say that these topics could certainly wait until daylight hours.

Gratified, I send a short email to Mayfield with the alien invasion date and time and a promise to reach out to him between classes. Classes. I see I'm running late and rush to catch the el to campus.

"What are you doing here?" Vinn smirks as she munches on a bite of my English muffin with lingonberry jam that I snuck past Manuel. "I thought you were working around the clock building a room worthy of receiving little green men from outer space."

"On a break," I mumble as I watch more of my breakfast treat enter the wrong mouth. "Seriously, I did let the team know that it's crunch time. They assure me that they'll all be ready in time for a dry run a couple days beforehand. I get the impression that Leo has them on a tight schedule."

"I heard that he promised the students discounts on catering for their wedding receptions if they put in some extra hours," Vinn says with a grin. "If only they knew what a disincentive that is. They do seem to like him, though, and are putting in extra effort to please him. There must be a side to his personality we don't see."

"We'll need to pull him away at some point," I remind her, "to go over as many possible scenarios we can think of for when this goes down. It's one thing to read a script for an advance recording and another to go live. We don't know what Veronica's reaction will be or what she'll say and he needs to be prepared to lead her into saying the magic words."

Vinn frowns. "I don't like having the success or failure of this whole plan dependent on so many nonprofessionals, but it was unavoidable. If this thing goes south, though, it'll do so in front of witnesses."

"Speaking of which, I guess I need to bring Mendez and Jenkins back into the picture. This isn't going to be an easy sell."

"Why not? I'm sure it's commonplace for cops to use untested technology to entice a confession out of a possible murderer with the promise of meeting aliens with whom she wants to have sex as a way of bringing peace to the citizens of Earth."

"When you put it that way, what would I ever have to worry about?" Besides everything, that is. I choose to leave that latter thought unsaid.

"Are you out of your freakin' mind?" Jenkins stares at me, mouth agape, a forkful of rice and beans halfway to his mouth. We're sitting in a small Puerto Rican restaurant in the heart of Pilsen that specializes in jibaritos, a sandwich that uses fried green plantains in the place of bread. Due to the nature of our conversation, I didn't want to meet too close to campus and risk being overheard by a student or faculty member, while Mendez wanted to be as far away from his district as reasonably possible.

I wait for Mendez to add his own helping of incredulity to the pile or to outright call me a fool, but he seems content to stare at me impassively without comment. I turn my attention back to Jenkins.

"The cops don't have one iota of evidence linking these killings to this woman and even after meeting with her all we have are a few vague verbal statements and our opinions based on our interactions, which I'll be the first to admit are colored by our dislike of her. The only way we'll tie her in is if she incriminates herself, which she's smart enough not to do. If we thought there was a more conventional way to corner her, we would do it. It's this way or give up."

Jenkins' animated hands indicate he clearly wants to respond, but a mouthful of pork gives the quiet Mendez a chance to intervene. "You're right that you don't have enough to even consider making this official. In those cases sometimes the only way to catch an insane killer is to take a ride on the crazy train yourself. I'm not saying this is something that we would have ever considered, and it's certainly not sanctioned, but I understand why you think this might work. A lot of things could go wrong, though."

I ignore Jenkins, who's now staring at Mendez like he's from Pluto. "Yeah, we know. Technical failures are the biggest concern. One little glitch and she'll see right through us. She might anyway. She may not take the bait and do or say anything you can use. Leo might mess up. I'd go on, but I'm depressing myself."

The smallest of smiles crosses Mendez' lips before disappearing. "Understood. And I appreciate the heads' up. What are you looking for from us?"

"For one, don't say anything to your superiors until right before it goes down. I don't want them to shut us down. It's up to you whether to make this official at all. But once it's clear we're moving forward, we could use some backup just in case. And of course if she says or does anything arrestable, you guys move in."

Mendez looks thoughtful. Jenkins looks baffled. "We can do that," Mendez says. "Myself and one or two others, probably all technically off-duty. And Jenkins if he wants in."

Both of us now turn our attention to the campus cop, only a few months removed from being cited as a hero for his role in tracking down the killer of the two youngsters. I wonder if his reluctance to participate here is related to not wanting to tarnish that moment of glory or due to the chance of reliving a fatal shooting.

"Yeah, I want to be there," he finally admits. "If for no other reason than to protect everyone involved."

That's probably not his reason and we know it, but it'll do. I place an order for a dish of tembleque, a coconut pudding, not because I want it but to give the two men in blue a chance to walk out together to discuss what an absolute pain in the ass I am. Five minutes later, stomach full of custard, I'm out the door.

"We have to wait on the parking lot until the last minute, but everything else is ready to go," Mayfield tells our group of three. Vinn, Rebecca, and I arrived together, pulling our rental car into the studio through a wide door and into a makeshift garage which effectively hid the rest of the soundstage from sight. "Ladies, you'll go through the door over here with the gold trim. That'll bring you to a small vestibule. Mal, once they're gone you'll go over this way"—he points to a hidden alcove next to the garage door—"where there's an opening to the AV room, as we call it. Let's look at that first."

It's only about ten steps from the car, but the dim light and slight inset from the wall, combined with the distraction of the boldly-painted door the women will use, makes the entryway virtually invisible. There's no door, a precaution against Veronica hearing it open and close. The room itself is pitch black as we enter, but as soon as we're all inside lights come on. I'm startled to see Leo and Malika already there. The room is fitted with a long table with four chairs abutting one side facing the wall, with two more chairs behind them. A computer monitor, several boxy electronic devices, and a headset with an attached boom and microphone are neatly arranged on the table.

"It'll be a tight fit, but there should be room for Leo, Malika, you, and me at the table. The other two chairs are for anyone else you bring along. More than two and they'll have to stand. Malika, why don't you take it from here."

A very nervous-looking Malika steps away from the wall by about three inches. "The room is mostly soundproofed, but any loud noises could still filter through into the reception hall so it's best to remain quiet, especially when Leo is speaking. We have seven cameras fitted around the hall to cover every angle and each view will appear on that monitor. I'll be in charge of those, zooming in when and where appropriate. I'll angle the monitor just a little so that you can see what's happening inside. I wasn't happy with the eighteen speakers so we added four more." She looks at me sheepishly. "Don't worry, Professor. They're borrowed so it didn't add to the cost.

"Anyway, so I'll be sitting here on the end. Mr. Mayfield will be here, where he'll be working the visuals. Then you, so that you can cue both him and Leo, who'll be on your right. We'll have pads of paper and pens for any necessary communication while the mic is live."

"One more thing before we go next door," Mayfield adds with a touch of pride. "If all goes well and you get what you want, or God forbid something goes wrong and the women are in danger, you're not going to want to go back through the garage to get inside. You'd lose precious seconds. On the other side of this panel here," he says as he walks to the corner of the room just past the table, "it looks like a seamless part of the wall in the room. But all you need to do is push it and you're inside." He leans against the panel and we all move over to look past him to get a glimpse of the reception area, but he lets it shut again before we see anything.

"No cheating," he tells us with a smile. "Let's go in the way your target will first see the room." As we're led away, I glance back to see Malika moving into Mayfield's seat and Leo donning the headset, readying for the all-important demonstration.

The vestibule is too small to comfortably fit all four bodies, causing us to stand awkwardly with shoulders touching. It's completely unadorned with only a single light bulb above, but the smell of fresh paint draws our attention to brightly colored walls.

Mayfield seems to read my thoughts. "We had to keep it simple due to time constraints," he explains. "And we wanted to focus more of our efforts on the reception room itself. We'll go inside in just a second. But first, I want to thank you again for asking me to be a part of this. It gives me the chance to try out a new toy while also helping to bring a little justice to the world. And," he continues with a grin, "it gave me an idea for an awesome short I want to film once this is all over."

With no further introduction to what we're about to

see, Mayfield swings the door inward and ushers us inside. I instantly freeze in place. A small gasp comes from Vinn at my side and Rebecca whispers "My god" at least three times. The place is astounding. Promotional materials prepared by the Raelists showed a fairly plain welcoming area but we, with Veronica's blessing, aimed for something a little more dramatic and aesthetically striking.

The room itself is dome-shaped, flattening out enough near the ground to allow for the placement of artwork. A few paintings of nature scenes adorn the walls, but most them as well as the ceiling are instead covered in painted representations of space, giving the room the illusion of extending off into the sky. An antique desk sits near the far wall under a giant three-dimensional Raelian symbol hanging from the ceiling. Modernistic seating and plush rugs fill out the remaining space. Lighting is provided by strings of tiny LED fairy lights strung liberally above, casting the room in a soft glow while giving the impression of thousands of stars in the room. Despite the large number of lights, it remains dim enough to hide any defects in the projection. The overall effect is one of being on a spacewalk in a particularly incredible part of the solar system.

All three of us are still in slow spins, eyes cast upward, when Sally approaches and breaks our reverie. "Do you like it?" she asks with a noticeable waiver in her voice. "Is it too much?"

"It's more than I ever imagined it would be," I tell her, with Vinn and Rebecca quickly adding their own similar views. "If we'd given you three months to put this together, I'd still be impressed."

"It was a collaborative effort," she insists as Blaire joins the group. "Chad has a midterm he needs to study for or he'd be here too."

"Don't let her fool you," Blaire adds. "Almost all of the decorative touches you see were hers. I helped give the ceiling a little depth but other than that, my focus was assisting Malika and Mr. Mayfield in making Casper's movements more natural."

"Which brings us to the main attraction," Mayfield calls from the other side of the room. He gazes at a point somewhere near the ceiling. "Malika, ready when you are."

We wait several moments until suddenly the room is awash in a bright, blinding light that forces us to cover our eyes. Seconds later the light disappears. As my eyes adjust, I have trouble believing what I see. Standing in front of us about ten feet away is the exact image of an Elohim as imagined by my student Lori, appearing as real as Vinn at my side. As we approach, it opens its arms and moves its head from side to side as if taking in each one of us. A long robe the same color of its green skin keeps the alien modest. True to Mayfield's promise, as we circle to the sides and rear, it is truly a three-dimensional image, sharp in its focus with the exception of its facial features, which are hard to distinguish in the dim light.

"Welcome," it suddenly says in the feminized manifestation of Leo's voice, causing me to jump. "This is a test." The voice does, in fact, seem to emanate from all portions of the room and has a slight echo effect.

Vinn approaches the being and reaches out. Her hand penetrates the image, smashing the illusion of solidity.

Mayfield quickly steps in. "Yes, you'll have to prevent her from getting too close. I assume you've considered that." Oops, no. As we step back and continue to stare, the Elohim messenger begins to flicker and even without intruding on its personal space, the illusion that it's an actual living creature is lost.

"Dammit," Mayfield curses. "Sorry, that's never happened before. Not sure what the issue is, but we'll have it fixed."

"And the flash of light? What was that" Vinn asks.

"We had trouble getting her to move in a natural way," Blaire responds. "So we couldn't show her walking from the door into the room." She points to a door in the corner I had overlooked which is labeled "Stairs to landing pad."

"That's another point." Mayfield adds. "Make sure she doesn't get curious enough while she explores to open that door. It doesn't lead anywhere."

The exhilaration I felt ten minutes ago has now been supplanted with an equal amount of anxiety. Doors to nowhere. Flickering alien. Rooms not completely soundproofed. An intelligent and unpredictable target. Nonprofessionals in key roles. What could possibly go wrong?

We'll find out in two days.

# THIRTY NINE

The students in each of my Friday classes either suffered from my inattention or had a great time deviating from the normal structure I maintain. I don't feel guilty about being distracted and promise myself I'll make it up to them next week with additional homework or some other draconian punishment teachers like to indiscriminately impose. Over lunch Vinn conveys that she hasn't been much better, a more serious circumstance when you're dealing with complex chemical formulas rather than with the difference between alliteration and consonance.

She drops by my office after her last class and we Uber to my place together. There's little for me to do before tonight's main event other than to remain available to the rest of the team in the event they need me and to make dinner for Vinn and Rebecca, who say they need hours to make themselves presentable and to fit into the robe-like dresses Veronica special ordered for them. Heather agreed to meet in Rebecca's apartment to recreate her magic while Vinn will do her own makeup at the same time. We learned the first time around that Veronica will only have eyes for Rebecca. Vinn could show up in a gorilla mask and get away with it.

Between dropping udon noodles into a simmering broth, checking my email every ninety seconds, and texting myself to make sure that my phone is working, time should be moving quickly, but it's dragging. Dinner is a silent affair, each of us barely tasting the food as we focus on the roles we have ahead of us. At least one of us is also stressing out over the possibility that an unexpected development could have dire consequences for one or more of us. Among other things.

After dinner the ladies go back down a flight to get dressed, leaving me on my own to brood as I wash the dishes.

The Elohim isn't due to arrive until 11:00 tonight. Even after succumbing to Veronica's insistent plea to get there early—negotiated down to thirty minutes from ninety—we still don't need to pick her up until 9:45. I run a mental checklist through my brain four times without discovering anything I need to do, so I settle onto the couch, phone on full volume in my hand, and do what comes naturally before dealing with a killer. I fall asleep.

I awake when I hear the key in the door and am immediately shocked into full consciousness upon seeing Vinn and Rebecca in dark blue, off-the-shoulder, floor length dresses with a tiered waist. Made of silk and obviously expensive, they give the unstylish observer the impression of a cross between a mermaid and a female gladiator. Rebecca is glowing while Vinn is clearly uncomfortable in something that doesn't have pockets and a hood.

Before I can say a word, Vinn sees my expression and anticipates my comment. "Drop dead, Winters," she snarls. "We didn't have any say in the selection."

"I think they're absolutely divine," Rebecca differs. "And the ultramarine shade just does wonders for my skin, don't you think? Of course, they might clash a bit with the alien but what color could you possibly find to complement that awful shade of green?"

"Can we just get on with this?" Vinn grumbles. For the first time since my nap, I look at the time. We're not late but need to get moving. We grab coats, and as we head down the stairs both women lift their dresses so as not to drag the hems in the snow. Rebecca chose ivory heels with crystals imbedded on the straps. Vinn's wearing orange sneakers. I choose not to comment. Time to focus.

It's a short walk to the rental, a newer Lexus, my concession to the assumption that when you're on your way to meet with a creature from outer space where the future of the world may be involved, you should travel with a little style. We also need a roomier back seat because while she doesn't know it yet, Veronica will be lying on the floor until we get to our destination. As the women struggle to maneuver into their seats, Vinn in back in case our guest gets feisty, I inspect the dark film I applied to the side and back windows last night. Still in place with no peeling or rips.

I send a group text stating that we're on our way and should be there in forty-five minutes or so then pull out. As we get within a couple blocks of Veronica's place, Rebecca sends her own text telling her that she can head out. Veronica's paranoid about being delayed and missing the encounter she's been anticipating for years. We obviously can't tell her that the alien will wait until we arrive to appear.

She's already outside when we pull up and heads quickly toward the car. Vinn spreads a clean blanket on the floor. Veronica makes a face when she sees who she'll be sharing the back seat with but still manages to blow a kiss to Rebecca. The large handbag she's carrying seems out of place for the evening and adds to my list of concerns. I consider finding a way to get her to leave it in the car once we arrive until I realize that it's as likely to contain what we hope she'll bring as it is a weapon.

We agreed that since I'm already considered a necessary annoyance by Rebecca, I'll play the heavy so as not to cause a rift among the women. Veronica no sooner closes the door and opens her mouth to speak than I turn around and address her. "You need to put this on. Quickly. No arguing. You don't wear it, you don't come with us." In my hand is a large opaque mask that will cover her eyes and most of her face. I wanted a hood but Rebecca insisted that Veronica would spend hours doing her hair, so it would be pushing our luck.

Veronica squeaks but before she can protest Vinn takes the mask and moves it toward her face. "Malcom's picked up some government chatter," she says in a semi-whisper. "Apparently they've been watching you for some time. They see you as the bait that'll bring them to the Elohim, and god knows what they'd do if they succeed. We made sure we weren't followed here but don't want to take any chances that they'll spot you. We need your face covered and you have to be out of sight. I'm sorry, but that's the way it's got to be."

Only when Rebecca apologetically confirms Vinn's absurd story does Veronica take the mask in hand, pushing away Vinn's help, and lower herself onto the blanket. I check to make sure she's unable to see anything, Vinn gives me a thumb's up, and off we go.

"We're going to take a more indirect route," I announce loud enough to carry to the floor in back. "We have to verify that we're not being tailed, and while the government is more than capable of stationing agents along the expressway, they can't man every little street in the city. I'm not new to this, I'll get us there unaccompanied and we won't be late."

Veronica mutters something that causes Vinn to raise her eyebrows, perhaps a salty epithet she doesn't know, but whatever it is doesn't carry to the front. I turn one way or another almost every two blocks or so to confuse Veronica as to the route since we're heading south this time instead of north, and the trip to the warehouse takes about one-fourth the time as to the park, but I'm gradually making our way in the right direction. The tension is palpable as I pull up to the edge of the parking lot, where I stop before entering.

"In the home stretch," I say for the benefit of the back seat. "We cleared a narrow path through the woods so that we can get the car closer to the entrance to the embassy. Once parked, Vinn will lead you into the anteroom. Once there and away from any unwanted eyes, you can take the blindfold off."

I slowly move into the lot, where Mayfield has set up a series of artificial bumps to simulate travel through the woods, some of them higher than others and a few angled so that the car leans to the side as we cross. The garage door sits open but I pause for a few minutes to feign waiting for it as well as to make sure that we've been observed by someone inside. As we drive in, I notice that he's also placed rough boards over the cement floor to hide it from view, but that may not be needed.

Rebecca sits frozen for a minute until I poke her harder than necessary, which gets her blood moving again. She may've been trying to remember her lines. "Veronica," she begins haltingly, "you can sit up but don't take the hood off yet. I'll let you know." Not so difficult after all.

I exit at the same time as the women, wait until the door to the vestibule closes behind them then hustle to the AV room, where the same crew from the run-through is already stationed in their chairs. Jenkins, Mendez, and an officer in uniform I don't recognize are against the wall. The uniformed cop must be down the ladder in rank, as he pulled the short straw and has to stand.

The video and audio feeds are already up and running. To my great relief, Veronica is impressed with the welcome area and appears content to stay in place while she turns to face every direction, for now staying away from the windows and the door to the nonexistent landing pad. It's a surrealistic experience watching the robed women seemingly standing among the stars.

It doesn't take long for Veronica's eyes to fall upon the ice bucket and crystal flutes prominently displayed on one of the tables. At one point Vinn suggested ways to have

Veronica inhale scopolamine, more popularly called "The Devil's Breath," a drug derived from the South American Borrachero tree which legend says makes the user powerless to resist any suggestion, even to the point of giving up all of their worldly possessions. While it might have been useful in encouraging Veronica to accept the image of the Elohim, it might also have made it difficult to have any confession stand up in court if she uttered it while under the influence of the drug. Once Vinn mentioned that even a tiny amount can also be fatal, we abandoned the idea. We then considered psilocybin, the ingredient found in magic mushrooms that makes them so fun and which is used by psychiatrists to raise mood and reduce inhibitions but rejected that as well.

In the end we went the old-fashioned way with champagne, a half bottle, figuring one glass will loosen her up just a touch or at least make her a little bit happy without also making her drunk enough to give a good lawyer support to toss out whatever happens next. Veronica hovers near the bottle, impatiently waiting until Vinn takes the hint, opens, and pours.

"To a successful interaction with the Elohim and a future of world peace," Veronica toasts as all three women touch glasses. Two glasses are quickly emptied of their contents. Vinn, who can down rivers of booze and still be functional, betrays her nerves by stopping after one sip and surreptitiously pouring the remainder into a nearby planter. It's still a few minutes from the anointed hour, but no one has watches and the less time Veronica is given to explore the better. Vinn senses the same thing and edges the group toward the center of the room. I give Mayfield the signal to commence the action. Leo clears his throat before turning on the microphone. I swivel and signal our observers to stay quiet.

All our eyes are fixated on the monitor. Slight movement from Mayfield's left hand and instantly the brilliant flash of light fills the view from every camera. Despite having lived through it once before and knowing what to expect, Rebecca shrieks right along with Veronica. During the distraction while the women covered their eyes and instinctively looked to the floor, Casper appears in all her glory. As Veronica looks up and first sees the specter, she momentarily freezes before instructing the other two to back up and let her approach the Elohim, which is realistically scanning the room.

I nod to Leo and mime to Mayfield to keep the alien's head aligned with Veronica. Leo leans into the mic and begins.

"You have done well," the creature tells her. It's eerie to hear Leo's gruff voice and indeterminable accent then a microsecond later listen to the same words repeated in the soft, lyrical, and feminine tone of the green image on the screen. "For now. But we will need much more when we return. We are not demanding but do expect great things from you and wish to be received in the proper manner. Do we have your understanding?"

So far, Leo is reading from a prepared script and hopefully he won't need to improvise. Our goal right from the beginning is to put Veronica on the defensive and so eager to please the Elohim messenger so that its next request, on which our whole plan relies, will be met without a second thought. I notice I'm clenching my hands so tightly that I'm cutting off circulation and force myself to relax.

"Yes, yes, of course," a rattled Veronica forces out as she cautiously moves to the side of the figure, checking to assure herself this isn't anything but what it appears to be. The alien's eyes follow her, forcing her to abashedly retreat. "My associates did not perform up to expectations today and I'll put them on task." I can almost hear Vinn's blood boiling. "Also, may I say that I am honored..."

I tap Leo and the Elohim interrupts what I assume is a prepared speech that Veronica stressed over for days. "Before we go any further, before I pass on the message for you to spread to the believers, you need to justify our great journey here. You must prove that we have chosen well. Not all that are with me are certain of your commitment."

Malika zooms one camera in for a close-up of Veronica's face. She's clearly shaken, uncertain if she'll take the required step to prove her worthiness. Without prompting, Leo intervenes. "Very well. We were mistaken. We will choose anoth—"

"No! No! I'm the one you want! I'm the only one, the chosen one. Wait, just wait and let me show you!" I give a thumbs up to Leo as the frantic woman rushes to retrieve her purse from a table near the entrance door. Malika brings that camera up as we watch her dump the contents out onto the table before grabbing onto a small paper lunch bag and dashing back to her former spot. With trembling hands she reaches into the bag and begins to pull out its contents.

At that very moment, the image of the Elohim begins to flicker. Everyone in the room gasps. Prompted by the change in light, Veronica looks up and stares at the alien, which has for the moment regained its lifelike appearance. But not for long enough. It again flickers, then waivers, then disappears entirely before the bottom half appears alone. Every real person both inside and outside the room is immobilized for a split second, mesmerized by the disaster unfolding in front of us. Then all hell breaks loose.

Veronica screams something primal as she turns toward Vinn and Rebecca. Before I can see what transpires next, I'm on my way to the hidden door, immediately behind Leo. As we enter the dim room, we can barely make out a twisting mass of bodies wrestling on the floor, crashing into the table holding the items from Veronica's purse. Leo slips as he approaches and I in turn tumble over him, landing on top of the pile.

"Wrist!" Vinn screams and I grab the first one I find. Rebecca squawks so I release and find another, which is holding a sharp and slippery blade. One twist, snap, and howl later, I have the arm belonging to the wrist bent behind Veronica's back. Leo is using his socks to tie her legs together, and Vinn is grabbing her hair. It's only then that I see the small puddle of blood that caused Leo to fall.

"I'm okay," Vinn says as she releases her hold on our captive. The gash in her arm is leaking badly. She's not okay. A shadow appears and I turn to see a humbled Mendez standing over the heap of bodies.

"Sorry," he says sheepishly. "It all seemed so distant, so unreal, like I was watching television. I moved too slowly. But better late than never."

"No, not really," I respond angrily. I don't move until the cop Mendez brought with him has Veronica's wrists secured in handcuffs. Only then am I able to offer Vinn a handkerchief to try to stem the bleeding. All doubts about whether Veronica was the murderer are now behind us, and she definitely just committed a few additional crimes, but Vinn's condition prevents us from hanging around to see if she brought the evidence to incriminate herself in the kids' killings to a cop's way of thinking. We wait until no one's looking in our direction and slip out the door.

# FOURTY

It isn't meant to be a party, which is good because no one present is in a celebratory mood. Still, being the ever-considerate host, I set out a spread of caramelized onion, spinach, and cheddar pastries, crab hush puppies, French dip sliders, and southwest baked eggrolls to munch on comfortably in my living room. Leo brought a variety of unlabeled bottles of booze, not trusting me to carry anything with enough punch to satisfy him. He appears to have sampled each one for freshness before climbing up the two flights. Rebecca contributed a special dip that she says is all the rage in Paris, which Leo and I take turns generously piling onto our plates before sneaking into the kitchen to scrape into the trash. Vinn begged off her share on the ground that she's crippled, an excuse that's also been used to get me to do her laundry, bring her breakfast in bed, and massage her feet.

Leo managed to disappear from last night's chaotic scene before Mendez could detain him, instinctively knowing that Vinn would appear at his door to take her place at my usual chair so that he could apply his colorful mystery salves to her wound before skillfully sewing her up. Rebecca stayed long enough to give a brief statement to the cops but couldn't tell us anything about what happened after we left other than the fact that Veronica was hustled out forcibly while engaging in a loud, one-sided diatribe not suitable for an Angel of any rank. A text from Mayfield stated that he discovered the glitch that gave Casper a case of the shivers and to say that he had already dissembled the welcome room. I left it to Malika to fill in the other students on what had gone down. I'll debrief them all later when I have something more substantive to say than "it was a disaster but thanks for your help."

When I invited my tenants and co-conspirators to eat with us tonight I didn't impose a prohibition on any mention of the prior evening's events, but it apparently wasn't something anyone cared to bring up. In fact the only conversation in the last thirty minutes has been Vinn quietly directing me to fill up her plate. More than one of us is startled, then, when there's a loud knock at the door.

"Open up in the name of the law!" a voice calls from outside. Jenkins. He hustles his baby face in out of the cold as soon as I open the door, followed closely by Mendez. Jenkins hands me a bottle of premium whiskey before shedding his coat. Not to be outdone, Mendez proffers a small gift bag. I peer inside just long enough to observe a few bags of loose tea from an online company I respect and another of locally ground coffee. Smart man to play both sides. I nod my acknowledgment and accompany the pair to the living room, where they find seats.

"This isn't an official visit," Mendez says. "Although we will want to take your statements at some point. Leo called to tell us we'd find you all together tonight. Jenkins and I both thought we owed you an apology, especially you," he says as he looks directly at Vinn. "Our delay in moving was unforgiveable. I'm just glad the result wasn't worse."

I notice Mendez eyeing the table as he talks, so I hand plates and napkins to he and Jenkins before going to the kitchen to retrieve a couple of glasses. Mendez pours a generous ration of a dark amber liquid into his glass, takes a sip, and winces. It must not be as bad as his expression implied, though, as he repeats the same action twice more before continuing.

"I'm sure you're curious about your alien-worshiping friend. Your setup was genius even if the execution went awry too quickly. Veronica did bring the holy grail to prove her worthiness to the green ghost. At the station she denied any connection to those murders until we put three bones from human foreheads in front of her and asked why we found them in that paper bag she brought. She sputtered something about their being relics she picked up in Italy until we wondered out loud if their DNA would match any remains we had in the coroner's office. That's when the gates opened. She tried to blame Crum, then you three, then the milkman, then Obama and whoever else popped into her mind. She went full-on crazy. We had enough to detain her without bond. It's early but my guys are confident they can build a case. I can sleep at night again and have a story to tell. It's already legendary around the station. So thank you."

Now the mood elevates so that the gathering does resemble more of a party. Mendez begs off soon, though, and Jenkins loses his ride if he stays, so he rises to go as well. Before he leaves he turns back to us. "You might also be interested to know that besides the bones, her purse contained a handgun and a bottle of batrachotoxin, one of the world's most deadly poisons. Comes from South American frogs I hear. A drop on your skin and its goodbye, world. From what I infer from our conversations with this madwoman, after her rendezvous with the alien she was planning on moving on with only one of you. The other two were expendable, something she intended to handle last night."

With those last words, he and Jenkins are gone and our gathering once again becomes somber as we reflect on how close we came to becoming victims ourselves. Not another word is spoken for the next hour. At that time Leo pulls himself out of his fog, raises his glass, which we all meet, and then we drink. Rebecca helps him out of his chair and they too exit, leaving Vinn and I alone once more.

It seems right to stay silent. We can communicate without words, which soon leads me to pick her up, the slash on her arm apparently affecting her legs, and carry her off to the bedroom. There's nothing like a brush with death to stimulate the hormones, and it would take more than a few stitches in her arm to stop what comes next.

# ABOUT THE AUTHOR

Never fond of even numbers, Thomas J. Thorson brings his characters back for a third installment in the series and marvels at how they seem to take control of the plot and bring it in directions he never anticipated. He recently followed Malcom into the city and now lives in a three-flat in the Ukrainian Village neighborhood of Chicago.